"Sweet are the uses of adversity…"
—Shakespeare, "*As You Like It*"

The Eddie Collins Series

Frog in a Bucket
Martini Shot
Velvet on a Tuesday Afternoon
Red Desert
Murder Unscripted

ROOM TONE

AN EDDIE COLLINS MYSTERY

Clive Rosengren

coffeetownpress

Kenmore, WA

A Coffeetown Press book published by Epicenter Press

Epicenter Press
6524 NE 181st St. Suite 2
Kenmore, WA 98028.

For more information go to:
www.Camelpress.com
www.Coffeetownpress.com
www.Epicenterpress.com
www.generontalbooks.com

Author website: cliverosengren.com

Design by Rudy Ramos

Room Tone
Copyright © 2024 by Clive Rosengren

ISBN: 9781684922123 (trade paper)
ISBN: 9781684922130 (ebook)

LOC:2024931751

ACKNOWLEDGMENTS

The author wishes to extend thanks to the fans of Eddie Collins, who have stuck with him over the course of five novels. *Room Tone* finds the intrepid private investigator at sort of a demarcation point. What next remains to be seen. I urge you to stay tuned.

Thank you to one of the practicing attorneys I happen to know, John Dickinson, who provided the author valuable information concerning all things legal.

Continued thanks to the folks at Coffeehouse Press for their ongoing support of the Eddie Collins novels.

And last, but certainly not least, my thanks to the members of Monday Mayhem, my steadfast writers' group. Jenn Ashton, Carole T. Beers, Sharon Dean and Michael Niemann are my first hurdle to clarity and plausibility. Without them, I wouldn't be able to see the forest for the trees. Thanks again, fellow scribes.

Praise for other Clive Rosengren books

(*Murder Unscripted*)

"Blasting out of a time warp, straight from the 1940s. It's set in modern Hollywood, but it's old-time California noir, right down to its Bakelite heart […] luscious."
—*Booklist*

"The plot purrs along fast and smooth […] the ending of *Murder Unscripted* delivers the reader a sweet surprise"
—*Mystery Scene*

(*Red Desert*)

"Enjoyable, fast and loaded with the author's trademark keen insights."
—Carl Brookins, author of the Sean Sean PI series

(*Velvet on a Tuesday Afternoon*)

"A contemporary mystery with a classic gumshoe feel […] Packed with action, romance, and intrigue…"
—Sarah E. Bradley for *InD'tale Magazine*

5 Stars: "The story is twisty and unpredictable, just what a mystery should be."
—Steve Aberle, Great Mysteries and Thrillers Blog

1

Hollywood Boulevard in the morning is always a treat, made even more so by falling rain, which, since Los Angeles essentially lies in a desert, is even more welcome. With a fresh cup of coffee in hand, I stood on the mini balcony outside my office and looked down as the Boulevard came to life. Metal shop doors rolled upward. Corrugated iron doors collapsed on themselves. The sounds signaled the dawning of yet another day of hawking tchotchkes and trinkets to visitors in Tinseltown. The rain had been steadily coming down since early morning, but by now had dwindled to a drizzle. Probably a good development; swimming pools in the Hollywood Hills wouldn't be sliding into neighbors' backyards.

Nevertheless, the wet street made Los Angelinos think the vehicles they drive are invincible, demonstrated by a red Mustang that plowed through an intersection and then a backed-up storm drain, soaking two young men waiting for the "walk" sign. One-finger salutes and curses followed the Mustang as it suddenly skidded to a halt behind a bus, narrowly escaping a collision. I fully expected the two drenched guys to continue the conflict by going after the driver. However, discretion prevailed, and they crossed the street.

I'd been standing on the balcony for only fifteen minutes. It was Easter Monday, April 21, 2019. The Mango Mussolini had been in the Oval Office for a little over two years. So far, the country had survived, but with this clown, anything was still possible. I'd been awakened by a phone call from Carla Rizzoli, an actress and my significant other, who was in Palm Springs shooting an episode of her television show, *Three on a Beat*. We'd spent Easter with her parents, Dominic and Helen, in Henderson, Nevada, after which we'd driven to the Springs, where I dropped her off and came back to Hollywood and rain.

Satisfied that all was well in my ersatz front yard, I was about to step back inside my studio apartment when my eye caught sight of a green Kia parking in front of a record shop on the other side of the Boulevard. My breath caught in my throat. I felt my heart rate increase and a tightness in my chest. I immediately flashed back to late last fall. My pal Reggie Benson and I had been instrumental in apprehending four slimeballs who had been running a snuff film operation north of LA up in Piru. One of them was a dreadlock-wearing young man by the name of Roger Iverson. He drove a green Kia.

Thinking it highly unlikely that this could be Iverson's vehicle, I nevertheless leaned on the balcony's railing and gripped it until my knuckles turned white as I watched the Kia squeeze itself into a space. The door opened, and I'll be damned if a mop of messy brown dreadlocks didn't appear—the same Roger Iverson. He plugged the parking meter and entered the store. Along with his three cohorts, Iverson had been indicted by a Ventura County grand jury. Given the seriousness of the charges leveled against them, I was surprised to see him walking around. Bail, I suppose. I hadn't heard how much had been set by the judge, but it had to be hefty. Reggie and I expected to testify against them when they were bound over for trial.

A bridge yet to be crossed, I thought, as I stepped inside and slid the glass door shut. Still, I was puzzled. Iverson lived in the San Fernando Valley. There were plenty of record shops up there. Why the necessity of seeking out one right across the street from me? Pushing aside my paranoia, I rinsed the coffee cup and dried my hands just in time to hear the front door open, signaling the entrance of Mavis, my girl Friday.

"Eddie, are you back?"

"I am. Be out in a minute."

After throwing the covers over Mr. Murphy's bed and stowing it, I parted the beaded curtain leading to my office and saw Mavis standing in the entrance to her domain, the front office of Collins Investigations. Mavis always brings a splash of color with her, and this morning was no exception. A bright red blouse and dark blue skirt complimented her shock of blonde hair. Fritz Werner, her husband, was a lucky man.

"When did you get back?"

"Yesterday afternoon."

"How was the desert?"

"Hot and dry."

We swapped a few more questions. Her Easter holiday was nice; so was mine. Carla was fine; so was Fritz. The telephone on her desk interrupted our interrogations. She picked it up and said, "Collins Investigations." After a pause she called out. "Tom Sanderson?"

I moved to my desk and picked up the receiver. "Hey, Tom, how ya doin'?"

"Right as rain, boss." I heard the click as Mavis hung up. "We still on for tonight?"

"We are. I don't exactly know what help I'm going to be to your students, but I'll give it a whirl."

"A working actor will set their little hearts all a-flutter," he said. "Seven-thirty, right?"

"Right."

"And you've got the address?"

"Got it."

"Outstanding. Afterwards the cold ones are on me."

"I'll hold you to that," I said, and we broke the connection.

Mavis had caught the tail end of the conversation. She had an envelope and a piece of paper in her hand and leaned against the door jamb leading to her office. "Who's Tom Sanderson?"

"I worked with him on *Terms of Power* last fall. He teaches an acting class and wants me to enlighten them this evening."

"Eddie Collins, the actor, enlightening? I'd like to be a fly on the wall."

"And well you should. I might surprise you. I've never told you about the years I spent studying the Method?"

She cocked her head and a smirk appeared. "I've seen the amount of some of your residuals, boss man. You might want to find another method."

Aside from bringing some color to the office and being an invaluable partner in my PI venture, Mavis never fails to be a worthy opponent when I attempt to be a smart aleck. She usually trumps me; this time was no exception. "So does that mean I shouldn't thank you when I accept my Golden Globe?" She chortled and held up what she had in her hand. "What's that?" I asked.

"The state of California wants to know if you're still interested in being a private eye. That is, if you're not too busy dispensing enlightenment."

I grinned, pulled my checkbook from a desk drawer and gestured for her to bring me the bill. As I wrote the check for my license, she walked into her cubicle containing office supplies and her coffee-making equipment.

"Have you heard anything about that audition you had last month?" she said.

"Not yet, but hope springs eternal." She and Carla had helped me upload an audition to a video file, which then had been emailed to the higher-ups. Mavis ran the camera, Carla fed me lines. I read the part of a bartender, a character with whom I could easily identify. The project was called *Burnt Hills*, and believe it or not, had a western setting, something almost unheard of in today's film industry. Gone were the days of sitting in a casting director's office, waiting to be examined like a specimen in a petri dish. Given the impersonal nature of most auditions I've attended over the years, I suppose the advent of the digital age was an improvement, but I had my doubts.

After signing my check, I put it in the envelope, sealed it and laid it on Mavis's desk to await postage, then sank into a chair in front of her desk. "Guess who I saw parking his car across the street just now."

"Who?"

"That dread-locked guy from the Piru incident. Roger Iverson."

"Good grief. What's he doing walking around?"

"Exactly my thought. Not who I wanted to see to start off the week."

She glanced at me and saw the frown on my face. "Bring up a flashback?"

"Yeah. Is it that obvious?"

"A bit. Try to let it go, Eddie."

"I'm working on it," I said, and walked back to my desk and flipped open my laptop. I located a couple of files concerning the actor's trade I'd saved and hit "print." The wireless printer next to Mavis's desk came to life and I walked into her office to retrieve the copies. She stuck her head out of her inner sanctum of office supplies.

"What are you printing?"

"Enlightenment."

"Let me see," she said, as she walked up to the printer.

"Nope. This is highly confidential material."

"I can always check the printer's history."

I handed her the two pages and walked back to my office. A beer mug sat on a shelf behind my desk. I use it as a depository of business cards I collect. I pulled out a handful and sorted through them until I found the one for Phil Ainsley, Assistant District Attorney for Ventura County. I dialed the phone number and after two rings a female voice answered.

"Phil Ainsley, please."

"I'm sorry, sir, he's out of the office. Can I take a message?"

"My name is Eddie Collins. I testified before a grand jury a few months ago and I was wondering if I could speak to Mr. Ainsley regarding one of the defendants."

"Give me your number, sir, and I'll pass along the message."

"Thank you," I said, and gave her my cell, then hung up.

Mavis walked in and laid the two pages on my desk. "This is good stuff. Are you going to share both of them with the students?"

"Not sure. I'll play it by ear."

"All kidding aside, Eddie, I think you'll wow them."

"Thanks, kiddo," I said. "I appreciate it."

"You're welcome, boss man," she said, as she playfully punched my arm and walked back into her office.

I looked at Ainsley's card for a moment and then stuck it in my wallet. If the sight of Roger Iverson suggested that these four creeps were out walking the streets, keeping the DA's number handy might be a good thing to do.

2

Tom Sanderson's acting workshop was located on Ventura Boulevard in Studio City. Looking for the address caused me to miss it on my first pass. Fortunately, the car's clock indicated it was only ten after seven. A swing around the block got me on track, and after finding a parking space on a side street, I texted Tom that I was in the vicinity. He'd told me his studio was on the second floor of the building. Street-level spaces were occupied by a deli and, of course, a Starbucks. Not sure how to get up there, I stood under an awning and waited for him to come down. A couple of minutes passed, and he pushed open a glass door next to the Starbucks front door and stuck his head out.

"Hey, Eddie, good to see you, man."

We shook hands and he ushered me inside and we started up a flight of stairs, the treads covered with well-worn carpeting. I could smell a faint trace of brewing coffee.

"Who came first? You, Starbucks or the deli?"

"I've been leasing my space for eight years. Starbucks was here already, and the deli came later. Word is there was a strip joint there some years back. Matter of fact, rumor has it a couple of the ladies used to hang out in the deli."

"Maybe they were homesick."

He chuckled and said, "Yeah, I never thought of that." We came to the top of the stairs where a hallway stretched out before us. "We're at the end down there. A few of the kids are already here."

"How many students do you have?"

"It goes up and down. Right now there are an even dozen. That's all I can handle."

"So, you meet what…once a week?"

"Yeah. I have to meet in the evening. That way, auditions don't interfere."

"And are there many of those?"

"Believe it or not, they crop up fairly often. One of the girls landed a pilot last year. Unfortunately, it didn't go anywhere."

"Been there, done that," I said.

"You and me both, brother." We passed a door on our right. "A photography studio in there. The guy gives my students a break on their headshots. He's got them plastered all over his walls."

At the end of the hall we came to a door with "Sanderson Studio" stenciled on the frosted glass.

"I'm impressed," I said. "Your own name on the door."

"Gimme a break. Don't tell me the private eye doesn't have his name on his office door."

"Yeah, but smaller letters than yours," I said.

He opened the door to reveal a small room with a half dozen canvas director's chairs scattered around the sides, giving the space the appearance of a lobby. Two black drapes constituted one wall. A gap in them indicated a corridor leading into the studio. Tom gestured for me to follow, and we entered a fairly large room with a four-inch platform covering most of the floor. Small spotlights illuminated the space. On either side of us were two levels of risers facing the platform, which I assumed was the performing space. Theater seats ran the length of the risers, which were separated by the aisle leading to the would-be stage. Two more director's chairs sat in the center of the platform, with a small table between them, on which sat two bottles of water.

Two girls and a guy sat in the seats. All three of them looked to be in their twenties, the latest entries in the quest for the Hollywood brass ring. Tom introduced them as Tony Carson, Nicole Patterson, and Beverly

Adams. We chatted for a couple of minutes and then Tom and I each grabbed a director's chair. He said he'd give me an introduction and the class would consist of a Q&A session.

"Heard anything about that film we did last fall?" he said.

"Nada. One has to wonder if the money they came up with is enough to get the thing on its feet." Financing for the *Terms of Power* project had disappeared, but the producers found a different source of backing, and we'd been able to finish it. "It wouldn't surprise me if it went straight to video."

"With a bullet," Tom added. "Or streaming. Christ, it seems like everything nowadays is winding up on Netflix or Amazon Prime."

"Thank God for residuals," I said. "You had any work since we wrapped?"

"Nah. I can't get arrested," he said. "You?"

"I'm waiting to hear about an audition. A film called *Burnt Hills*. Some kind of Western, I guess."

"Really? I thought oaters were a thing of the past."

"You and me both," I replied.

"Well, good for you. Land that sucker." Two more students entered the room and Tom exchanged greetings with them, then turned back to me. "Hey, what about that case you were working on? What happened?"

I took a pull from a bottle of water and filled him in on what had gone down with the events up in Piru.

"Christ, Eddie, sounds like you came close to buying the farm."

"Believe me, it was touch and go there for a while. It still fucks with my head."

"You got anyone to give you some help?"

"Yeah, I see a guy once a week. He put me on Zoloft. It seems to help."

"That's good. In the meantime, I hope they throw the book at those assholes and then throw away the key while they're at it."

I agreed and we watched the studio space fill up with young hopefuls. And almost all of them were young, save for a couple of women who looked like they might have signed up for the class on a dare, or maybe were empty nesters who needed something to identify themselves other than housewife.

All the chairs being full, Tom got their attention. "Evening, people. Last time I told you we were going to have a conversation with a bona-fide working actor. This gentleman fits the bill. Say hello to Eddie Collins." Some hand waves and a few hellos welcomed me. "And I might also add that in his spare time he's also a licensed private eye. Eddie and I worked together on a picture last fall called *Terms of Power*."

"Hopefully coming to a theater near you," I said.

"Your lips to God's ears," Tom said. "So, let me get things rolling. How long have you been in Hollywood?"

"I got here in nineteen ninety-one, after two years in the Army."

"And how did the private eye come to be?"

"Well, I was a military policeman. Early on when I got here, I worked as an armed security guard for a gated community out in Bel Air. That background met some of the qualifications for me to get my license."

Tom then turned the questioning over to the students, and for the next half hour or so I told them about some of the projects I'd worked on; gave them advice on how to get an agent and/or a manager; whether or not I thought both of them were necessary. I said I'd never had a manager, but that didn't mean they weren't helpful; however, I also told them that a manager is going to want another slice of their paycheck.

A young woman raised her hand and said, "Hi, Mr. Collins. My name's Emily Garrison. I've got a question."

"Hi Emily," I said. "I hope I have an answer."

"We hear a lot about an actor's 'process.' What's yours, or do you even have one?"

"I try to remember Spencer Tracy's advice. Learn your lines, tell the truth and don't bump into the furniture." The comment got a good laugh, and several heads nodded in agreement. I reached into my shirt pocket and pulled out one of the pages I'd printed earlier, then continued. "But seriously. I think part of my process is to not let the business dominate my life. You have to strive to be a well-rounded person." I unfolded the sheet of paper. "Anybody here ever heard of Stark Young?" Blank looks from everyone. I turned to Tom. "You know who he is?"

"I've heard the name. Critic, wasn't he?"

"That's right. He was also a playwright and a teacher who died in nineteen sixty-three. A director I once worked with gave me this quote. I don't know where it comes from, but I think it makes a lot of sense when talking about 'process.' Here's what Stark Young said." I started reading from the page in front of me. *"The actor's business is to remain himself forever, but to cause to grow in himself such flexibility and fluidity and eloquent magnetism of body, and such sympathy of the imagination, as may be translated into compelling presentations of human character and living. Only through this translation of the given character into himself can an actor profess to be an artist at all and lord of another's soul."*

I laid the piece of paper on the table next to me. "So, what the hell's he talking about?"

Tony Carson, the young man Tom had introduced earlier, raised his hand and said, "Don't give up your day job."

His answer got a round of laughs and I said, "Well, that's good advice, Tony, but I think Mr. Young had something a little more serious in mind." I again referred to the piece of paper in front of me. "Listen to what else he had to say. *Actors remain artists, therefore, in proportion to the extent to which they remain themselves and translate into the terms of themselves the thing to be created. They are firmly fixed at centre. They remain themselves even though it may not be their immediate selves. The greatness of a man's acting will depend on the extent to which the elements of life may be gathered up in him for the spring towards luminous revelation, towards more abundant life."*

I laid the piece of paper on the table next to me. "Anybody have an idea what he means?"

After a few moments of silence, a young Black man raised his hand. "Lamar Paxton, Mr. Collins."

"Go ahead, Lamar."

"He seems to be saying that you've got to marry the life you lead with the material you're presented with."

"Exactly." I referred again to the Young passage. *"They remain themselves even though it may not be their immediate selves.* I don't think you're going to be a good actor if you're buried in your cell phone all the time and react to other people only through Facebook, Twitter, Instagram, TikTok, and Snapchat. Did I miss any? Turn off your cellphones and observe the life around you. Become a people watcher. Spend an afternoon at Venice Beach and I'll guarantee you'll find a wealth of character traits you can use in your work."

Tony Carson again raised his hand and said, "Isn't that sort of what the Method is all about?"

"Partially, I think. The problem I have with the Method is that you're taught to immerse yourself in your character to the exclusion of everything else around you. I'm not a big fan of taking your character home with you and being that person twenty-four seven. Tony, are you married."

"Yes."

"What if you're playing a serial killer and you take the character home with you? You think your wife wants to go to bed with a serial killer?"

"Sometimes she doesn't want to go to bed with me now," he said, which drew a chorus of laughs, mine included. "I get what you're saying, but the Method seems like it worked for Brando."

"Yeah, until he started mumbling and pissing away his career. Now, I know in some quarters that statement will be considered heresy. Anyone here seen *The Missouri Breaks*? A film he did with Jack Nicholson?" One hand went up. "There's a scene where Brando comes riding up dressed as a pioneer woman. Now, if anyone can explain to me how that choice syncs with the screenplay, I'll buy you dinner at Musso and Frank's."

I got a few more chuckles, this time even from Tom, who chimed in with "And I'll spring for dessert."

"Look," I said. "I'm not knocking Brando and the rest of the Actor's Studio crowd. Whatever works. They've obviously influenced a great number of actors. All I'm saying is don't get hung up on technique. As Lamar just said, use what's inside you and create a symbiotic relationship between you and what the writer has given you. If that demands you dress up as a pioneer woman, well then, go for it."

A slender Hispanic man raised his hand.

"Yes, sir?" I said.

"Armando Ruiz, Mr. Collins."

"Shoot, Armando."

"Whose work do you think best illustrates what you're talking about?"

I thought for a moment and took a sip of water. "Okay, let's look at Dustin Hoffman. Armando, what film put him on the map?"

He thought a minute and said, "I suppose *The Graduate*."

"Right. That was in nineteen sixty-seven. And two years later he did what?"

Nicole Patterson raised her hand and said, "*Midnight Cowboy*."

"Exactly. From Benjamin Braddock to Ratso Rizzo is quite a quantum leap. I've never sat down with Hoffman, but it's obvious he soaked up a lot of what he saw and heard from his struggling years in New York. And then later on he did *Tootsie*. Extraordinary."

Beverly Adams raised her hand and said, "And who on the actress side of the business?"

"Easy," I replied. "Look at Meryl Streep. I may be going out on a limb here, but for my money, she's the best actress Hollywood has ever produced. Look at her movies. I've never seen her do anything that's dishonest, where she looks like she's phoning it in. That woman she played in *Sophie's Choice*, for example. Somehow, she found within herself what it took to make a choice about which one of her children she would sacrifice. She couldn't find that on Facebook or Twitter."

Several heads nodded in agreement and then a young woman in the front row raised her hand. "Mister Collins, my name's Wendy Jackson."

"How you doin', Wendy? What's on your mind?"

"I'd like to know your advice in dealing with the rejection."

"Embrace it," I said. "But don't obsess over it. I had a roommate at one time who kept bugging me about every audition I went on. How did it go? On and on. I finally had to tell him that I'd left it at the door. Do the best you can when you audition, but then go home and get on with your life. I'm waiting right now to hear about an audition I had last month. If I get it, that's great, but if I don't, my life goes on."

"But you've got your PI business to fall back on," another young man said.

"Fair point. And each one of you has to have something to fall back on. Any waiters or waitresses in here? Uber drivers? Bartenders?" Several hands went up. "You have to be the best waitress or Uber driver you can be, while at the same time using all those experiences and bringing them to your acting. As you guys well know, this is a tough town. I've always had the belief that you've got to treat rejection as not being personal. Unless, of course, you throw something at the director when you're auditioning. And believe me, there's been times when I've wanted to do just that. But you can't let the business be the only reason you get out of bed every day. You've got to have a life. If you've got a partner, or children, you've got to be present in their lives as well as your own."

One of the potential empty nesters raised her hand. "Janet Tomlinson, Mr. Collins. I've been lucky enough to get an agent, and she keeps telling me to get involved in theater. Do you agree?"

"First of all, Janet, you getting an agent was due to more than just luck. You brought something to the table. So, congratulations. That's an important first step. Now, no disrespect to my buddy Tom here, and what he's teaching you, but I think one of the best avenues to hone your acting chops is to get onstage and do plays, scenes, workshops. Granted, there's little or no money involved, but you just might get seen by somebody who's got some clout. Believe it or not, it does happen. I've done a couple of plays in these small theaters all over town. I didn't make a dime doing it, but I wouldn't have traded the experience for anything."

I pulled the second printout from my shirt pocket. "Let me share another little gem I picked up somewhere. I think I got this off the Internet somewhere, so it must be true, right?" A few chuckles drifted up to me. "You all know who Arthur Miller is, right? Other than being one of Marilyn Monroe's husbands?"

A brief silence, then a young man said, "He wrote *Death of a Salesman*."

"Bingo. Here's what he said," and I started reading. "*There is a certain immortality involved in theater, not created by monuments and books, but through the knowledge the actor keeps to his dying day that on a certain afternoon, in an empty and dusty theater, he cast a shadow of a being that was not himself but the distillation of all he had ever observed; all the unsingable heartsong the ordinary man may feel but never utter, he gave voice to. And by that he somehow joins the ages.*"

I folded the paper and put it back in my pocket. "Believe me, you'll know when that happens, and it'll knock your socks off. It's happened to me a couple of times." I turned to Tom. "And I bet it's happened to you too, right?"

"Once," he said, "and it scared the crap out of me." His remark provoked laughs from his students.

"It's a wonderful moment," I said. "That moment when you know you're hitting on all cylinders. When you've touched an audience, made a difference in their lives. When you've reached immortality, as Miller said. And you'll find it. Each and every one of you. I'm convinced of it. So go out there and 'join the ages.' But don't mumble."

Another laugh and a hand shot up. "Where can we find those quotes?"

"Tell you what," I said. "They're on my computer. I'll email them to Tom and he can make copies for you."

"Anything else?" Tom said. No hands were raised. "Okay, that's a good note to end on. Let's give it up for Eddie Collins."

The class burst into applause. I raised my hand in thanks and took another swallow of water.

Tom and I stood up and he shook my hand. "Good stuff, Eddie."

"I'll shoot those links to you in the morning."

"Great. These guys should hang on to those words."

A few students lingered to thank me. Lamar Paxton walked up and stuck out his hand. "Thank you, sir," he said. "I saw you in a show a couple of years ago. I forget the name, but you played a disgruntled teacher, I think."

"Oh, yeah, *Class in Session*," I said.

"That's it. That was nice work, man."

"Thanks, Lamar. I had a nice arc there. Thought it would go longer, but they wrote the character out. Writers. What the hell do they know, right?"

"Comes with the territory," he said.

I pointed a finger at him. "As Linda says over the grave of Willy Loman. You know the play, huh?"

"I played Biff in a workshop project awhile back."

"Terrific," I said. "How's things going for you, Lamar?"

"Oh, you know, up one day, down the next."

"I hear you, man. But just hang in there."

Lamar said he would, shook my hand, and walked off. Tom finished his conversation with a couple of his students, then turned to me as the class filtered out.

"Ready for a cold one?" he said.

"Lead on, Macduff," I said, as he started toward the studio's front door.

He stopped and turned around. "I should make you turn around three times, but I've never believed in those damn superstitions with the Scottish Play. Have you?"

"Well..." I said, leaving the thought hanging in the air.

"What?"

"I was in a production once where Macduff's broadsword broke and fell in the lap of a lady in the front row."

"Oh, crap," Tom said. He shut off the lights; we went out into the hall, and after he locked the door, he looked at me for a moment. We simultaneously turned around three times and then burst into laughter as we headed for the stairs down to Ventura Boulevard.

Despite our adherence to superstition and without getting overly pedantic, I almost felt like I was leaving a temple, some sort of shrine. I hadn't felt like that in some time.

3

Eclectic best describes my neighbors at Collins Investigations. Peggy Stafford is the mother hen of the Elite Talent Agency, whose clientele makes me wish the birthdate on my driver's license could miraculously be changed to indicate a younger age. And then there's Lenny Daye, the editor and publisher of *Pecs 'n Abs*, a magazine devoted to the appreciation of those body parts of the male persuasion. Leonid Travnikov, a Russian medical doctor, completes the roster of neighbors.

Fresh from a breakfast of Moons Over My Hammy at my favorite Denny's, I encountered said doctor waiting for the elevator in my building. As usual, he wore a black overcoat, complemented by a black fedora on his head. He was gaunt of face, deep furrows on either side of a prominent nose. I've never had extensive conversations with the good doctor, so I don't know how long he's been in this country. My guess is he left Russia after the fall of the USSR. The elevator door opened and he held it for me when he saw me approach. After it closed, he pushed the appropriate button, and with a shudder, we began our ascent.

"Good morning, Mr. Collins."

"Morning, Doctor."

After a moment or two he continued. "Life insurance. You have?"

"I do. Why do you ask?"

"Every time I am in this elevator, I am glad for life insurance."

"Me too," I said. The car groaned past the second floor and I said, "Nice rain we had yesterday."

"Very nice. Good for the sinuses. Hot, dry, not good for sinuses."

We continued upward. I thought I'd get more free medical advice, but none was forthcoming. The car jerked to a stop on our floor, and we exited and headed for our respective offices.

"Have a good day, Doctor," I said.

"You the same," he replied. "Remember. Eat your vegetables."

I nodded and pushed open the door to see Mavis at her computer, brow furrowed in concentration.

"Morning, Eddie."

"Morning. You look like your dog died."

"Fritz and I don't have a dog."

"Maybe you should get one."

She looked up at me. "Why?"

"You could put pictures of the dog on your screen and you wouldn't have to frown."

"Was I frowning?"

"Big time. What's the matter?"

"This yahoo out in Rancho Cucamonga hasn't paid me for an order I sent him."

Mavis supplements her second-in-command status at Collins Investigations by buying and selling gewgaws, collectibles, and other forms of doodads on the internet, an enterprise that sometimes results in furrowed brows for her and muted grins of amusement for me. "What did you send him?"

"Bobbleheads."

"Of whom?"

"Elvis, Jimi Hendrix, and Janis Joplin. He's got some sort of dead rock and rollers thing going."

Shaking my head, I said, "Where do you find this stuff?"

"Commerce, Eddie, commerce." She rose from her desk, grabbed her coffee cup and went into her off-limits-to-me alcove for a refill. "Who were you talking to out in the hall?"

"The good doctor next door. He told me to eat my vegetables."

"Smart advice," she said, as she came back to her desk with a fresh cup of coffee. "What did you have for breakfast?"

"Ham, eggs, and hash browns." She set the coffee down and turned to me, eyebrows arched, a smirk on her face. "Don't give me that look," I said. "Last time I checked potatoes were a vegetable."

"If you say so. How did the class go last night?"

"Terrific. I wowed them."

"As I knew you would, boss man."

I entered my office, hung my porkpie on its peg and sat behind my desk. When my laptop booted up, I found the Stark Young and Arthur Miller quotes and emailed them to Tom Sanderson, along with thanks for a good evening in front of his students. Just as I was about to paw through the beaded curtain leading to my apartment, the phone rang. "I'll get it," I said.

"Collins Investigations."

"Good morning, *bubbeleh*, this is your agent."

"I gather that, Morrie. You've probably got that term next to my name in your Rolodex."

"You're correct. Under 'b.'" He laughed, then, as usual, coughed, while I moved the receiver away from my ear. "Good news. You're booked on that picture...what the hell's the name? *Burnt* something?

"*Burnt Hills*, Morrie."

"That's it. *Oy vey.* Somewhere on this desk of mine is the booking memo." Sounds of more coughing and rustling of paper. "Ah, here it is. Right in front of me, for crissakes." One final cough. "Three weeks. Maybe more. Above scale. They wanna see you in wardrobe tomorrow. You can do?"

"I can do."

"Fabulous. Here's where you're going."

I grabbed a pen and jotted down the address and more details of the booking. Then Morrie hung up and I framed myself in the doorway to Mavis's office. "Good news. I booked a job."

"Great. From that audition tape Carla and I helped you with?"

"That's the one. Your camera work sealed the deal."

"Does that mean we get a percentage?"

"I'll take it under advisement. After Morrie takes his ten percent."

She uttered a derisive snort, and I went through the beaded curtain to answer the call of nature. That done, I sent a text to Carla informing her of the booking and thanking her for her help. No sooner had I finished with that than the phone again rang.

This time Mavis picked up and called out, "Eddie, it's a Phil Ainsley."

I picked up the phone and said, "Good morning, Mr. Ainsley. Thanks for returning my call."

"No problem, Mr. Collins. Sorry it took me so long. I was in court all day yesterday. What can I do for you?"

"Well, I'm just a little curious about those four individuals you indicted last fall. Relating to that incident up in Piru?"

"Yes, of course. What do you need to know?"

"I saw one of them, Roger Iverson, yesterday, and got to wondering if he's out on bail."

"Pulling up the case right now. Give me a minute." I heard keys clicking and then he said, "Iverson was granted bail, which he couldn't meet initially. He then agreed to cooperate with the DA's office. The judge subsequently reduced bail and made him wear an electronic bracelet."

"How about the other three? Thompson, Benedetti, and Forbes?"

More clicks on a keyboard. "In all three cases, real estate was offered as bail. Forbes also agreed to cooperate, and his bail was reduced."

"So, they're all out on bail?"

"That's correct."

"Are they also wearing electronic bracelets?"

"Yes, to the best of my knowledge."

I was silent for a moment and Ainsley said, "Let me broach this with you, Mr. Collins. Are you by any chance harboring thoughts of them retaliating against you?"

"To be honest, yes."

"Given what they put you gentlemen through, I can understand your concern, but let me assure you, that, first of all, any action against you would be incredibly stupid. They're under constant monitoring. If they in any way violate terms of their bail, those electronic bracelets will be removed immediately, and they'll find themselves waking up to iron bars."

"That's good to know."

"If you feel threatened at all, a call to Ventura County Sheriff's will have a deputy knocking on their door."

"Do you know when they're scheduled to go on trial?"

"Let me check." More clicks. "Their lawyers are throwing a lot of pre-trial motions at us, so I don't have a definite date for you yet."

"I see. Well, thanks."

"But we can still count on your testimony, Mr. Collins, and that of Mr. Benson's?"

"Absolutely. We'll be there."

"Outstanding. I'll keep you posted. Anything else I can do for you, please feel free to reach out."

I told him I would, and we ended the call. I leaned back in my chair and stared at the opposite wall, tapping my pen on the desktop. I knew that seeing Roger Iverson yesterday was pure coincidence, but his appearance nevertheless nagged at me. Would he, or any of the other three have the *cojones* to seek retribution against me and Reggie? I doubted it, but considering how blatant they had been in their obscene undertakings, it wasn't out of the realm of possibility.

4

My wardrobe call for *Burnt Hills* the next morning was located at what looked to be some sort of former warehouse out in Reseda. The fact that the call wasn't on one of the studio lots stirred the flutter of a red flag in me, but then I reasoned that these days all kinds of independent movies rent space wherever they can find it. Last fall's experience with *Terms of Power*, the film both Tom Sanderson and I had worked on, was another example of how sometimes an actor can get caught up in a fly-by-night enterprise that doesn't end well. Fortunately, that wasn't the case. After the initial funding for the film disappeared into thin air, the producers were able to find alternative financing and we completed the picture. Also, our SAG-AFTRA union guarantees that if a production does indeed go belly-up, the actor will be paid the salary negotiated on the contract.

So, with those thoughts in my head, I pushed aside my paranoia and pulled up next to a security person sitting under an umbrella in a gap of chain-link fencing surrounding the building. He looked up from a paperback book as I pulled in. He wore an ill-fitting uniform, a look of boredom and carried a clipboard in his hand as he walked up to my window. "Help you?"

"Eddie Collins. I'm here for a wardrobe fitting."

He ran a pencil down the clipboard. "Right." He pointed to the left side of the building. "Take any empty space you find. Better lock your doors."

I thanked him and drove off as he returned to his chair and paperback. About two dozen vehicles sat on a paved slab that had seen better days. Concrete cracks and weeds covered the surface. After parking next to a

Ford 150 pickup, I locked my car and started for the front of the building, which I figured was seventy-five yards long and maybe half that in width. Windows spaced ten feet or so from each other ran the length of the building. Air conditioning units protruded from most of them.

Nailed to the wall next to the front door was a cardboard sign that said, "Windward Productions. Come on in." And so I did. The door opened to a small room with chairs shoved up against three walls to my left. Through a wide central portal I could see large tables with wardrobe crew hunched over them, and others bent over sewing machines. From the far end of the building and behind another wall I heard the sound of power tools, a sign that set construction was underway.

Occupying one of the chairs was an elderly lady, gray hair tied up in a bun, small earrings dangling from lobes on either side of a face that still held traces of a very attractive woman. She wore an insulated leather vest over a red blouse. A denim skirt completed her ensemble. She glanced up from her phone and smiled. To my right sat a small desk, flanked by a four-drawer, gunmetal-gray file cabinet. On the desk were strewn piles of paper and three inboxes stacked on top of each other. A phone occupied one corner and in a chair behind the desk sat a young red-haired woman, fingers with crimson nail polish clicking away at keys on a laptop. She looked up as I stepped in front of her.

"Hi there," she said. "Here for a fitting?"

"I am. Eddie Collins."

She consulted a clipboard and said, "Gotcha. Have a seat. Mitzi will be with you in just a bit."

I sank down into a chair four away from the elderly lady. She shut off her phone and dropped it into a huge tote bag draped over one shoulder, then crossed her legs, revealing Birkenstocks on her feet.

"Here for *Burnt Hills*?" she said. I nodded. She stood and moved to a chair next to me. I couldn't help but wonder what the hell was wrong with the other chairs, but didn't think it wise to get up and move. "What role?"

"A bartender. Can't remember the guy's name, come to think of it."

She picked at a piece of lint on her calf-length skirt. "Have you read the script?"

"Not yet. They were supposed to messenger a copy to my office this morning, but it hadn't arrived by the time I left."

"Office? You have another job?"

"Yeah," I said, as I turned to look at her, again wondering why she had to be so inquisitive. "I'm a private investigator."

"No kidding. A gumshoe?" Again I nodded and she stuck out one hand. "I'm Lois Maxwell."

"Eddie Collins," I said, as I shook a hand with a firm grip.

"I was married to a gumshoe once. On screen, that is. Years ago at Metro. A real potboiler. *Some Things Never End* was the name of it. Sort of described the job, too," she said, and punctuated her statement with a hearty laugh.

"I think I've probably seen you in some things," I said. "You've been around a while, haven't you?"

"That's putting it mildly, honey. I was kicking up my heels before there was such a thing as residuals." She rooted around in her tote bag, came up with some lip balm, squeezed a dollop on one finger and applied it to her lips. "That's why I keep doing stuff like this. Gotta pay the mortgage, you know."

"So I take it you don't think much of the script?"

"Aw, it's okay. It ain't John Ford caliber, but it might be fun."

"Who are you playing?"

"Dolly Blaine. She runs a hotel. It's really a whorehouse, but she doesn't tell anybody that." She laughed and said, "She refers to it as a finishing school, especially when the sheriff comes around."

We shared a laugh as a young woman appeared in the portal and said, "Lois, we're ready for you."

She tapped me on the shoulder and said, "Good to meet you, Eddie."

"Same here, Lois," I said.

"I look forward to working with you. My goodness, a real live gumshoe, no less. Makes my heart go pitty-pat." She stood, fanned her face in ultra-dramatic fashion, and with another laugh sauntered off into the wardrobe room.

I grinned and decided she would be a fun colleague to work with on this project, even if it didn't pass muster with the late, great John Ford. Just for kicks, I pulled out my phone, opened the IMDB website and found "Lois Maxwell." A quick glance through her list of credits revealed that she had indeed been around a while, going all the way back into the late fifties. Before I could peruse the list any further, a young Black woman walked through the portal.

"Eddie?"

"That's me," I said.

"Come on back." I walked toward her and she stuck out a hand. "I'm Mitzi."

"How you doin', Mitzi?" I said, as I shook her hand.

"Good." She led me into the wardrobe room, which I saw had windows on the other side of the building. Whoever had toiled in this space, if indeed it was a former warehouse, at least had the pleasure of windows and sunshine. Mitzi led me past a long table that had patterns laid out on it. Racks of clothes lined the walls of the room, hats and bonnets on shelves above them. Lois was in a far corner, trying on one such head piece. "You're playing Chet Cassidy, the bartender, right?"

"I'll take your word for it. Damned if I haven't forgotten the guy's name since I sent them the audition tape. They haven't gotten a script to me yet."

"Chet Cassidy is what my list says."

"Then Chet Cassidy it is."

She smiled and ushered me into an opposite corner from where Lois was being attended to. We were up against the rear wall of the room and from the other side I heard the buzz of a saw.

"Those power tools bother you after a while?" I asked.

"Sometimes," Mitzi said. "The secret is to have ear buds with the loudest music you can tolerate. We don't have any control over it. Fortunately, the sawdust doesn't get through that wall." She pawed through some costume pieces on a clothes rack and pulled out a pair of black trousers, a white shirt, and a black vest. "Try these on. I hope you gave us the right sizes."

"Oh, yeah. I learned a long time ago not to get off on the wrong foot with wardrobe."

"Good man," she said. "You'd be amazed how many people, guys mainly, come in and not a damn thing fits. Vanity running rampant." She handed me the costume pieces and pointed to drapes hanging from a metal bar running between two light stands. She pulled one of them aside, then handed me a pair of western boots and ushered me into the makeshift dressing room.

I took off my coat and porkpie, hung them on a coat rack, then got down to my skivvies and put on Chet Cassidy's costume. Everything fit perfectly. The boots gave me a little trouble, until I decided not to make a fool of myself and sat on a chair to pull them on. Dressed, I pulled back one of the drapes and stepped out to where Mitzi was waiting.

"Hey, pardner, you look pretty good," she said. She had a pair of black arm garters in her hand. "Pull these up the sleeves." Then she handed me a string tie and helped me fix it around my neck. When I was in full regalia, she stepped back, looked me over, and pulled out her cell phone and snapped a couple of pictures.

"You don't use Polaroids anymore?" I said.

"It's a brave new world. I email these to the costume designer and she weighs in after looking at them. Cheaper than buying Polaroid film, I guess."

"If you can even find it anymore."

"That's true." She took the garters off my shirtsleeves and the string tie from around my neck. "This is your first look. We'll have you in later for a couple of other fittings. You'll need a hat and a different getup for some exterior scenes you're in."

"Great. So I'm good to go?"

"Good to go. Thanks for coming in."

I disappeared behind the drapes, got dressed and handed Mitzi the costume pieces. She put them back on hangers as I started walking back to the front door. Lois was nowhere to be seen. The receptionist checked me out and I went through the front door. The sun peeked through a cloud bank and I squinted into it, trying to look like a Chet Cassidy. I don't think I matched Clint Eastwood's signature squint, but I'd give myself an "A" for effort.

When I rounded the corner of the building and headed for my car, I saw Lois Maxwell standing next to a Volkswagen a few spaces beyond mine. She was engaged in conversation with a young man, and it didn't appear to be pleasant. Both their voices were raised in anger, and as I got nearer, the man shoved her against her car. He was probably a foot taller than her, wore a denim jacket and a baseball cap. His face sprouted a mustache and goatee.

"Everything okay, Lois?" I called out.

Both of them stopped and turned to me.

"I'm fine, Mr. Collins. No problem."

"You sure?"

"Yeah, nothing to worry about. See you at the table read."

I had an urge to walk over to them, but decided it wasn't any of my business, so I unlocked my car and backed out. As I headed for the entrance to the lot, I looked in the rearview mirror and saw that the conversation had continued, and it still looked pretty heated.

Apparently the jaunty side of Lois Maxwell I'd met inside had another aspect.

5

I'd no sooner merged onto the Ventura Freeway, headed east back to Hollywood, when my stomach started growling. For a moment I thought about pulling off and grabbing a bite, but I was hoping that the screenplay of *Burnt Hills* had been delivered. I needed to read it and find out who this Chet Cassidy character was. At the Van Nuys exit, the growling became part of the soundtrack of *Jurassic Park*, especially annoying, since the noise was interfering with Tom T. Hall's *"Old Dogs and Children and Watermelon Wine"* coming from the disc player.

With stomach growls and Tom T. for company, the Cahuenga Pass was clear sailing. I nudged my car into my assigned parking space and stood waiting for the elevator. It pinged and the door sidled open to reveal a mane of blond hair and Peggy Stafford, the den mother of the Elite Talent Agency.

"Eddie, just the person I wanted to see."

"What did I do now?"

"Have you ever had a conversation with our landlord about that God-awful carpet in our hallway?"

"Not lately. I think he's ignoring it, or else he's left the country. What's the matter?"

"Yesterday one of my girls came into the office sick to her stomach after being confronted with that Jackson Pollock-wannabe."

"You sure it was the carpet, and not something she ate?"

"She's a vegan, Eddie. I don't think so."

"What do you want me to do about it, Peggy?"

"Oh, hell, I don't know. Maybe start a petition or something." She threw up her hands and stomped off, her high heels clicking on the parquet floor. "I'm late for lunch. See you later. Think about it."

I did. For about ten seconds, until the door started to close. On the ride up, I thought maybe her client should get some good animal protein into her. The carpet would soon become benign. It worked for me.

Our Jackson Pollock-wannabe didn't surprise me, but what did was Charlie Rivers sitting in a chair in front of Mavis's desk. Charlie is my steadfast link with the LAPD, having cut some red tape for me from time to time. I hadn't seen him in a while; his presence in my office was rare.

"What's going on here?" I said. "Am I under arrest?"

"Not unless you've done something wrong," he said.

"Then what brings you through my portal, Lieutenant?"

"I've got something to share with you, which is going to result in you buying me lunch."

"You got it. How you doin'?" I said, as I stuck out my hand. "Long time no see."

"It has been," he replied, and shook my hand. "Mavis tells me you're still trying to be an actor."

"Yeah, just got booked on a picture."

Mavis held up a large envelope. "And your screenplay has arrived, sir."

She handed it to me and I opened it. "How about this, Charlie? A Western."

"And who might you be?" he said.

"Chet Cassidy. A bartender."

"Well, you know the territory." He chuckled and added, "I've seen you in action."

"If you're going to bust my chops, you can buy your own lunch," I said, as I walked into my office and tossed the script on my desk. When I came back, Charlie had gotten to his feet and was checking his phone.

"Norm's?" I said.

"You read my mind." He stretched his hand across Mavis's desk and she took it in one of hers. "Good to see you, Mavis. Glad to see you're keeping him on the straight and narrow."

"Believe me, it's a challenge," she said.

I shook my head, Charlie slapped me on the back, and we were out the door and onto Jackson Pollock territory.

Norm's is a Los Angeles landmark on La Cienega Boulevard, a little north of the Beverly Center. Charlie and I had frequented the place many times. I waited by the front door while he parked his car. The place wasn't very busy, and a waitress led us to a booth in one corner.

We stuffed ourselves in and she laid menus in front of us, then asked if we'd like something to drink. We both ordered iced tea, and she walked off as we opened our menus.

"So how's things with LA's finest, Charlie?"

"About the same. I find myself getting to be a short-timer, so my feet don't get as wet as they used to."

"What do you mean?"

"That's what I wanted to share with you. I'm turning in my shield in eight months."

I folded my menu and looked at him, surprised. "You're retiring?"

"Yup. Twenty years. That's enough."

"Wow," I said, which is about all I could think of saying. "What the hell are you going to do then?"

"Maybe I'll work for you. Since you're all of a sudden this hot-shot actor, you're probably going to need a sidekick shamus."

"Not a bad thought. You work cheap?"

"I'm negotiable," he said, with a chuckle. A waitress arrived with two iced teas. Her name tag said she was Fran. She was all business, welcomed us with a broad smile and asked if we were ready to order. We were, and did so: a corned beef sandwich with slaw for Charlie, a BLT and fries for me. He tore open two sweetener packets and poured them into his glass.

"Charlie Rivers retiring. I can't believe it. The man, the cop, the legend."

"Yeah, right," he said. "After twenty years the legend dies, Eddie. I'm just going to be another ex-flatfoot living on a pension."

"But you're my 'in,' Charlie. Who the hell's going to cut through the red tape for me?"

"You're gonna have to find somebody else. I can introduce you to a couple of guys. In a moment of weakness, they've both told me they admired you private guys. Where the hell they came up with that feeling beats the hell out of me." He grinned, then picked up a long spoon and stirred the sweetener in his glass. "I haven't seen you in a while. In addition to my news, I wanted to talk to you about that case you were working on last fall. How'd that shake out?"

I gave him a recap on the incident up at Piru and the four creeps Ventura County indicted.

"Come to think of it, I did hear about those indictments," he said. "Pretty serious stuff. Sounds like you stumbled onto a real shit-show."

"That's putting it mildly." I sat back as Fran appeared with plates full of our sandwiches.

"Here ya go, fellas. Can I get you anything else?" We both shook our heads. "Enjoy," she said, and walked off.

"Matter of fact, I saw one of those creeps the day before yesterday," I said. "Across from my building."

He lifted up two pieces of bread and squirted mustard on the corned beef. "So they're out on bail?"

"And wearing ankle bracelets." I filled one corner of my plate with ketchup and dipped a fry into it. "Let me ask you something. You ever run across a situation where somebody you brought to trial tried to get revenge against you?"

"Nope. One time a guy hurled insults at me when I was on the witness stand. But they hauled his ass out of the courtroom. He wound up doing a dime up at Folsom." He dabbed at the corner of his mouth with a napkin. "Why? You think one of these guys is gonna come after you?"

"To be honest, the thought has crossed my mind."

"From what I gather they had some pretty stiff indictments thrown at them. Seems like that'd be a dumb-ass move."

"That's what I'm thinking."

"However," he said, then put a forkful of slaw in his mouth.

"However what?"

"If they are stupid, as it appears they are, nothing prevents them from hiring someone else to do it."

I bit off a corner of the BLT and chewed while looking at him, then said, "Are you suggesting I keep watching my back?"

"I'm not suggesting anything. All I'm saying is if something happens to the DA's prime witness, a big hole opens up in their case. Where do they live?"

"Thompson's in Hollywood. The other three are out in the Valley."

"Did you talk to the DA?"

"Yeah. He told me to call Ventura Sheriff's if I feel the need. They'd revoke bail and haul their asses in."

Charlie swallowed some sandwich and sipped his iced tea. "Then I don't think you've got too much to worry about."

"You're probably right. Paranoia, I guess."

Fran appeared with more iced tea. "Got some fresh cherry pie over there, guys," she said, as she filled our glasses.

"None for me," Charlie said. I echoed his words and she walked off.

I shoved my plate to the edge of the table and said, "You looking forward to retirement?"

"I don't know exactly. But I'll tell you one thing. I'm sure as hell going to enjoy getting out from under the bureaucratic bullshit. It's getting harder and harder to be a good cop." Fran reappeared and left the check, then whisked away our plates. "Maybe I should become an actor," he continued. "Think there's room for a handsome guy like me?"

"No offense, but I don't think Clooney and Pitt have anything to worry about."

"Naw, forget about those pretty boys. I'm thinking more along the lines of De Niro and Pacino." I laughed, and after a feigned look of hurt washed over his face, he joined in with the laugh.

"Seriously, though," I said. "You could always make yourself available as a technical advisor."

"Hmmm," he muttered. "Not a bad idea."

We sat and gabbed for a few minutes: Lakers, Dodgers, and other pressing issues. He looked at his watch and said he'd better get back to his desk. I slipped twenty percent of the tab under my iced tea glass and we pried ourselves out of the booth. Charlie stood outside with a toothpick in his mouth as I paid the check. I pushed open the door and felt a couple drops of rain.

"Thanks for lunch," he said. "Good luck with the movie."

"Thanks. Let me know when your retirement party is. I'll spring for the strippers."

"Fat chance of that. They'll shove me out the door after making sure I haven't taken any paperclips."

We shook hands and I started for my car.

"Hey, Eddie."

"Yeah?"

"Don't get your knickers in a twist over those guys."

"Nah, I'm good. Thanks for listening."

He flipped me a two-finger salute and crawled into his car. I waved as he drove out of the parking lot. It was going to be strange to think of Charlie Rivers without a badge. But the times they are a-changin', as someone once said.

Mavis had left me a note saying she'd run to the post office and would be right back. I hung up my porkpie, answered Mother Nature's call, nuked a cup of this morning's coffee, then put my feet up on my desk and dug into the envelope containing *Burnt Hills*. The cover sheet revealed that a table read would be held next Wednesday at a studio up in North

Hollywood. It seemed a little strange that they would have a table read of the screenplay. Usually, it's been my experience that you get the script, learn your lines and show up for the first day of shooting. Maybe the director intended to shed some light on how he was going to shoot the picture. More power to him, I thought.

Burnt Hills proved to be a pretty standard oater. A tyrannical rancher was trying to buy up land outside of town to gain water rights for his cattle. Smaller ranchers had banded together to throw a monkey wrench into his plans. The big operator owned the bar where Chet Cassidy served drinks and had him under his thumb. As I progressed through the script, I was pleased to see that my character had a mean streak in him, and also that he had a few dustups with Lois Maxwell's character.

After a half hour or so, Mavis came back into the office. "How's Charlie?" she called out.

"He's retiring in eight months."

"Really," she said, as she appeared in the entry to my office. "What's he going to do then?"

"Well, either work for me or become an actor."

Her response was a typical Mavis guffaw. "That'll be the day."

"I agree. You're eating up all my payroll as it is."

Another guffaw. "How's the screenplay?"

"Not bad. I've got some pretty good stuff."

"Great," she said, and went back to her desk.

After another hour, I'd read through the script and found myself eager to get in front of the camera. I looked over the cast list and above-the-line people. A couple of the actors' names, in addition to Lois Maxwell, I recognized from other projects. The director was a man named Pete O'Brien. An IMDB search revealed he'd put together a fairly decent list of credits.

Further internet searching was suddenly interrupted by a chirp from my cellphone. The screen said it was Carla. "How's my favorite television star?"

"Desperately missing you," she replied.

"I feel the same. Things going okay?"

"No problems. And it's not even that hot out here."

Are you shooting this weekend?"

"Nope. In fact, I was thinking I might rent a car and drive back."

"I've got a better idea. Why don't I drive out there?"

"Really?"

"Yeah, really. I need some sunshine and the film starts next Wednesday, so who knows how much I'll be tied up after that."

"That's the best idea I've heard all day. Come on Friday, okay?"

"That's what I was thinking."

"Can you stop by my place and pick up a few things for me?"

"Give me a list." I jotted the items down. "Maybe you can help me with my dialogue?"

"You got a deal." She paused, then continued in her best Marilyn Monroe voice. "Maybe I can help you with something else, Shamus. What do you say, big boy?"

"I say keep those thoughts in your head."

"I will. And some others too. See you Friday." She made the sound of a kiss and hung up.

A weekend in Palm Springs. Whatever would I do, I wondered, as answers started whirling around in my head.

6

Conventional wisdom dealing with California freeways is to leave early. That particularly applies to the 405 going through the Sepulveda Pass. Never mind the time of day, it's always a virtual parking lot. I was beginning to think Interstate 10 eastbound to Palm Springs had become the same thing. According to my computer, the trip was only a hundred and six miles, which factored out to a two hour, six-minute drive. It was now two o'clock and traffic had dwindled to a crawl around the intersection of I-15 heading north to Vegas. Everybody on their way to an ambush by one-armed bandits, I suppose.

At noon I'd swung by Carla's condo to pick up the list of things she wanted. One item was a red bikini bathing suit that looked to be no bigger than two band aids. I'd never seen her wear it and could only imagine how nicely she would fill it out. Once I got beyond the I-15 interchange I pulled off, stopped at a gas station to answer the call of nature and bought a Snickers bar and a large soda to wash it down. Before continuing on my way, I sent her a text and told her where I was and the condition of the traffic. She responded after a couple of miles and said she was still shooting but would wrap in an hour or so.

Ample compact discs and random thoughts provided relief from the slow pace. I found myself thinking back to the meeting I'd had with Charlie Rivers and the news of his impending retirement. Charlie and I first crossed paths a few years ago when I got involved in the investigation into the murder of my ex-wife Elaine Weddington. Being a private eye, I was technically prevented from sticking my nose into a homicide.

However, an insurance company that had a financial stake in the movie she was working on at the time had hired me, which gave me access to the investigation. Charlie and I struck up not only a professional relationship, but one that developed into a personal friendship as well. I took comfort in the fact that he hadn't said anything about leaving Los Angeles, so our occasional get-togethers over lunches and ballgames would continue. But I had to admit that his connection with the LAPD and my reliance on it would be factors I would miss.

Charlie, however, had injected a bit of angst into our meeting when he said that even though Roger Iverson and his three pals were tethered by ankle bracelets, nothing prevented them from hiring someone to eliminate Reggie and me, thus ruining the Ventura County's DA's case against them. I've never been one to harbor much fear in the various cases I've been involved in over the years, but I had to admit this one had upped the ante.

Clinically speaking, I came away from the incident with some PTSD. Both Carla and Mavis had suggested I consult someone to deal with it, but stubborn animal that I am, I'd initially disregarded their advice. When difficulty in sleeping continued and the noise from a car backfiring made me cringe, I surrendered and sought help. I'd been making progress, but spotting Roger Iverson had spooked me and unleashed a surge of paranoia. Then when Charlie opened up the possibility of the quartet of creeps hiring someone to take me out, my insecurity ticked up considerably. Granted, hit men and murder for hire are great topics for the Hollywood fiction factories, but police blotters provide tangible evidence of their existence—all the more reason to distance myself from those thoughts by an escape to the desert and the welcoming arms of a soul mate.

I came up over a small incline on the freeway and saw what was probably the cause of the traffic slowdown. A jackknifed big rig jutted into one lane and traffic was being diverted onto the left shoulder; and, of course, the inevitable rubbernecks added to the slowdown. As I drifted by, it didn't seem as if there'd been any injuries, only a frustrated driver who leaned against his overturned cab talking to a highway patrolman.

Traffic picked up after the accident and it wasn't long before the valley of wind turbines appeared, signaling the approach to Palm Springs. A layer of brown smog lay over the city, an anachronism that destroyed any semblance one would have of the purity of the desert. Back in the Hollywood heydays, the Springs was the playground of the great and would-be greats. Hope, Crosby, Sinatra, and anyone of that ilk you could think of relaxed and cavorted in this oasis. I suppose the environment gave them freedom from the eyes and ears of the public and the press. Inhibitions were dropped; parties were everywhere, and misbehaving was the rule, not the exception.

For reasons that escape me, Palm Springs nowadays doesn't have that same reputation. The population of the city has a higher percentage of same-sex unions than any other city in the country. That same freedom from press and public apparently has the same appeal for the gay community that it had for the Hollywood elite. Snowbirds still flock to the area, but the chance sightings of entertainment A-listers on the golf courses aren't commonplace anymore.

Speaking of Bob Hope, the hotel Carla said the production was staying at was located on Bob Hope Drive. I pulled into the parking lot and shot her a text saying I had arrived, then cracked the windows on the car and waited to see if she'd respond promptly. A warm cross-breeze wafted through, nothing like the inferno I would have encountered six months earlier. After a few moments of watching Hawaiian-shirt clad snowbirds climb on a tour bus, the cell rang.

"Eddie, I'm just getting changed. I'll be there in a few."

"Okay. I'll get out of the heat and be in the bar."

"See you there."

She hung up and I closed the windows, then grabbed my empty soda cup and made my way to the front door of the hotel, depositing the cup in a trash receptacle on the way. A welcome blast of air conditioning greeted me as the electronic doors slid open. The success of Carla's television show, *Three on a Beat*, was reflected in the lodging for the cast. The hotel was plush; no Motel 6 for this outfit. Desert hues dominated the walls and area rugs were sprinkled over the floor of the lobby. Cushiony beige chairs and sofas sprawled in every corner. I spotted a door to my left with a neon sign above it that read "The Oasis," obviously meant to lure a thirsty traveler.

As I headed for the door I glanced to my right and saw the inside of a small casino, slot machines beeping and lights blinking. The hotel was actually located in Rancho Mirage, on tribal lands of the Coachella Indians, thus the legality of gambling. The Indian gaming industry hadn't yet made an inroad into Reno and Vegas enterprises, but certainly provided an alternative to several hours of driving to satisfy one's urge to lose a paycheck or two.

I climbed onto a stool and a young man wearing a white short-sleeved shirt under a red vest put a coaster in front of me and said, "Afternoon, sir. What can I get you?"

"What's on tap?"

He looked at his watch and said, "My shift's almost over. You want the whole list?"

I cocked my head, slightly taken aback by his comment.

He caught my look and leaned on the bar. "I'm just pulling your leg, sir. Craft beers rule. We've got almost anything you can come up with."

"That include plain old Budweiser?"

"Absolutely." He pulled a frosted mug from a cooler and stood behind the stick as the mug filled, then set it on the coaster in front of me. "On me, sir. Sorry for trying to be a smart ass."

"No worries. Why don't you include a shot of bourbon while you're at it?"

He reached behind him for a bottle of Jim Beam and poured a healthy shot in a smaller glass and set it beside the beer.

"Gonna have to charge you for the bourbon, though."

"Fair enough."

I sipped some of the Beam as he rang up a tab and laid it in front of me. "Welcome to Rancho Mirage."

"Thanks."

"Are you a guest at the hotel?"

"Just visiting a friend."

"Well, enjoy your visit. Let me know if you need anything else."

He ambled down to the other end of the bar. I chased the bourbon with a pull from the frosted mug and glanced around the bar. Dim lights revealed six tables occupied with guests. Four guys sat around one of them. They wore polo shirts and shorts, looking like they were fresh off one of the many golf courses that were fanned throughout this desert oasis.

My attention focused on a television screen hanging above the bar. A CNN talking head was detailing some crisis happening in the nation's capital. Since the sound was muted and the closed-captioned transcript made it impossible to follow, I soon lost interest, and instead ordered another frosted mug. A burst of voices from the lobby made me swivel around and see Carla coming through the door. Behind her, people working on the production poured out of a van.

Wearing sandals, shorts, and a tank top, she came striding toward me and wrapped her arms around my shoulders, then planted a huge kiss on me. "Hi, sailor. New in town?"

"Yes, ma'am. Know where I can find a good time?"

"Room eight-fourteen." She giggled, then plopped her shoulder bag on a stool and crawled onto one next to me. After another kiss, she said, "I am so glad to see you."

"Right back atcha," I said, as she took a sip of my beer. "You want one of those?"

"Later. What I want is a shower, preferably one with you in the stall."

I mustered my most lascivious grin, then tossed back the rest of my bourbon. "Let me get the bags out of the car and I'll meet you up there. Oh, by the way. Do you think it's warm enough for that red bikini?"

"Absolutely." She kissed me, picked up her bag and walked out of the bar, swiveling her hips and looking back at me with a come-hither grin on her face. When Carla and I had first started seeing each other she was working as an exotic dancer at a gentlemen's club, a time that had definitely left its mark on her.

The fleet is in, I thought, as I settled my tab and headed out to my car.

When I knocked on the door of 814, it slowly swung back to reveal a bare leg, which, as I continued to push, eventually gave way to Carla in her birthday suit. I closed the door behind me, dropped the bags I carried and she pressed herself against me. I barely managed to toss my clothes on the bed before she grabbed my hand and pulled me into the bathroom. The hotel obviously had an ample supply of hot water, since we cavorted under the shower head for a considerable amount of time.

Refreshed in more ways than one and wrapped in a complimentary bathrobe, I lay on the bed and watched her—still in her birthday suit—as she walked to the mini-bar and pulled out a bottle of beer and a small bottle of wine. Wide open drapes provided a view of mountains and the San Bernardino National Forest. She stood by a table close to the window, opened both the wine and the beer, poured the contents of each into glasses, then sauntered over to where I was propped up by a pillow.

"Aren't you concerned that someone's going to perv on you with those drapes open like that?"

She handed me the glass of beer. "I'm eight floors up. They'd need a telescope. If someone goes to that much trouble to spy on me, they've earned what they see, say I."

"Fair enough."

We clinked glasses, and after a nice wet kiss she sat on the bed, legs crossed. "So, tell me. Except for landing the movie, anything else exciting happen since I saw you last?"

I told her about Tom Sanderson's class and the Stark Young and Arthur Miller quotes I'd used. She was duly impressed, even to the point of suggesting I should maybe entertain the idea of teaching.

"No way," I said.

"Why not?"

"The old adage. 'Those that can, do. Those that can't, teach.'"

"Oh, that's silly. From what you've described, you know what you're doing."

"Maybe so, but I'm not sure I can explain it." I took a swallow of beer and leaned over to put the glass on the nightstand. "The story goes that Laurence Olivier, when he was doing *Othello* onstage, was particularly brilliant one night. The cast lined up backstage after the curtain call and applauded him. He stormed into his dressing room and slammed the door behind him. Finally one cast member knocked on the door, went in, and said, 'What's the matter, Larry? It was brilliant.' Olivier replied, 'I know it was, but I don't know how I did it, and if I don't know how I did it, I won't know how to do it again.'"

Carla looked at me, bemused. "Is that true?"

"Yeah, I think it's somewhere in one of the books about him."

"No disrespect, but you're not Olivier."

"I know that, for crissakes, but the point is he didn't know how he did it. So how is he supposed to tell someone else how to do it?"

She sipped from her glass of wine, set it on the nightstand, then leaned in and kissed me. "Well, I'd take a class from you, honey. But only if you let me be teacher's pet."

I pushed her back on the bed and kissed her. "Done." I reached over to retrieve my glass, as she did hers. I went on to tell her about seeing Roger Iverson and how the sighting spooked me. I then went on to tell her about my phone conversation with the Ventura County DA and finally my get-together with Charlie Rivers. She laughed when I told her about his suggestion that he was going to work for me or become an actor.

"But you know," she said, "with all the cop shows being shot, he could probably do a lot of consulting on police procedures. Did he take your suggestion seriously?"

"I'm not sure. But come to think of it, I should talk to Morrie and explore the idea of possibly getting him some representation." I took a pull on my beer and leaned over and put the glass back on the nightstand. "He did put one little hint of gloom in me, though."

"What?"

"I admitted my paranoia in finding out that those four guys are out on bail."

"But that's natural, isn't it?"

"I guess."

A moment of silence came between us. Then Carla said, "Wait. You think they'd come after you and Reggie?"

"I can't deny it."

"But you said they're wearing ankle bracelets."

"They are, but Charlie went on to suggest that that doesn't prevent them from hiring someone to go after us. With Reggie and me out of the picture, the district attorney is up a creek without you know what."

She finished off the last of her wine, set the glass back on the nightstand, and stretched out beside me. "Oh, Eddie, I don't think you've got anything to worry about."

"I hope you're right, kiddo."

She drew my face to hers and kissed me deeply. Two pairs of hands started groping and eventually threats of retribution disappeared from my mind.

After another heated interlude, with Carla being particularly zealous, we lay in each other's arms like we hadn't been together in months. Her fingers traced random patterns on my cheeks and lips. Her eyes bored into mine, suggesting that she was in my corner.

Our canoodling came to a sudden end when she jumped out of bed and bounced up and down. "I know how to cheer you up," she said. She pounced on the bag with the things I'd brought her and pulled out the red bikini. "You brought a bathing suit, didn't you?" she said, as she began covering strategic places on her body with the two band aids.

"I did."

"Come on, the sun's still up. They've got a gorgeous pool." She stood in front of the bathroom mirror and made final adjustments as I ditched the robe and found my swimming trunks.

"What do you think?" she said, as she went into her best runway pose.

"Is that thing legal?"

"You better believe it, Buster. What I do wearing it may be questionable, though." She grabbed two towels from the bathroom, tossed one to me and wrapped the other one around her hips. "Surf's up, sailor."

The sun was in the wrong hemisphere, but we did manage to catch some of its heat. Carla swam a few laps in the pool, her red bikini clinging to her in desperation. I tried to keep up with her but failed miserably. After another shower we both had a little nap and went downstairs for dinner. Several members of the *Three on a Beat* company were in the restaurant, and after some delicious surf 'n turf, we joined them in the bar. Before heading up to the room, we stuck our heads in the casino and Carla squealed with delight when she hit a hundred-dollar jackpot on a one-armed bandit. I got no argument when I told her she was buying breakfast.

Saturday dawned with plenty of sunshine and thin, wispy clouds that slowly drifted across the desert. We took a drive up into the San Bernardino mountains and soaked up plenty of fresh air, laced with the scent of pine trees. I couldn't help but remember the last time I was in the woods, north of Piru, prior to setting foot in a chamber of depravity and evil.

Today, however, those thoughts were pushed aside by the company I kept. One of Carla's assets is that she whole heartedly embraces any environment in which she finds herself. She was like a little kid, chasing squirrels and peppering me with pine cones. For two people who lived in the concrete jungle of Los Angeles and endless freeways, the getaway was euphoric. We caught a glimpse of deer and smaller creatures; sat under a pine tree and had a picnic lunch we'd brought with us. Saturday night we caught a movie: Annette Bening in *Film Stars Don't Die in Liverpool*, the story of the last days of the quintessential film noir actress Gloria Grahame. We both thought it to be a bittersweet story, and also that it was high time for Miss Bening to be awarded an Oscar.

I may be wrong, but I think it's inherent in the female of the species to thrive on that most primal of urges—shopping. On Sunday,

Carla was no exception. We prowled the business section of Palm Springs proper, me tagging along and offering my approval of the various items of clothing she felt compelled to buy. Mid-afternoon found us sitting on a bench with ice cream cones: chocolate for me, strawberry for her.

She pawed through one of the bags at her feet. "I've been looking for sandals like these for ages. Even on Rodeo Drive, for cryin' out loud. Cute, huh? What do you think?"

"Yeah," I replied, my eyes fixed on a green Kia parked across the street from us.

She nudged me with an elbow, then saw what I was looking at. She grasped my hand and said, "Let me ask you something."

"Yeah, what?"

"How many green Kias do you think there are in Southern California?"

"I don't know. Hundreds, I suppose."

"Exactly. You can't think every time you see one that Roger Iverson is behind the wheel."

"I know, dammit, but the sight of one takes me right back there."

She wrapped an arm around my shoulders. "Eddie, you've got to try and let it go."

"Yeah, yeah."

"Your doctor and the medicine are helping, aren't they?"

"For the most part."

"I'm glad. And I'll bet that Kia belongs to some little old lady from Pasadena out here visiting her grandchildren." That provoked a grin from me and she leaned in and kissed me on the cheek. A drop of strawberry ice cream landed on my trousers.

"Oops," she said, and dabbed at it with a napkin.

"Watch where that hand goes. We're out in public."

"Don't care," she said, and squeezed me someplace other than where the ice cream landed.

Early Monday morning I stood at the front door of the hotel and watched the *Three on a Beat* crowd climb into the company van. Carla put her arms around me and kissed me.

"We're due to finish by mid-week, so I'll see you soon."

"Thanks for the company this weekend," I said. "Just what I needed."

"Me too. Do me a favor and forget about green Kias, okay?"

"You got it."

"You need to look forward to *Burnt Hills* and this Chet Cassidy guy."

"That's my plan."

She kissed me again and climbed into the van. I watched it pull away from the hotel, then picked up my bag and crawled into my car. As I pulled onto I-10 and headed west, I told myself this paranoia I had was stupid.

I hoped I was right.

7

Wednesday morning dawned cloudy and drizzly. Random drops of rain pelted my windshield as I made my way through the Cahuenga Pass into the San Fernando Valley. The 9:00 AM table read for *Burnt Hills* was to take place at an office complex in Studio City. I still harbored a question or two as to why a table read was even necessary, as opposed to just showing up for the first day of shooting. But mine was not to question why, just show up and be ready to go—a lesson I've learned many years ago.

The address I'd been given was a nondescript building across the street from a strip mall. A deli, a check-cashing outlet and a stationery store were the main tenants. Parking was to the left of the structure and with script in hand, I walked through the front door and saw a sign with "*Burnt Hills* Company" on it and an arrow pointing down a corridor. There were offices on both sides of the hall with people hunched over computers, others on phones. About thirty yards in I came to another sign saying "table read" with an arrow pointing to an open door.

Inside, a horseshoe configuration of tables was spread out. Against one wall sat two more tables, filled with coffee urns and craft services snacks. Clumps of people were clustered around the tables. A young lady walked up. She had a clipboard in one hand and wore a red flannel shirt and jeans.

"Good morning," she said, as she stuck out a hand. "I'm Debbie Merton, one of the second assistant directors. And you are?"

"Eddie Collins."

"Hi Eddie. Welcome aboard. Help yourself to coffee and nibbles if you'd like. We're almost ready to start."

I poured myself a cup of coffee and gazed at the people gathered around the horseshoe grouping of tables. Several of them I recognized from previous projects I'd worked on or auditions I'd gone to. Lois Maxwell was talking to a couple of actors. She caught my eye and walked toward me.

"Morning, Eddie. Good to see you."

"Same here."

"Ready to strap on your sidearm?"

"If that's what they want me to do."

"Did you get a chance to read the screenplay?"

"I did."

"And?"

"I thought it was okay. Glad to see we've got some scenes together."

"Me too. Should be fun."

Our conversation was interrupted by a burly, bearded man dressed in khakis and a black vest over a plaid shirt. "Good morning, everyone. Gather around the table and we'll get this show on the road. No assigned seating. Just pick a chair." Everyone jockeyed for a seat, and I managed to sit next to Lois. "I'm Brad Foster," he continued, "the first AD. My two assistants are Debbie Merton and Paul Laxton." He pointed to the two of them and they raised their hands in greeting. "First things first. Please mute your phones. Put them on airplane mode, or even take a drastic step and turn them off." I chose airplane mode, and Foster then proceeded to introduce below-the-line people, such as cinematographer, sound engineer, production and costume designer, etc.

I was glad to see him also introduce the screenwriter, a person that is all too often invisible on movie shoots. This particular scribe, Andrew Watson, was a young man who seemed genuinely pleased to be given an introduction. For years writers and directors have engaged in a debate as to whom the term "a film by" refers. Too often, the director as "*auteur*" philosophy prevails and leaves the screenwriter out in the cold. I don't have a dog in this fight, but common sense tells me a film begins with what's on the page. The two respective guilds will probably never come to an agreement over that particular screen credit. It's sort of a chicken versus the egg debate.

Introductions over, Foster said, "The daily call sheet will be emailed to you, so check with me, Debbie or Paul to see if we've got your correct contact information. Any questions, hit me up at the break. That's it from me. I'll turn it over to our director, Pete O'Brien." He gestured to a Black man seated at the head of the horseshoe. O'Brien stood and pushed his chair back. He was a tall, slim man, who wore granny glasses and had a finely sculptured beard and sprinkles of gray hair at his temples. He had on a tan safari jacket, pens clipped to one of the breast pockets.

"Good morning, people. I'm glad to see everyone, and I hope we're on the threshold of something special here. Most of you probably aren't used to having a table read, but I thought it important for everyone to get to know one another off the set." He went on to tell us in broad terms why he chose the project, admitting that the Western is often regarded as a dying genre in Hollywood. He thought we could set out to prove those people wrong. He revealed that the picture was going to be shot with a digital camera, which would save time, not only in setting up the various shots, but also make the editing in post-production much smoother than with traditional film.

"I'm also glad to report to you that our film is going to be shot at Sunset Ranch up near Acton, just off the Antelope Freeway. If that sounds unfamiliar to you, it's because it's a brand-new facility and we're the first production to be shot there." Postive murmurs floated around the tables, and a few hands were clapped. "Yes, I know, I'm excited by that fact alone. A local investment group put the money together and made the producers an offer they couldn't refuse. It's got everything we need. Complete western street scene, soundstages with saloon, hotel, sheriff's office, everything right at one location." He turned to his Brad Foster, his 1st AD. "I miss anything, Brad?"

"Don't think so, Pete," he said. "Give yourself a good hour to get up there. We'll be getting directions to everyone when we're done here."

O'Brien continued. "Okay. I'd like to go around the table and have everybody introduce themselves and who they're playing."

I kind of had the feeling that we were at the first day of camp, but if the introductions led to some esprit de corps, so be it. The town's mayor, the cattle barons, the sheriff, all relayed their names and roles.

When it came time for Lois, she said, "I'm Lois Maxwell, and I play Dolly Blaine, the owner of the Empire Hotel. At least that's what the sheriff thinks it is. Y'all come on upstairs and you might think differently."

She succeeded in breaking the ice and elicited hearty laughs from the company. O'Brien said the second ADs, Debbie Merton and Paul Laxton, would split up reading the stage directions, and without further ado, we were off and running.

The exact location of *Burnt Hills* was not revealed, except that it was set in the 1880s, somewhere in the West. The Kincannon cattle ranch had been running roughshod over the town of Twin Forks for some years. Two smaller ranchers were squabbling with the big outfit over water and grazing rights. The twist here was that one of the smaller ranchers was a Black man, Jeremiah Rawlins. Off hand, I couldn't recall a film with that dynamic, thereby giving credence to O'Brien's feeling that the film might be something out of the ordinary. My character, Chet Cassidy, was not only a bartender in the saloon owned by Kincannon, but was also a former ranch hand of the cattle baron and still in his employ.

At one point during the reading, I heard Lois's cell phone buzz. She looked at the screen. It was a text, and after reading it, a frown broke out on her face. She didn't respond and angrily stuffed the phone back into her bag. She shook her head and I leaned over to her and whispered.

"Everything all right?"

"Yeah. Just somebody who keeps buggin' me. No big deal."

She turned to me, smiled, and picked up her coffee cup. The smile was forced, and I had a feeling the text bothered her more than she let on. I couldn't help but wonder if the text had anything to do with the guy she had argued with the other day at the costume fitting. Something, or someone, had obviously put a burr under her saddle.

My first scene was set in the saloon, where a bunch of cowboys had come to wet their whistles. A couple of them started to get a bit rowdy, and the script called for me to withhold any more whiskey. That didn't set right with them, and it looked like a major donnybrook was going to happen, until Bart Kincannon, their boss, came in and told them to knock it off.

After another half hour, Foster announced a fifteen-minute break for refreshments and bathroom runs. Before I could ask Lois if she wanted more coffee, she quickly pulled her phone from her bag and headed for a far corner of the room.

I refilled my cup and took a bite from a doughnut as Hugh Danton walked up to me. He was a big man, barrel-chested, with a ruddy complexion. He was playing Bart Kincannon, the main heavy of this film. I'd worked with him a few years back, but hadn't seen much of him lately.

"Hey, Eddie, long time no see," he said, as he stuck out his hand.

I swallowed the bite of doughnut and said, "That it has, Hugh. How you been?"

"Hangin' in there. Glad to be working."

"Same here."

He stuck his coffee cup under the tap of one of the big urns on the table. "Last time I saw you, you told me about some case you were working on as a private eye. Still got the license?"

"Yup. My name's still on the door."

"Good for you. At our age, we all probably need a day job."

"Absolutely."

We chatted for a few moments, catching up on what both of us had been doing in the acting arena. At one point I glanced at the corner of the room where Lois had gone. She was on her cell phone, engaged in what appeared to be a heated conversation; at least that's what her body language told me. One arm sawed the air, emphasizing what she said into the phone. I couldn't make out what she was saying, but she obviously wasn't talking about the weather.

Foster announced the break was over and everyone took their seats. Lois was silent, her demeanor telling me the phone call hadn't gone well. The upbeat, out-going personality she'd displayed earlier had disappeared.

The table read continued, and, as expected, Kincannon and his cohorts got their just due by the end of the film. Before dismissing the company, Foster and O'Brien conveyed some general announcements. Directions to Sunset Ranch were handed out, as well as call sheets for tomorrow's first day of shooting. Before Lois and I left the room we sought out Debbie Merton and confirmed that the production had our correct contact information. My watch said it was ten to one.

"Hey, Lois," I said. "I spied a deli across the street. Feel like a sandwich? My treat."

She looked at her watch. "Good idea. Their craft services didn't do much for me."

"My sentiments exactly. I'll meet you there."

The deli was simply called "Earl's." Lois stood by the front door, doing something with her phone as I parked my car. We found a little table in one corner, ordered sandwiches and iced tea from a middle-aged guy with curly black hair and a stained apron wrapped around an impressive midriff. In response to Lois's question, he identified himself as Earl, and bid us welcome.

"What did you think?" Lois said.

"About the script? I like it. Some interesting dynamics going on."

"I agree. And it sounds like a good company."

"Especially that gal playing Dolly Blaine," I said. "She sounds like a firecracker."

Lois laughed and swept a strand of hair behind one ear. "Oh, heck, I always figure a giggle or two never hurts anything."

"Me too. Hugh Danton, the guy playing Kincannon? I've worked with him before. He's a solid actor."

"Oh yeah, I've seen him in a ton of stuff."

Earl appeared with two huge glasses of iced tea, set them in front of us and grabbed a sugar caddy from a nearby table. "Sandwiches comin' right up, folks."

We both tore open sweetener packets and stirred the contents into our glasses.

"So, Sunset Ranch," I said. "From what O'Brien described, the place sounds a lot like Melody Ranch."

"Yeah, right. You ever work up there?"

"Once," I said. "A few years back. I'm not sure that it's used for filming anymore, though.

"Didn't Gene Autry own that place at one time?"

"That's right."

"Supposedly he needed a place for his horse," she said. "Silver, or something like that?"

"Nope. Champion. Silver was the Lone Ranger."

"Aw, crap, that's right," she said. "I can't keep my horses straight."

We shared a laugh as Earl brought our sandwiches. A moment or two elapsed as we slathered mustard and mayo on them and dug in.

Lois dabbed at the corner of her mouth with a napkin. "O'Brien didn't say anything about shooting the exteriors, though, the ones out on the range. Any scuttlebutt about where the actual 'burnt hills' will be?"

"I haven't heard anything. I don't think either one of us will be riding the range, though."

"Good thing," she said. "I haven't been on a horse since I can't remember when."

"You're one up on me."

"Wait a minute," she said. "I thought every actor says he can ride a horse and a motorcycle, shoot a gun, or rassle a rattlesnake."

"Shoot a gun, yes. Horses, motorcycles, and rattlesnakes, nope. The question has never come up."

A young couple came through the front door and sat at a table. I took another bite of my pastrami sandwich and Lois's cell phone rang. She ignored it and sipped from her iced tea.

"You need to get that?" I said.

"Nope. I know who it is." She didn't elaborate and bit off a corner of her sandwich.

I debated whether or not to let it go, but my curiosity got the better of me. "Hey, listen, this is none of my business, but is someone harassing you in any way?"

"I don't know if I'd call it harassment, but he is bugging the crap out of me."

"The same guy you were arguing with the other day?"

"At the wardrobe fitting?" I nodded. "Yeah, someone from my past."

"Anything I can do to help?"

"You're a sweetie, Eddie, but it's nothing. Thanks, though."

She bit into her sandwich. I didn't pursue it any further. Our conversation turned to her years in Hollywood. I told her that I'd checked her out on the Internet, but as she talked, I realized I had no idea as to the extent of her career. I was impressed at the number of television shows she'd done and the list of celebrities she'd worked with. She had no reservations about telling me she was pushing eighty, but had no thoughts of retiring. Our iced teas turned into a second as she recounted a few tales of the people she knew. Every once in a while she asked me if I knew so-and-so and I had to tell her that I didn't land in Hollywood until 1991.

"Oh, for cryin' out loud, you're just a pup," she said.

"It feels like I've been here forever."

"Not an easy town, I'll give you that. But I don't know what else I'd do. Good for you, having that PI license. Does it keep you busy enough?"

"For the most part," I said.

Earl came up to the table and collected our plates. "Anything else for you folks?"

We both declined and he left the check.

"Thanks for lunch, Eddie. Been fun talking to you. Sorry if I ramble on too much. Next time just give me a kick under the table."

We stood, pushed back our chairs and she stepped outside while I stopped and paid Earl. I came out of the deli. Lois was again looking at her phone, but dropped it into her bag when she saw me.

"Are you called tomorrow?" she said.

"Nope. Day after tomorrow. You?"

"Ten o'clock. One scene."

"Okay. I'll catch up with you later."

"You will. Thanks again," she said, and walked to her car.

I always enjoy talking to self-described "old timers" who've been around this crazy business for far longer than me. Lois Maxwell fit the bill in spades, and I couldn't help but be a little concerned that a successful career was maybe being tarnished by someone bugging her.

Given her longevity, I suppose it was possible that a bridge or two had been burned over the years—reason enough for someone to be harassing her.

She'd said that that wasn't the case, but I wasn't convinced.

8

My *Burnt Hills* call for Friday was 7:00 AM, so it was still dark when I rolled out of my Murphy bed. Carla had returned from the Springs yesterday, but given the fact that I had to get up before the crack of dawn, we agreed that I should bunk by myself. Even though we spend most nights together, I still have the option of my studio apartment behind my office. Mavis never knows if I'll be there when she comes to work, which prompts her to loudly announce her entrance. A time or two, on a lark, I've not answered and sneaked up on her. I get a giggle out of my prank. She, however, isn't amused.

Carla and I have discussed moving in together from time to time but we've always sidestepped a decision. Mavis has hinted that such an undertaking would provide more space for the trinkets and tchotchkes she deals with, a prospect which always brings a gleam to her eyes. But unless my building is razed, I see no reason for uprooting Collins Investigations. Besides, it would break up my little family of neighbors. I've become fond of Lenny Daye and his sartorial splendors. The winsome clientele of the Elite Talent Agency and even the dour Russian doctor always provide a breath of fresh air. However, truth be told, the gentrification of Hollywood Boulevard always raises the threat of a move.

Food for thought, I decided, as I merged onto Interstate 5 from the Hollywood Freeway. When I passed the turnoff for the 126 leading to Santa Paula, Fillmore and Piru I immediately pushed aside the deplorable memories of last autumn and concentrated on not missing the exit for the Antelope Freeway and Sunset Ranch.

I've never been able to comprehend a GPS system, so with printed directions propped up on my steering wheel and the dome light on, I managed to find my way to the front gate, flanked on both sides by adobe bell towers. The usual uniformed security guard was stationed under the one to the left. I turned off the light, pulled up and opened the car's window.

"*Burnt Hills* company?"

"Right. Eddie Collins."

After consulting a clipboard, he acknowledged my legitimacy and placed a sticker on one corner of the windshield. "Good morning, sir. Leave the sticker on the window. It'll make it easier for you to get on the lot."

"Thanks. Where do I park?"

He pointed to an area off to the right. "Cast and crew parking where you see the sign. Welcome to Sunset Ranch."

The glow of a rising sun provided enough illumination to reveal a roped-off section of the lot where another security guard with a flashlight ushered me to a parking space. I got out of the car, zipped up my windbreaker and walked in the direction he pointed toward the dressing trailers, where he said I'd find a production assistant to check in with. To my left, I caught a glimpse of a classic western street laid out in all its 19th century splendor, giving one the feeling of traveling back in time.

Back in the present, a young Black woman with all the accoutrements of a PA walked up to me. She wore a denim jacket, jeans, and had a radio clipped to her belt and a headphone spanning a cap with "*Burnt Hills* crew" stenciled on the front. "Good morning. Are you Mister Collins?"

"That's me."

She stuck out a hand. "Hi. I'm Cheryl, one of the production assistants. Let me show you to your trailer." We started walking and she keyed her radio to relay that she had me in tow and was directing me to my dressing room. She listened to the response and said "Roger that" as we came to the door of the trailer. A strip of masking tape with "Chet Cassidy" written on it signified we had found the right one. It's commonplace to have an actor's character name, rather his street name, on one's trailer.

I guess it's easier for the crew to ride herd on everyone; or, I suppose, if you're inclined to be a devotee of the Method, it gives you the opportunity to immediately start getting into character. Since I don't adhere to that school of thought, there was no need for me to scrape the horse-pucky from my boots as I crossed the threshold.

"Craft services is set up, and the coffee is hot," Cheryl said. "I'll come and find you when hair and makeup are ready for you. You should have sides for what you're doing first thing, so welcome to *Burnt Hills*."

"Thanks, Cheryl." She walked off, talking on her radio as I closed the door to the trailer. I was pleased to see that, unlike other dressing rooms I've had, this one was big enough to where I didn't have to go outside to change my mind. It was a small RV, complete with television set, mini-kitchen, bath and bedroom. Chet Cassidy's wardrobe hung in the latter's closet. The day's call-sheet and the afore-mentioned "sides," lay on a fold-down table. They're 5x8 miniaturized pages of the screenplay containing an actor's scene, still able to be read, but small enough to be stuffed into a pocket out of sight of the camera.

I carry a small "survival bag" with me on film shoots: crosswords, a magazine or two, maybe a book, and a yellow Magic Marker to highlight my dialogue. I tossed the bag on the table, found the marker, but decided I needed some fuel first.

I stepped out and walked toward a roach coach and an adjoining tarp with tables set up underneath it. The line was small and in no time I had a plate filled with scrambled eggs, bacon and two slices of toast. I siphoned a cup of coffee out of a large urn and straddled a chair at a long table. Two crew members were finishing up and I had the distinct feeling I had butted into an argument of some sort.

One of the men, a grizzled elderly gent with a full beard and wearing a heavy down jacket, leaned over the tray in front of him. He accused somebody in the sound department of not knowing what the hell they were doing. The guy across the table from him was younger and wore a hooded sweatshirt underneath a heavy denim jacket. He disagreed with his partner and maintained that it wasn't that person's fault, but rather that of the director. The two men went back and forth without paying any attention to me. After ten minutes or so they finished their breakfasts and continued the debate as they bussed their plates and walked off toward the set.

Interesting: it was only the second day of shooting and already there's a rhubarb among the crew? Film shoots can sometimes become territorial, what with unions and proprieties. And of course, flaring egos always add fuel to the fire. I didn't have a clue as to what the two men were arguing about, and figured it was none of my business, so I polished off my breakfast, refilled my coffee cup and walked back to my trailer. After highlighting my lines in the short scene that was due up first, I finished my coffee, settled onto a sofa and worked on my lines.

There weren't that many in the first scene to be shot. A bunch of cowpokes push into the saloon where I'm the barkeep. A couple of them get rowdy. I quit serving them whiskey. Tempers flare, until the sheriff comes in and restores order. I went over the lines several times until they were firmly in my head.

I must have dozed off, because the next sound I heard was a knock on the trailer's door.

"Mr. Collins?"

"Yeah," I said. "Come on in."

Cheryl pulled the door open and stuck her head in. "Makeup's ready for you."

"Okie doke," I replied, as I hauled myself off the sofa. "Getting any warmer out there?"

"A little, but I'd slip on your jacket."

I put on my hat and the windbreaker I'd worn and followed Cheryl. "This place is amazing. Really puts you back in time."

"I know. It's bound to grow on you sooner or later. I've got an uncle who crewed on *Deadwood* for a season or two. Now he wears nothing but cowboy boots and a Stetson." We shared a laugh as we walked to the makeup trailer. Cheryl pulled the door open and stepped up. "This is Eddie Collins, guys. He's playing Chet Cassidy."

There were four chairs. The "guys" turned out to be one guy and three ladies. One of the latter, a small Black woman, rose from a chair, swiveled it around and said, "Good mornin', honey. I'm Wanda. Sit yourself down here and let's have a look at you. You can hang your stuff on the wall there."

I took off the windbreaker and my porkpie, hung them on a peg and sat down.

"How you doin' this mornin', darlin?"

"So far so good."

"But it ain't over yet, right?" She uttered a healthy laugh and stuck tissues under my collar. She then pointed to the far chair next to the wall, occupied by a woman with a full head of jet-black hair. "That's Darla down there at the end. She's gonna look after your curly locks." Wanda then pointed to a tall redhead at the chair next to her. "That carrot top there is Melanie and the dreamboat next to her is Blake. But you better watch out for him." She laughed as Blake blew her a kiss, not disguising the fact that he was a gay man. I raised my hand in greeting to all three of them and they all said hello.

Wanda swiveled the chair around to face the mirror. "I'm likin' that porkpie you're wearin', honey. My ol' man wore one of them for a while. Said it made him feel macho."

"Didn't work, though, did it?" Blake said.

"That's what you think, sugar. I got no complaints."

All four broke out in laughter. They obviously knew each other and might even have worked together before. It's not uncommon for film crews to be somewhat incestuous—friends taking care of each other, loyalties abound. Being this jovial this early in the day pointed to the fact that they enjoyed their work and their camaraderie. In the past, I've always liked being around the below-the-line people, the ones who aren't in the limelight, don't get the glory, but nevertheless strive to take care of actors and, in turn, ask only that you respect them. I've never done anything less. The *Burnt Hills* contingent was good company.

Wanda and I continued to chat as she dabbed some pancake makeup on my face, darkened my eyebrows a bit with a pencil, put a little line under the eyes, and told me I was good to go. I got out of the chair and walked down to Darla's.

"Good morning, sir," she said, in a voice that could melt ice cubes. She ran a comb through my receding hairline, snipped a few errant strands from around my ears, and pronounced me fit for filming.

I reseated the porkpie, slipped on my windbreaker and bid the gang good morning.

Once back in my trailer, I donned Chet Cassidy's costume, checked myself in a mirror and decided I could pass muster as a 19th century barkeep. After another go at Chet's dialogue, I pulled the morning paper from my survival bag and checked to see what was going on in the world. I was almost through it when there was another knock on the door and Cheryl's head again appeared in the portal.

"They're ready for you on set, Eddie. Hop into the van."

"Okay. I've got a question."

"Shoot."

"What does one do with valuables? Wallet, etcetera?"

"Glad you asked." She reached into a pocket and pulled out a cluster of keys. "I'm going to give you a key to the trailer, and you can leave it on the table at the end of the day. Transportation will give it back to me. For future reference, it may be more prudent to leave your wallet in your car when you report in the morning."

"Thanks."

I checked the time on my cellphone and saw it was almost ten o'clock. "What about this?" I said, holding up the phone.

"If you've got a pocket to hide it and power it down, take it with you." I slid the sides into a hip pocket, turned off the phone, stowed it into the other one and stepped out. After locking the door, I turned to see a van idling nearby, wisps of exhaust floating upwards. Cheryl pulled open a rear door for me. I climbed in and saw Melanie and Darla on the rear bench. Cheryl slammed the door shut, hopped into the front seat and we set out for the soundstage.

"Mr. Collins is on the way," she said into her radio.

My face broke into a grin. Nice way to make a guy feel important on an early morning in the high desert.

The van's route took us down the Western street. All the elements were there: livery stable, saloon, dry-goods store, hotel, sheriff's office. I half-expected to see Gary Cooper on his lonely walk to a date with Frank Miller…or Burt Lancaster and Kirk Douglas striding toward the O.K. Corral and a clash with the Clantons.

My reverie ended when the van turned right in front of a small white church and deposited me outside the soundstage. Cheryl led us to the door, opened it, and I entered to find a three-sided saloon set, taking up most of the floor space of the vast stage. It was replete with all the trimmings: brass cuspidors and bar rail, round poker tables, a small piano on a pedestal, and a couple dozen cowpokes, extras dressed in every variation of western attire one could imagine.

Cheryl keyed her radio saying I was on the premises. Brad Foster, the 1st AD, stood next to the camera and turned when he heard Cheryl's transmission. He walked over to me and stuck out a hand.

"Good morning, sir. Any trouble finding the place?"

"No problem."

"Great. Follow me and we'll get you in place." He led me through the tables and up to the bar. "Pretty easy blocking. You're just behind the bar serving drinks. Pete will fill you in on more details."

He walked off and I surveyed my bar. The production spared no details. Both Pete O'Brien and Brad Foster had indicated that a full stock of props was available. It was evident they'd found everything they needed. Two rows of bottles filled to various levels with fake whiskey occupied a back shelf. On the wall above the bar was a mural showing a wagon train threading its way through a valley. There was a beer tap in the center of the bar. I gave the stick a slight pull, and sure enough, amber liquid spurted out. Mugs and shot glasses sat on a towel below the bar. I felt at home. God knows I've seen a few of these places in my time. The only difference here was that the customers were packing sidearms. I pulled out my sides, laid them on the bar and said the lines to myself. After a moment, Pete O'Brien, the director, walked up.

"Good morning, Eddie."

"Morning."

"Glad to have you with us. I've seen some of your work. Especially liked the FBI agent you did on that HBO series a while back. Damned if I can remember the name of it offhand."

"Oh, yeah. *Executive Action.*"

"That's it. Nice work."

"Thanks. You've got a great place to shoot here."

"I know. It's amazing, isn't it?" He went on to describe in more detail what the scene entailed. The stage was already rigged with lights, so he didn't foresee many delays waiting for the scene to be lit.

At one point, he called to one of the cowboys and beckoned him over. "Eddie, this is Andy Tyler. He's playing Luke Baxton, the cowpoke who gets in your face." We introduced ourselves and O'Brien walked off.

"Great set," Tyler said. "Really gets you in the mood. Have you done a Western before?"

"Few years back. Didn't amount to much, though."

We chatted for a couple of minutes until a sound technician walked up and wired both of us with microphones. When we were live, the director signaled to his AD he was ready to go. Foster called for touchups and Melanie and Darla hustled up to Tyler and me, gave us pats of powder and final looks at hair, then scurried off.

Foster took control of the set and explained to the extras what was going to happen. Debbie Merton and Paul Laxton, Foster's 2nd ADs, placed extras at the tables and strung out some of them along the length of the bar. The digital camera was mounted on a dolly at one end of the bar. Glasses were filled with fake whiskey. Andy Tyler was across from me. It was magic time.

O'Brien said, "Call it, Brad."

"Everybody, settle," Foster said. Conversations stopped.

"Roll sound," Foster continued.

"Speed," the sound man responded.

"Roll camera," again from Foster.

"Rolling," the camera operator answered.

"Background," Foster shouted, which was the cue for extras to begin muted conversations and movements.

"And action!" O'Brien shouted.

That was the cue for the scene to start. I filled a mug with beer and set it in front of one of the extras, at which point Tyler's character started to get in my face. I shouted back at him and we started a pretty good donnybrook, with lots of adlibs added to our scripted dialogue. After a few minutes, with Tyler about to jump over the bar, O'Brien called "Cut!" and everybody relaxed.

O'Brien and Foster quickly looked at the scene on a small monitor plugged into the camera. They made a few adjustments and after more touchups, we did another take. Another look at the monitor, and O'Brien said he was satisfied. The camera then moved to get coverage of both Tyler and me. With closeups, some added lighting was needed to fully illuminate our faces. Two grips placed white boards to reflect existing lighting that lit our faces. For the next hour or so, O'Brien moved the camera to get different angles of coverage. Foster then called for a break while they set up the sheriff's entrance to restore order.

We resumed the shoot with the camera in a different point of view. They'd cast the sheriff with authority in mind. Sheriff Haynes was played by Lou Anson, who must have stood 6 feet, 4 inches, give or take an inch. I'd seen him before at auditions. He shook hands with both Tyler and me and we did the scene. It went off without a hitch. O'Brien shot a couple more takes for safety's sake, then added some coverage, and after a consultation with Foster and the film's cinematographer, the AD announced that they had the sequence.

Before the scene was wrapped, the sound man called for sixty seconds of "room tone," a peculiarity of every film and TV shoot where absolute silence on a set is recorded for a specific amount of time. It basically records ambience, which is then used when the film undergoes the editing and sound mixing process. I've never been exactly sure why it's needed, but that's beyond my pay grade.

Foster shouted, "quiet on the set."

The sound man called "room tone," and identified the scene by number. Silence began, with everyone looking at each other and resisting the urge to cough, giggle, or break wind. Truth be told, I've been on sets where all three of those utterances have occurred. Fifteen seconds elapsed when a commotion was heard from behind the back wall of the set.

"Hold the roll!" Foster shouted.

"What the hell is that?" O'Brien asked.

Paul Laxton darted off to the area behind the set. I heard shouting. Some of it came from Laxton. It sounded like bodies crashed into furniture. A lot of four-letter words were exchanged, and I heard the unmistakable sound of fists hitting faces. It went on for several minutes, and at one point both Brad Foster and Pete O'Brien joined the fray. When that happened, Tyler and I moved to the end of the saloon's wall to take a look at what was happening.

The two men who earlier had been arguing at the breakfast table were flaying away at each other. Laxton was between them, trying to pull them apart. They were having none of it. The AD took a couple of punches and Foster grabbed the big guy with the beard and tried to pull him away from the fray. He succeeded in getting him to back off a couple of feet, but the bearded guy shook him off and Foster stumbled back into a light stand, both him and the light hitting the floor. Then bearded guy again lit into his opponent. O'Brien jumped between the two men, and Tyler and I looked at each other.

"You think they need help?" Tyler said.

"I doubt it. Reinforcements are on the way," I said, as I drew his attention to four crew members rounding the far corner of the set.

A few more fists flew and shouts continued, but finally the additional crew were able to separate the two men and drag them ten or fifteen feet away from each other. The shouting stopped and the two combatants settled down. Foster ordered the four crew members to get them the hell out of the soundstage. Two of them grabbed the bearded guy and escorted him to the door I'd come through earlier, while two more shoved the other guy toward a door on the opposite side of the stage.

Foster bent to pick up his headset, which had been dislodged during the fight. Laxton pulled a handkerchief from his back pocket and wiped a spot of blood off his chin. O'Brien asked if he was okay. The 2nd AD replied that he was.

Foster and O'Brien walked back toward the camera.

"Who the hell are those two?" O'Brien said.

"The guy with the beard is Tom Hanson," Foster said. "He's a gaffer. The other one is Wally Ahmanson. I think he's on the sound crew."

"What's their beef?" O'Brien continued.

"Damned if I know," Foster said.

I overheard them arguing when I was having breakfast," I said.

"What about?" Foster said.

"Far as I could tell, something having to do with the sound department."

The director and his AD exchanged puzzled looks and O'Brien said, "Get somebody from production to talk to them." Foster turned to Laxton and relayed the director's order. Laxton keyed his radio and walked off a few steps, as O'Brien and Foster walked to the camera. Tyler and I returned to our places.

Obviously embarrassed, O'Brien addressed the set full of extras. "Sorry, people. That's not what we had in mind when we called for room tone. Let's try it once more."

Again the sound man said, "Room tone," then the number of the scene, and "Take two."

This time the full minute elapsed before the man with the headphones said, "Got it. Thanks, folks."

Foster announced that we were broken for lunch—one hour.

My immersion into *Burnt Hills* was underway. Barring an argument that interrupted the sanctity of room tone, the results seemed to be positive. One could only hope the dustup was a one-time event. Time would tell.

9

In my humble opinion, sleeping late is one of life's unheralded pleasures. I recommend it for every red-blooded American male, especially if he has the added perk of being curled up next to someone like Carla Rizzoli. That's where I found myself mid-Saturday morning: two working actors with no early call, no angst over remembering dialogue and hitting your mark for the camera. Just the warm, fuzzy feeling of being next to someone with enticing curves. I was in the process of exploring one of those curves when she stirred, grabbed my hand and placed it over another curve and then uttered what could best be described as a purr of contentment.

"Are you awake?" I said.

"I am now." She turned over, flipped a strand of raven hair from her eyes and started her own exploration with her right hand. "Did you sleep well?"

"Aside from a snore or two, just fine."

She stopped her exploration and slapped my chest. "I don't snore, if that's what you're implying."

"Hmmm. Something woke me up. Must have been a leaf blower."

She propped herself up on one elbow and pinched my nose between her thumb and forefinger. "You're not exactly as quiet as a church mouse yourself." She leaned over and kissed me. "We'll have to coordinate our snores."

I returned her kiss and she rolled over on top of me. "What do you want to do today?" I asked.

"Go to the beach."

"With all the wind?"

"So? Put on a jacket. It ain't gonna blow away the water. The tide rolls on eternally, Shamus."

"Oooh. Such philosophy so early in the morning."

She glanced at the alarm clock next to the bed. "It's not early. The day is wasting away. Come on," she said, and crawled off me and pushed the covers back. I'll start the coffee. You jump in the shower."

I did just that and was drying off when she came into the bathroom with two fresh cups. She handed me one and set the other on the sink before stepping under the water. I thought about joining her but realized we'd never get anything accomplished if I gave in to that temptation.

"A nice walk on the beach and we'll be ready for a good brunch," she said. "What do you say?"

"Sounds like a plan," I said, and went back to the bedroom and started to get dressed.

As I finished tying my shoes Carla came in, wrapped in a towel and drying her hair with another. "Have you got a warm enough jacket?" she asked.

"I've got a windbreaker in the trunk of my car. I don't think I'm going to be able to keep my porkpie on, though."

"Oh, my God, crisis time," she said, and pulled open a drawer, poked around and tossed me a red stocking cap with a white puff ball on top of it. I pulled it on to just above my ears. "Very cute," she said, as she draped a plaid woolen scarf around my neck. "That should help too." She dropped her towel and began pulling on underwear as I walked into the kitchen and topped off my coffee.

Carla's wardrobe contributions were welcome. She, too, had a stocking cap on and wore a hooded sweatshirt. A stiff breeze greeted us as we got out of the car next to the Santa Monica Pier. The beach was fairly full of people. Most of them walked along the shore. A few sat on blankets. If they expected sunshine, they were disappointed. Heavy cloud cover filled the sky. We walked north from the pier. To our left we saw the outline of a tanker slowly inching its way south to either San Pedro or Long Beach. A couple of diehard surfers sat on their boards waiting for a wave. Better men than me, Gunga Din, I thought. We walked about half a mile and came to a sizable log that had washed up. We sat down and I removed some sand from one of my shoes.

"You ever get the urge to move up there?" Carla said.

"Where?" I turned to her and saw she was looking further north. "What? Malibu?"

"Yeah."

"I dunno, kiddo. Kind of out of my league."

She wrapped an arm around my shoulder. "If my show continues, we could maybe buy something."

"Are you serious? You better hope for syndication."

"Marsha, Alison and I think about it all the time. Believe me."

Marsha Bailey and Alison Jackson were Carla's two co-stars on her show *Three on a Beat*. My mention of syndication referred to the fact that after five seasons a show on one of the broadcast networks normally goes into syndication and the money starts to roll in. They weren't there yet, but if the ratings held up, they could start seeing some serious money.

"Well, I don't know," she said. "Food for thought."

"Come to think of it, might not be a bad idea. I don't know about Malibu, though. Maybe we should start inland and move west. Don't forget I've got that money Ben left me." A while back I'd helped Ben Roth, an elderly actor, locate his son. After he passed on, I learned that he'd left me two hundred and fifty grand for my efforts. Part of it had gone to Kelly Robinson, my daughter, to help with her education. The rest I'd put it in the bank where it has stayed, gathering interest.

"That's your nest egg," Carla said. "Your mad money."

I grabbed one of her gloved hands and gave it a squeeze. "Yeah, well, like you said, food for thought."

"Yup. You hungry?"

"I could eat."

She kissed me and bounded to her feet. "Follow me, Shamus."

The Bubba Gump Shrimp Company was spawned in the wake of the Tom Hanks film *Forrest Gump* and one of its branches subsequently landed on the Santa Monica Pier. A bubbly young hostess showed us to a four-top looking out over the water. She handed us menus and said our wait person would be right with us. References to the movie and its characters dominated the bill of fare. A young lady with a blond ponytail and piercing blue eyes appeared. Her name tag identified her as Bonnie and she asked if we'd like something to drink. Not shying away from the movie tie-ins, we both ordered *Lt. Dan's Pomegranate Punch*, consisting of Cruzon Coconut rum and De Kuyper pomegranate liqueur. She affirmed that was an excellent choice and said she'd be right back.

"Good thing you're driving, Eddie. I might be getting more punch than I need."

"But don't forget, we get souvenir glasses."

"Whoopee."

I chuckled and flipped to the list of appetizers and entrees. "All right, since we're in the mood, how about an order of *Bubba's Far Out Dip?*"

"Let's go for it," she said. "And continuing with the mood, I'm going to have *Lt. Dan's Surf & Turf.*" I glanced at her with a skeptical look on my face. "What? The ocean has invigorated me, man. I need to be fed!"

"You got it. I'll match you with the *Ping Pong Chicken Pasta.*"

"Yes!" She drummed her forefingers on the table and said, "We're both working, and we deserve it!" A woman at an adjacent table turned and gave us a smile and a thumbs-up.

Bonnie appeared with two huge glasses filled with the potent punch. She took our orders, said she'd be right back with the Far Out Dip, then moved off as we raised our glasses in a toast.

"Here's to gainful employment and more of it," Carla said.

"Hear, hear."

"And to no more green Kias," she added.

I paused, saw her wink with a smile and said, "Amen."

We'd no sooner taken off our jackets and deposited them on the extra chairs when Bonnie arrived with the appetizer. We started scooping up the dip with tortilla chips. It was a tasty mix of spinach, artichoke, tomato and jack cheese. A perfect complement to the punch and it didn't last long.

With the arrival of our entrees, rather than a second round of pomegranate punch, Carla switched to a glass of white wine and I settled on a Budweiser. We sampled each other's choices and pronounced them delicious.

"Do you think Gary Sinise had to sign off on using his character's name?" Carla said, as she sliced a bite off her turf.

"I doubt it," I said. Sinise, of course, was the actor who portrayed Lieutenant Dan in the film. "Whoever owns the copyright to the movie maybe had to. In this case I think that's Paramount."

Silence settled over us as we dug into our food. At one point the lady who'd earlier turned to Carla and given her a thumbs-up leaned over as she and her companion were leaving and said she was glad to see her eating a hefty lunch.

We finished stuffing ourselves and Bonnie appeared to ask us if we'd like anything else. We both passed on desserts but ordered coffee.

My cell phone buzzed, announcing the arrival of a text. The screen revealed one from Kelly Robinson, my daughter who lives with her adoptive parents in Cincinnati. There was a photo attached that showed her wearing a tee shirt Carla and I had recently sent her for her birthday.

"Hey, look at this," I said, and handed her the phone. The picture depicted Kelly wearing a red shirt that had a pair of black horned-rimmed glasses on its front. Above the glasses were the words *Does this shirt*, followed by *make me look smarter* underneath the specs. Kelly's text read "Your opinion, please."

Her message provoked giggles from both of us. "Damn, but she looks more like her mother all the time," I said, and texted back, *you don't even need the glasses.* We both looked at the picture for a moment until I said, "I've got to hit the head." I handed Carla the phone and stood up. "Send her your reply. Be right back."

When I returned Carla had the phone in her hand and was gazing at the picture. She had kind of a wistful look on her face as she handed it to me.

"Do you think about her a lot?" she said.

"All the time. I've got a picture of her on my desk."

"I don't mean her. I mean Elaine."

Her comment caught me by surprise. Carla knew all about my previous marriage and the circumstances surrounding our breakup and Elaine's subsequent murder. I stirred some cream into my coffee and nodded. "Sometimes. Why?"

"I don't know. Once in a while I feel kind of jealous of her. That she had you, and that she had Kelly."

I sipped some coffee and said, "Well, she didn't have me very long, honey. I did my best to screw that up. Now you've got me, and I'm through screwing up. Where is this coming from?"

"From watching you and how you react to Kelly. Makes me wish I had the same thing."

I glanced over at her and she returned my gaze with eyes that looked like they were searching for something. What? Reassurance? Validity? I leaned back in my chair as Bonnie walked up and poured more coffee.

"Sounds like we need a talk. About serious stuff," I said. "This have anything to do with what we talked about earlier? Moving? Buying property?"

"Sort of. I don't mean to scare you off, Shamus. But there comes a time when we girls need to talk about that kind of…stuff." She raised her coffee cup and took a sip. "But right now I need to walk off some of this surf and turf. Let's table it for the time being, okay?"

"Okay," I said, still a bit surprised about what had prompted the topic. But then, given the fact that I'd been clueless as to how my behavior had soured my relationship with Elaine, I took her comments as a sign I had better not take for granted my feelings about Carla and what she expected of me. Maybe it was time to think seriously about turning my back on my tendency to be a lone wolf. As I donned my windbreaker and settled the bill, that prospect looked pretty good to me.

With our souvenir glasses in hand, we walked south from the Pier, the wind at our backs and a sun that periodically broke through the cloud cover. We talked about our respective film projects. Carla revealed that *Three on a Beat* was starting a new episode on Monday, the final one before hiatus. I remarked how different today's television network schedules were. Back in the day—or even further back—a show's season lasted for thirty-nine episodes. Then thirteen became the norm, with an additional "back nine" making the total twenty-two. Now, if you started to get hooked on a show, you were subject to an "autumn hiatus," then a few more episodes before a "winter hiatus." It's no wonder cable and streaming platforms have begun to make deep inroads into broadcast television.

"What time is your call on Monday?" Carla asked.

"Seven."

"You think you'll have any more fistfights?"

"I hope not."

Our walk brought us to the edge of a small gully where tidal flows had formed a little creek. The sand looked wet and capable of doing damage to a pair of shoes, so we turned around and started back to the car.

"Hey, how about a movie?" Carla said.

"I'm always up for a movie. What'd you have in mind?"

"Let's get back to the car and out of this wind. I'll check my phone."

With the wind slicing through our clothing, we found refuge in the car and the heater on full blast. Carla pushed buttons and came up with a list of options at Grauman's Chinese Theater, which, since 2013, has been called TCL theater, in the wake of a Chinese company purchasing the landmark. There was a late afternoon showing of *Green Book*, the story of classical musician Don Shirley's journey through the deep south and the racial tensions he encountered. Mahershala Ali had just won his second Supporting Actor Oscar for his portrayal of Shirley and was ably supported by the wonderful young actor Viggo Mortensen, who played his chauffeur.

We had plenty of time before the movie started, so we detoured through Beverly Hills and fantasized about the mansions that filled every street. Carla pointed to one where a tour bus had stopped, one of many ferrying gawkers to the homes of the stars.

"Dahling, what do you think about that one?" she said, in a spot-on imitation of Zsa Zsa Gabor.

"A bit provincial," I replied, trying my best to sound like George Sanders or James Mason. I don't think I was very successful with either one.

We laughed uproariously and made our way eastward on Sunset. Since parking in Hollywood on a Saturday night was scarce, I slid the car into my allotted space behind my building. Without the biting wind of the beach, we felt it prudent to eliminate the stocking caps and scarves. I rescued my trusty porkpie from the back seat, but Carla decided to stay with her hooded sweatshirt. It was only a few blocks to Grauman's and we had time to take in the hand and feet impressions in the cement courtyard of the Hollywood landmark. We both thought it wise to forego popcorn but shared a big cup of soda and settled in to watch Ali and Mortensen strut their stuff.

The movie was a fascinating story of the two men and their relationship. An actual "green book" did exist back in the Jim Crow days, providing guidance for Blacks about where to go to avoid racial tension and violence.

Darkness had descended when we emerged from the theater. There was a slight nip in the air, and Carla slipped her arm through mine as we walked eastward on the Boulevard.

"What did you think?" she said.

"I thought it was excellent. Ali is a hell of an actor."

"Viggo is no slouch either," she said. "He's sexy."

"How so?"

"Well, he's got that classic cleft in his chin. You know, like Mitchum and Kirk Douglas."

I ran my fingers over my chin and said, "Hmm, guess I'm out of luck."

"Oh, honey, you're already sexy. Besides, I don't know how those guys manage to shave with those canyons in the way."

We laughed and stopped for the light at Highland and Hollywood. She leaned over and kissed me on the cheek. "Thanks for a nice afternoon, Shamus."

"My pleasure."

The light changed and we continued walking. Halfway down the block, we stopped to look in the window of one of the many stores that catered to tourists. The shop was still open. Huge plate glass windows were on each side of the front door. The owner, who looked to be of some Middle Eastern ethnicity, beckoned for us to come in. We smiled, shook our heads and waved to him. Everything imaginable having to do with Hollywood was displayed in the most garish manner possible. We moved to the other side of the door as a young Asian couple came up behind us to start their own rubbernecking.

"Look at this stuff, Eddie. Mavis would go nuts in this place."

"Believe me when I tell you she's probably already combed through this entire store." I pointed to a pair of action figures in the guise of Superman and Wonder Woman. "For instance, those two have already crossed her path."

Traffic on the street was heavy and from behind me I heard what sounded like a vehicle back firing.

But I was wrong.

The window in front of us suddenly exploded and shards of glass rained down upon us. I pushed Carla to the sidewalk and shielded her with my body as another shot flew over my head. As I glanced toward the traffic, two more shots rang out. One of them shattered the glass window in front of the Asian couple. The second struck the woman, who fell to the sidewalk. Her companion screamed and sank to his knees beside her. Further down the street pedestrians dropped to the sidewalk at the sounds of the gunfire. I looked at the flow of traffic and saw there was a red light at the intersection. A dark SUV was behind two vehicles. It suddenly veered to the right, jumped over the curb onto the sidewalk, and destroyed a wire trash can and a newspaper box in its path. The SUV squealed around the corner, scattered pedestrians and headed north on Highland Avenue to the Hollywood Freeway.

I fumbled for my cell phone and frantically punched in the 911 digits.

10

After I relayed the information to the 911 dispatcher I sat back on my haunches and turned Carla so I could look at her. Her face was etched in fear and shock. Bits of glass were caught in her hair. One of them had landed on her forehead and resulted in a small trickle of blood seeping toward her left eye. I held her head in my hands and forced her to look at me.

"It's okay now. They're gone. I'm here. You're safe."

"Are you okay?" she said.

"Yeah." I pulled a handkerchief from my hip pocket and pressed it against the cut. "Keep pressure on this. You caught a piece of glass on your forehead. It doesn't look too bad but keep the pressure on." I helped her rearrange herself so she sat with her back against the building. "I'm going to check on the other couple. I'll be right back."

The shopkeeper came through his front door as I scrambled over to the young Asian man who knelt next to his female companion.

"I called nine-one-one," the shopkeeper said.

"I did too," I replied. I put my hands on the Asian man's shoulders and told him help was on the way. The woman on the sidewalk had taken a bullet through her right shoulder and her clothing was soaked in blood. I turned to the shopkeeper and said, "Can you bring a blanket of some sort to put over her?"

"Yes, yes, right away."

"Maybe a towel or two also?"

"Yes, absolutely," he said, and scurried back into his shop.

"Ambulance should be here soon," I said to the Asian man. He moaned and rocked back and forth on his haunches. The shopkeeper reappeared with a couple of hand towels and a blanket. I pressed the towels to the wound and we draped the blanket over the woman. "Stay with them, will you?" I said to the shopkeeper. "Until the ambulance gets here?"

"Yes, of course," he said.

I clapped him on the shoulder and went back to Carla. She'd pulled her knees up and had one arm around them. The other one held the handkerchief, which by now revealed a splotch of blood in the center.

"Have you got a handkerchief or some tissues in your purse?" I said.

"I think so. Have a look."

I pulled her handbag off her shoulder and started rummaging around inside. She had one of those pocket-sized packet of tissues. I pulled several sheets out and replaced the bloody handkerchief with them. She pressed the tissues to the cut and looked up at me.

"Did any land on you?"

"No. My porkpie took the brunt."

She managed a smile and said, "Now I know why you're so reluctant to take it off."

I kissed her cheek, pulled her toward me and held her.

"Hell of a way to end a nice day, huh, Shamus?"

"Yeah. I'm damn glad it wasn't worse."

In the distance we heard the sounds of sirens. I looked down the sidewalk and saw a tableau of chaos and confusion. We held each other tightly and watched two ambulances screech to a stop amid shouts from bystanders petrified with fear.

It's amazing how quickly police and emergency services can take control of a situation. We watched as two police cars blocked off the lane of traffic next to the curb along the entire block. Lights flashed. Yellow cones popped up. Two officers directed west-bound traffic to the center lane. With siren blaring and lights flashing, an ambulance bumped over the curb and stopped next to the Asian woman who lay on the sidewalk. She was quickly put on a stretcher. The collapsible legs went up and it rolled to the rear of the ambulance. The legs folded again as she was slid into the rear of the vehicle. An EMT helped her companion inside, the door slammed shut and with siren wailing again, it nudged its way through the intersection of Hollywood and Highland.

Carla sat on the rear bumper of a second ambulance while two paramedics attended to her. One was a young Black man whose name tag identified himself as Tyler. He first asked Carla for her name and then told her his name was Jerry. He wrapped her arm with a blood pressure cuff and took her pulse. The second EMT was Helen Wilson, who busied herself with cleaning the cut on Carla's forehead.

"Blood pressure's a little high, Carla," Tyler said. "And your pulse is racing a bit, but I guess that's to be expected. Aside from the cut on your head, how do you feel?"

"I'm okay," Carla said.

"The bleeding's stopped," Wilson said. "The cut is only superficial. I put a couple of butterflies on it, which should do the job. Keep it clean, and if it bothers you later tonight or tomorrow get yourself to an emergency room, okay?" As tears rolled down her cheeks, Carla nodded and grabbed for my hand.

"Just sit here for a bit," Tyler said. "Police are probably going to want to ask you a few questions."

As if on cue, Charlie Rivers walked up from the front of the ambulance. He wore a newsboy-style cap on his head and as per usual, his suit looked rumpled and lived in. His face registered complete surprise when he saw Carla and me.

"Even short-timers work on weekends, Charlie?"

"Yeah, I got the call. No rest for the wicked." He showed his badge to the two paramedics. "Surprised to see you here, Collins. What happened?"

I pointed to one of the shattered plate glass windows on the shop.

"Carla and I were standing in front of that store. Somebody opened fire from behind us."

"Are you all right?" he said.

"Carla got cut, but I'm okay."

"Good thing he was a lousy shot." He turned to Tyler. "You done with these two?"

"They're good to go, Lieutenant," Tyler said.

"Let's get in my shop," Charlie said. "Bring me up to speed."

Both Carla and I thanked the two EMTs and we followed him to the front of the fire truck where an unmarked police car sat with a flashing blue bubble on its dashboard. A few scattered drops of rain fell as Carla and I climbed into the back.

Charlie stopped and gave instructions to a detective, then climbed behind the wheel, turned in his seat and pulled out a pen and a notebook. "Okay, start from the beginning," he said.

We did, from the time we left the theater.

"Tell me about the shooter's vehicle."

"An SUV. Black, or dark blue," I said. "It all happened so fast I couldn't get a good look at it."

"The make? A plate number, maybe?"

"Nope. Sorry. Maybe one of the higher-end SUVs? Navigator? Escalade? It squealed around the corner and headed up Highland before I could get a good look at it."

"Well, maybe someone caught a glimpse of it." He jotted down a note. "If it got on the freeway, it could be anywhere. Up in the hills, Burbank, the Valley." His radio crackled and he picked it up. "Yeah?"

"Lieutenant, we've got somebody who thinks they've got a partial plate number."

"Thinks?"

"The guy's pretty sure. He was waiting for the light to change. Saw the SUV coming right at him."

"Okay, see if you can get some corroboration from someone else."

"Roger."

He hung up the handset and turned to us. "Well, a partial is better than nothing."

"He was in front of somebody before he went up over the curb," I said.

"Unless the shooter has a vanity plate on his vehicle, chances are whoever was behind him probably didn't pay any attention. And then the light changes and he's through the intersection before we get here. Not much help there." He jotted something down in his notebook. "Okay. Couple of things. You think you were his target?"

"I'd bet on it."

"Why?"

Carla and I exchanged glances and I said, "Well, not to get all paranoid here, Charlie, but remember what we talked about the other day?"

"That somebody's trying to silence you so you can't testify?"

"Exactly."

"Then why did he miss?"

"Hell, I don't know, Charlie!" I said, my voice rising. "Maybe he's a piss-poor shot! Moving vehicle? It's night?"

"Okay, okay, point taken," he said. Carla put an arm around my shoulders. There was silence for a moment as Charlie looked through the windshield, then turned back to us. "Then why shoot at the other couple?"

I didn't have an answer, but Carla did.

"To draw attention from Eddie being the victim?" she said. "Make it seem more like a routine drive-by?"

"Good point," Charlie said, and nodded. "Did either of you know the other couple?"

"No," Carla said. "They just walked up behind us as we looked through the window."

He made some more notes in his book and then flipped it shut and put it back in his pocket. "Okay, that's it for now. Give me a buzz if you think of anything else. We'll get to work on this possible partial plate."

I opened the door and Carla and I got out.

Charlie climbed out and leaned over the top of his car. "Hold up a minute. Where's your car?"

"At my building," I said. "We walked to the theater."

"Let me get someone to give you two a ride." He reached in and grabbed the radio. "This is Rivers. Any available officer come to my twenty." He replaced the radio transmitter and shut the car door. "Eddie, one more thing. You said there were four of those guys that were indicted, right?"

"Right."

"And they're all on ankle bracelets?"

"Yeah, according to the DA."

"We'll reach out to Ventura Sheriff's. Have them give us their whereabouts tonight."

"Appreciate it, Charlie."

"You got it."

A uniformed officer approached the car. "What you need, Lieutenant?"

"Take these two to wherever they need to go."

"Yes, sir," the cop said. "Follow me, folks."

The uniformed cop dropped us at my car behind my building. We climbed in and headed for Carla's condo. Both of us were silent for several minutes, trying to assess what we'd just been through.

"How you doin'?" I said.

"Okay, now. But I was scared to death."

I reached over and clasped her hand. "Me too, honey."

Further words weren't needed. I parked the car in her lot and with arms around each other, we rode up the elevator to her unit. She said she was going to have a cup of tea and asked if I wanted one. I opted for a cup of coffee. We sat on the sofa in front of the television set. I turned it on, but every channel was mindless. She finally turned it off and we sat next to each other, lost in our thoughts.

Mine weren't very pleasant, and I'm sure hers weren't either.

11

Sleep proved elusive, not only for me, but for Carla as well. It had nothing to do with our mutual snoring, but rather with dreams of sounds and sights: gun fire, windows shattering, a bleeding woman laying on a sidewalk, a dark SUV careening around a corner. I was awakened several times, once when Carla moaned. She woke when I folded her into my arms. We finally managed to fall into some semblance of uninterrupted sleep and didn't rouse ourselves until well after ten o'clock.

I sipped on a cup of coffee and watched her as she scrambled some eggs. Her face was drawn and her eyes were puffy. She pushed the eggs onto two plates, added some bacon and set them on the kitchen table. I spread a dollop of grape jam on a piece of buttered toast and handed it to her.

"Thanks," she said.

I pointed to the cut on her forehead. "Looks like a scab is forming."
"Yeah, I saw that."

"Makeup will probably cover it okay."

"Either that or I'll wear some kind of a hat."

We shared some silence as we chewed on bacon and eggs.

"What are you going to do?" she said.

"How do you mean?"

"If someone is really after you? How are you going to deal with that?"

I swallowed a forkful of eggs and saw her dark eyes boring into me. "I'll probably have to carry my gun."

"You can legally do that?"

"Yeah. I have to have it as part of the license." She nodded and sipped some orange juice. I reached over and squeezed her left hand. "That doesn't do you any good, though."

"Well, I'm going to be around a lot of people, so I don't think it's the same problem as it is for you." She set the orange juice down and returned the hand squeeze.

"You should probably stay away from me," I said.

"Nice try, but you're stuck with me, Shamus." She raised my hand and kissed it. "But let me run something by you."

"Shoot." I winced and shook my head. "Ooops. Wrong choice of phrase."

"What if you weren't the object of the shooter?"

"It sure looked like I was," I replied.

"But why shoot at that Asian couple?"

"Well, like you said. To draw attention from me."

"But then why fire a second time and shatter the windows?"

I laid my fork on my plate and took a sip of coffee. "And your point is?"

"All right, follow me here. What if the shooter had a beef with the owner of that store? And we and that other couple just happened to be in the wrong place at the wrong time."

"I suppose it's possible," I said, as I put my knife and fork on the plate and shoved it to the side of the table. "Do you remember the name of the place?"

"'All things Hollywood' or something like that."

I pulled my cell from my pocket, found a number and punched in the digits.

"Who are you calling?"

"Mavis. Maybe she knows the owner." After two rings, she picked up.

"Isn't it part of my contract that the boss doesn't hassle me on my days off?" she said.

"You've got a contract?"

She chuckled and said, "What's up, boss man?"

"Have you dealt with the owner of a shop on Hollywood? North side of the street, between Highland and McCadden Place?"

"Yeah. Nice guy. Akeem Farouq or something like that. Why?"

I briefly filled her in and what had happened the previous evening.

"Good God, Eddie, are you all right?"

"I'm fine."

"And Carla?"

"She caught a piece of glass on her forehead, but she's okay. So, this Farouq, is he difficult to work with? Anything that would cause somebody to take a pot shot at him?"

"Oh, gosh, I don't think so. He's always been up front with me. Very friendly. Always glad to see me when I go in there. Even gives me some good discounts on stuff."

"Okay, that's good to know."

"Any witnesses?"

"Somebody apparently got a partial license plate on the shooter's vehicle. LAPD's going to run it down."

"You think it's got anything to do with those four creeps you ran into up in Piru?"

"I don't know. Charlie's going to ask the Ventura Sheriff's Department to track their whereabouts last night."

"Good grief, right in the middle of Hollywood Boulevard? Whoever the heck did it has some kind of *cojones.* "

"Yeah, and fortunately poor aim."

"Are you filming tomorrow?"

"I have to be there at seven."

"Well, look, I'll stop by Farouq's store and see if he's got any ideas about who might have destroyed his windows."

"Good idea. Thanks. I'll try and check in with you sometime during the day."

"Sounds good. Glad you're okay, Eddie."

She hung up and I went for more coffee. "Mavis knows the owner. She's going to talk to him tomorrow to see if he's got any idea who might have it in for him." I topped off our coffee cups and set the pot back on its perch. "What do you want to do today?"

"After last night absolutely nothing." She picked up the plates and opened the dishwasher. "There's got to be some mindless television on somewhere. Find something and I'll clean up the dishes."

I tapped her on the shoulder. She turned and I wrapped my arms around her. "I'm sorry you had to be confronted like that last night, honey. You shouldn't have to deal with that kind of danger."

"Yeah, but wasn't it Willy Loman who said 'it comes with the territory'?"

"Different context, but you've got the right character."

She draped her arms around my neck and looked into my eyes. "You're my territory, Shamus. I wouldn't have it any other way." She bent my head down and covered my lips with hers, a kiss that carried more significance than any we'd shared in a long time. "Find a game and I'll be right in."

I picked up my coffee and walked into the living room. Channel surfing found a Dodgers and Mets game. I leafed through the Sunday paper, but put it aside when Carla sank into the sofa next to me.

She set her cup on the coffee table, tucked one leg under her and turned to me. "When's your next appointment with your doctor?"

"You mean my head guy?"

She pursed her lips and said, "Yes. Your head guy. Your PTSD counselor."

"Not sure. We've got to work around my shooting schedule."

"After last night, you shouldn't stay away from him for too long."

"No, I won't. We've obviously got a lot to talk about."

She nodded and picked up her coffee cup, took a sip and looked at the television. Silence filled the room for several moments.

I leaned forward and set my cup down on the coffee table. "But there's a new wrinkle."

"What?"

"You. Last night you were also in the line of fire."

She sipped and turned to me. "Okay, turn about, fair play. After what happened, I don't mind telling you I was scared shitless. I've been thinking about it. And maybe I should see someone too."

"I think that's a good idea. We could go together."

"I kind of like that," she said. "His and hers PTSD counselors."

"How Beverly Hills of us. What's next? Plastic surgeons?"

We looked at each other, and, despite the seriousness of the topic, broke into laughter.

"How should I go about finding someone?" she said.

"I can call my guy and get you a referral. Or better yet, you've got medical people attached to your show, don't you?"

"Yeah, both a doc and a nurse."

"Talk to them. They'll probably know someone right off the bat."

"Yeah, good idea," she said, and scooted over on the sofa and nestled herself into my arms.

So there we were, two unsuspecting victims of violence seeking comfort with each other. I damn well knew I was glad she was there for me…and I was also glad I was there for her.

12

For the rest of our Sunday Carla and I tried every possible way to put some distance between us and what had happened in front of Akeem Farouq's store on Hollywood Boulevard. We devoured the Sunday paper, tried to get involved in a baseball game and helped each other with dialogue for our upcoming scenes; we napped, ordered Chinese food, and finished off the day with Turner Classic Movies and a breezy, frothy Cary Grant and Doris Day film, *That Touch of Mink.*

Since I was again called to Sunset Ranch before sunup, I thought it best to bunk in my apartment. We held each close before I left and did our best to reassure ourselves that we wouldn't encounter any further mayhem directed toward us.

I parked the car in its assigned spot behind my building and opened the trunk. My Beretta 21 Bobcat was kept in a metal box stashed under a ratty beach towel. I opened it and took out the gun. Once the office door was locked behind me, I set about cleaning and oiling the firearm. Not in the habit of carrying it all the time, I nevertheless thought it wise to make sure it was fully operational.

There was one message on the answering machine: AT&T informed me that my account was eligible for huge discounts. Good to hear, I thought, if I had such an account. But I didn't, so I quickly deleted it. After pulling down Mr. Murphy's bed, I brushed my teeth, undressed, and climbed into the sack. I thought about delving into a new Lee Child novel I'd picked up, but my mind was cluttered, so I doused the light and left Jack Reacher for another time.

The security guard at Sunset Ranch easily spotted the tag in my windshield and waved me through the gate. The sun was only a glow to the east, but it looked like movie activity was already underway. I stuffed my wallet and the Beretta into the glove compartment, locked the car and headed for the honey wagons. The door to my dressing room was unlocked and the day's call sheet and sides were on the table. I picked them up and went looking for chow. The breakfast roach coach was nestled up next to a soundstage, but in deference to the morning's high desert chill, tables had been moved inside. With a plate full of scrambled eggs, bacon and toast, I came through the door and spotted Lois Maxwell sitting by herself.

"Morning, Lois. Mind if I join you?"

"Pull up a chair. Good to see you."

"Let me get some coffee," I said, as I set down my plate. "Can I get you anything?"

"I wouldn't say no to another cup of coffee. Just black."

"You got it." I walked over to a table where coffee urns sat, along with cream and sugar. Coolers full of juices and milk sat next to the table. I grabbed a bottle of orange juice, stuck it in the pocket of my coat and filled two cups with coffee.

"Looks like we're working together today," she said, glancing up from the call sheet she was scanning. "I hope you're going to take it easy on this ol' senior actress."

"Something tells me you're not going to have anything to worry about," I said, as I sprinkled some pepper on the eggs. "How was your weekend?"

"Pretty quiet. I hit a couple of good yard sales. Amazing what people decide to get rid of." She held up one end of a scarf that was around her neck. "Got this. A buck and a half." Then she adjusted the cap on her head, which could best be described as a newsboy hat. "How 'bout this? Five bucks. A steal."

"You look downright Bohemian," I said.

"That's me. The orginal Bohemian," she said, and let loose with a laugh, then sipped on her coffee and glanced around the soundstage. "Heard you had some fisticuffs the other day."

"Yeah. Couple of the crew."

"Were they fired?"

"I don't know," I said, as I glanced around the soundstage. "I don't see them."

"Probably argued over who moves a light from A to B." She chuckled, then sipped some coffee. "Aw, hell, I shouldn't be so snarky. Those guys work their butts off."

"They do indeed." I let it go with that statement. While I did concede that union protocols sometimes create little fiefdoms with their job descriptions and divisions of labor, I also knew that in most cases, film crews are the backbone of the movie business and I wasn't in the habit of bad-mouthing them.

"And how was your weekend, Mr. Private Eye?"

"I've had better."

"I'm sorry. Feel like sharing?"

On one hand, I thought it was none of Lois Maxwell's business, but on the other hand, she'd started to become sort of a pal on *Burnt Hills* and, as my counselor had been telling me, I was better off talking about what happened, rather than keeping it bottled up. So I related the events of Saturday night to her. When I finished, she sat transfixed, her eyes wide with surprise.

"My God, that's terrible. Were there witnesses?"

"Plenty. The cops were able to get a partial license plate. Hopefully, they'll come up with something."

I finished my breakfast and we chatted for a few minutes. She told me about a time where she'd been held up at gun point by someone in the middle of the day when she was walking to her car. We both acknowledged it was part of life in the big city, but she went on to tell me that the incident caused her to get a handgun and take training in the proper use of it. I complimented her on her decision and got up to refill our coffee cups.

When I came back to the table we ran the dialogue for the scene we had until a production assistant walked up and said they were ready for both of us in makeup.

Lois knew Blake, one of the makeup people, from another job. Their back-and-forth stories and items of gossip provoked lots of laughs and made the time in the chair fly by. I was through before her, told her I'd see her on the set and walked back to my dressing trailer. Chet Cassidy's clothes still fit me to a tee, despite the weekend's foray into the Bubba Gump Shrimp Company and takeout Moo Goo Gai Pan. Satisfied with what I saw in the mirror, I was ready to go when the knock on the door summoned me to reel magic before the camera.

The scene between Lois and me took place in one of the upstairs rooms in the Empire Hotel. Dolly Blaine, her character—owner of the hotel—tries to pry some information from Chet Cassidy as to what the sheriff plans to do about complaints he's been getting from Jeremiah Rawlins, a Black rancher. It seems Rawlins is being harassed by Bart Kincannon, owner of the largest spread in the valley over water and grazing rights.

The hotel room was built on a soundstage different from the one where I'd filmed my previous scene. In the van on the way to the set, a production assistant revealed that indoor scenes were being shot earlier in the day, to allow for the morning's chill to disappear.

Lois and I were the only two characters in the shot. After morning greetings between actors and crew, we ran through the scene a couple of times, then shot it. Pete O'Brien, the director, liked what he saw and started shooting coverage—closeups of both of us. We wrapped the scene a little after 10 AM and were told to standby for further shooting later in the morning.

It had warmed up enough for me to decline a ride back to my trailer. Instead, I started walking and once again began to daydream about striding through some dust-encrusted hamlet in the middle of nowhere. At one point I saw a group of tourists being escorted along part of the main street. Then I recalled being informed at the table read that Sunset Ranch offered guided tours, but the production had been assured that they would in no way interfere with the *Burnt Hills* shoot. Right, I thought; if you believe that, I've got some waterfront property in Pasadena you might be interested in.

The morning hadn't warmed up as much as I had thought, so I was glad I'd left the heat on in my trailer. I kicked it up a notch and powered up my phone. There was a text from Mavis, which read: *Stopped by Farouq's shop on my way to the office. His windows are boarded up, but he was open. He couldn't think of anyone who'd have a grudge against him. I told him I worked for you, and he said to tell you he's sorry about the whole incident. He wanted to know if I knew anything about the woman who was shot. I said I didn't and would ask you. Have you heard anything?* I replied and said that I didn't, then texted Charlie Rivers and asked him if LAPD had been able to learn anything about the condition of the Asian woman from Saturday night.

I looked over the next scene to be shot. This also was with Lois and consisted of the two of us walking from her hotel room to the sheriff's office. I'd leafed through the morning's paper and was into a crossword when Cheryl, the production assistant, knocked on the door and said they were ready for us. After powering down the phone, I donned a Stetson they had given me and stepped outside. Cheryl had commandeered a golf cart that had Lois in the front seat. I climbed in the back and we headed out for the main street of this fictional hamlet.

"Do you golf, Eddie?" Lois asked.

"Never had the pleasure. I think I'll stick with Mark Twain on that."

"Oh, yeah. What did he say?"

"'Golf is a good walk ruined,' or words to that effect."

She burst into laughter and turned to me. "Hah! Good one. I'm going to remember that."

Cheryl pulled up to a hitching post outside a building designated as the Empire Hotel. Across the street, about twenty yards away, a group of tourists gathered to watch the proceedings. O'Brien described the action to us. We were to come through the front doors of the building, turn to our right and walk along a sidewalk of planks running along the street. The cameraman, strapped to a Steadicam, was to follow us as we engaged in conversation. At one point, Lois was to stop and speak to a woman who'd stuck her head out of a dry goods store, while I went two or three steps ahead of her. After the women's conversation, she was to catch up with me and we continued another ten yards and entered the sheriff's office.

After we got our directions, a soundman wired us up and O'Brien turned to Brad Foster, his 1st assistant director. "What about that crowd?" he said, pointing to the group of tourists across the street.

"I've been assured they aren't going to be a problem," Foster said.

"I hope you're right. All right, people, let's try a rehearsal."

Lois and I went through double doors of the building and Foster called for silence and for everyone to settle. After a moment the director hollered "Action!" and I pulled one of the doors open and we started down the planked sidewalk. Our conversation went on for about fifteen yards until a woman stuck her head out of the dry goods store and Lois stopped to talk to her. Just as directed, when the conversation ended, she rejoined me and we continued on to the sheriff's office.

O'Brien yelled, "Cut," and asked if the Steadicam operator had any problems. He said he didn't. The Steadicam is a cantilevered camera strapped to the operator with a harness. It provides much more flexibility and a smoother image than a typical hand-held. Our operator was a tall lanky gentleman, whose spindly legs—along with the harness—made him look almost like a huge bug. The sound man also reported he had no problems. O'Brien then asked if everything was okay with the two of us. We said we were good to go and he said, "All right, folks, let's lay one down."

Lois and I went back behind the double glass doors, settled, and listened to Foster's litany of directions for the shot. When we heard "Action," we started through the doors and repeated the action until we heard O'Brien call, "Cut." We huddled with him and Foster and they said they'd like a second take just for safety's sake.

Before Lois and I repositioned ourselves he gave us a couple of tweaks and we went back through the doors. On cue, we came out of the building and started our action. Lois stopped to talk to the woman in the dry goods store, and as she turned to rejoin me, the scene suddenly stopped—not because of a direction from O'Brien. He hadn't called "Cut!"

The action came to a screeching halt after a shot was fired and Lois Maxwell collapsed to the planked sidewalk.

13

As it had two days ago, chaos erupted around me. When I heard the gun shot, I immediately hit the planked sidewalk and saw Lois collapse in front of me. A chorus of shouts came from across the street where the group of tourist onlookers had congregated. As I crawled over to her, I heard O'Brien order Cheryl, the PA, to call the production's on-set doctor. Brad Foster, O'Brien's first AD, immediately got on his cell phone and called 911. When I reached Lois, I saw a red strawberry of blood soaking her costume on the upper part of her right arm. I turned her on her back and rested her head on my thigh.

Her eyes fluttered open and she looked up at me. "Damn it, Eddie, I thought it was you that someone was gunning for, not me."

"Looks like you've joined the club," I said, as O'Brien and Foster dropped to their knees beside her.

Foster whipped out a bandana from his hip pocket and wrapped it around her arm above the wound. "Hang on, Lois, help is on the way."

O'Brien took off his jacket and wadded it up, then placed it under her head as I sank back on my haunches. Another crew member took off his denim jacket and draped it over her.

Lois stayed conscious, but her face registered a look of panic as the reality of what had happened washed over her. I glanced toward the opposite side of the street and saw two security guards begin to herd the onlookers away from the scene.

The production's doctor rushed up and asked everyone to step back to give him room. He started attending to her and I retreated to the wall of the building that served as the sheriff's office. Foster asked me if I was all right and I assured him I was.

But that wasn't true.

As I leaned against the wall and sat down, I felt my heart race and I was short of breath. Being this close to gun fire in the space of a few days filled me with panic and outright fear.

Pandemonium continued to bubble as word of the shooting reached the entire crew. Several of them ran to the other side of the street and helped the security guards with the crowd that was being ushered to the rear of buildings away from the set. Off in the distance I heard the sound of an approaching siren.

The doctor ripped open the seam of the sleeve on Lois's costume and pressed gauze on the wound, which, to my untrained eye, didn't look all that serious, but I'd have to leave that opinion to someone who knew what the hell they were doing. O'Brien grabbed her left hand and Foster and the doc helped her sit up. After a moment, she said she was okay, and they guided her to a bench that sat next to the wall of the set. I had to admire her pluck and the way she kept telling them she was all right.

An ambulance tore around buildings at the end of the street and skidded to a stop. Two EMTs rushed to Lois, and after peppering her with a few questions, they helped her walk to the rear of their vehicle. One of them climbed in after her, the other one informed Foster that she'd be taken to the Antelope Valley Medical Center in Acton. He then got behind the wheel and they roared off, leaving behind a stunned crew.

I watched O'Brien huddling with his assistant directors. The crowd of onlookers had disappeared. While I couldn't be absolutely sure, I thought the gun shot had come from that direction. Which made no sense whatsoever. It stretched credulity to think that someone had brought a gun with them, but when I thought about it, I hadn't seen a lot of security prowling the set. If someone wanted to smuggle a firearm into a guided tour and nobody was going to screen them, have at it, I guess.

Then another thought occurred to me: was the shot intended for Lois, or was I once again in someone's crosshairs? As I dwelled on that prospect, more paranoia started to seep into my head, which was all I needed.

I pushed the thought aside when Debbie Merton, one of O'Brien's second ADs, walked up and leaned over in front of me.

"You doin' okay, Eddie?"

"Yeah. What's the plan?"

"Well, obviously, we've been thrown a curve ball here. Why don't you head on back to your trailer and let us sort some things out, okay?"

"You got it."

"You need anything? Coffee?"

"Yeah, some coffee would be good, and some water."

"Cheryl's here with a cart. I'll tell her to swing by craft services for you."

"Thanks."

I crawled into the front seat of the golf cart and was whisked away, wondering what the fate of *Burnt Hills* was going to be.

Fortified with coffee and two bottles of water, I hopped out of the cart in front of my trailer. Cheryl told me she'd keep me up to date on any schedule changes and drove off. Inside, I took off my Stetson, laid it brim-up on the table, then gulped some coffee and pulled out my cell phone. There was text from Charlie Rivers: *No word yet on the Asian woman. But heard from the Ventura Sheriff. Hit me back.*

I punched in his number, and he picked up after three rings.

"What's the word from Ventura?" I said.

"They tell me all four of those guys were nowhere near Hollywood and Highland Saturday night."

"But that doesn't mean they weren't behind it."

"No, you're right, if you want to go there."

I took a beat, surprised at his comment. "You don't think they could have hired somebody to put a hit on me?"

"That's not what I'm saying."

"Then what are you saying?"

"I'm saying let us get evidence. Once we get a make on the shooter's vehicle, let's see where it leads us."

"So, any progress on that front?"

"Some. But there's a hell of a lot of dark SUVs in the county. We're narrowing it down." He took the phone away from his ear and talked to somebody in the background, then said, "Can you drop by the station today? We need to get a statement from you."

"I'm up at Sunset Ranch, working."

"All day?"

"Not sure. We had an incident a few minutes ago."

"What kind of incident?"

"An actress got shot," I said, and went on to give him the shortened version of the events of the morning.

"For crissakes, Collins, can't you ever stay out of trouble?"

"I'm trying, Charlie."

"Well, swing by when you get the chance."

"Roger that."

"And, hey?"

"Yeah?"

"Don't worry, Eddie, we're workin' it."

Easy for him to say, I thought, as I broke the connection. I took a swallow of coffee, then splashed cold water on my face. When I sat down and looked in the mirror of my dressing table, the image I saw was of someone who looked scared. I sent a text to Carla, relating the news. There wasn't an immediate response, so I called the office and Mavis picked up.

"Hey, Eddie, how's it going up there?"

"You're not going to believe it."

She didn't. "You have got to be kidding me. Is the lady all right?"

"It didn't look that serious to me, but they took her to a hospital to be sure. I'm waiting to hear what the production's going to do next. If they can work around her."

"Did you find out anything about the lady wo was shot outside Farouq's shop?"

"Yeah," I said. "Just got off the phone with Charlie. They haven't heard anything. You might want to tell Farouq he can call Cedars Sinai. That's where they took her. I don't know if they'll give him any information, but it's worth a shot."

"I'll go over there around lunch time and tell him."

"Right. I'll check in with you later."

I hung up and took another hit of my coffee. With nothing to do but wait on the director and his crew, I pulled the *Burnt Hills* screenplay out of my bag. The day's call sheet I'd looked at earlier had me in one more scene, which Lois was also in. Obviously, some change in the schedule was necessary, but far be it from me to figure out what the people in charge were going to do. Not my bailiwick, I thought, so I laid down on the sofa and started committing to memory what lines I had.

After a half hour or so I hadn't made any progress; I couldn't get the sound of gunfire and the sight of Lois falling to the sidewalk out of my mind. I sat up when someone knocked. Cheryl pulled the door open a crack and stuck her head in.

"Ready for some lunch, Eddie?"

"You bet."

"Come on. I'll run you over there."

I stuck my phone in a hip pocket, folded the sides and grabbed the Stetson. Hugh Danton and Lou Anson were in the golf cart. Danton was playing Bart Kincannon, the valley's biggest rancher, and Anson was Sheriff Haynes.

"Hey, Collins, I heard what happened earlier," Kincannon said. "That's some bad shit. Were you in the scene with her?"

"Right next to her," I said. "Hell of way to spend a morning."

"No kidding," Anson said. "Any word on her condition?"

"We'll find out after lunch," Cheryl said, as she turned a corner and headed for the soundstage where the roach coach sat. "Pete and the production manager will talk to everyone after chow."

She stopped next to the food trailer and the three of us got out and stood in line. Hopefully, a good lunch would take off some of the edge that the morning's events had caused.

14

Despite the noise from crew members working on a set on the other side of the soundstage, chatter around the lunch tables was unusually subdued. News of the event with Lois had obviously made the rounds of the entire company. Pete O'Brien and Preston Bridges, the *Burnt Hills* production manager, circulated among the tables. I couldn't hear what was being said, but from reactions of people at the tables, some decisions had been made about what was going to happen in the wake of the shooting.

I sat with Hugh Danton and Lou Anson, both of whom I was scheduled to work with later in the day, if indeed the production was going to proceed as normal. Danton and I had crossed paths on a TV movie a few years back, but Lou Anson I'd never met. He was a small, thin man with a head of closely cropped gray hair and a Clark Gable pencil-thin moustache. A gold star was pinned to his vest that identified him as the sheriff of our reel town.

He sliced into a hefty pork chop and pointed his knife at something over my left shoulder. "Look sharp, guys, five-o is here."

I turned around and spotted a Los Angeles County Sheriff's deputy talking with O'Brien and Preston Bridges. "What do you think?" I said. "He's going to want to talk to us?"

"With you for sure," Danton said. "You were in the scene with her."

"You ever work with her before, Collins?" Anson said.

"No, I just met her the other day at the wardrobe call. Either one of you?"

"We did a TV episode together one time," Danton said. "The name of which I can't remember. But she was a pretty feisty lady, as I recall."

"Yeah, that's the impression I get too," I said.

O'Brien and Bridges walked up to our table. Bridges was a solidly built Black man who wore a leather jacket over a light red turtleneck and jeans. He stuck out his hand and all three of us shook it.

"Well, obviously, we got thrown a curve ball," he said. "In light of that, Pete and I think it best we wrap you guys for the day and sort some stuff out. We'll give either you or your agents more information as soon as we've made some decisions. When you're done with lunch, sign out with one of the PAs. And thanks for your patience, guys."

Bridges then sat down next to me and said, "As you can see, Eddie, sheriff's personnel are here. Since you were in the scene with Lois, the deputy needs to ask you a few questions."

"Sure thing," I said. "Where would you like to do it?"

"He's got an SUV parked outside," Bridges said.

"Right now?"

"That would be best. Soon as you're done with lunch."

"I'm done. Just let me bus this tray," I said.

"I'll get it, Eddie," Hugh said.

I thanked him and followed Bridges to where the deputy stood. He wore an insulated black jacket that ended just above his Sam Browne belt. His trousers were creased to perfection and his black boots had a high shine. He introduced himself as Luis Ramirez and ushered me through the door of the soundstage to a black and white Ford SUV. He directed me to the passenger seat while he got behind the wheel.

"Thanks for your time," he said. "Mr. Collins, right?"

"Correct. Eddie."

A slight grin crossed his face. "Not to be confused with the ballplayer, I assume?"

"No, but I've memorized his stats. He was a hell of a second baseman."

"That he was. Despite all that Black Sox mess."

"I take it you're a baseball fan?"

"Dodger blue, through and through." He pulled out a notebook and flipped it open. "I figured we'd talk here instead of competing with the noise inside."

"Fine with me."

"I understand you were in close proximity to Miss Maxwell when she was shot?"

"That's right. I couldn't have been more than two, three feet away."

"Any idea where the shot may have come from?"

"I can't be entirely certain, but it sounded like it came from across the street where we were filming. There was a group of tourists watching the scene from there."

"Right. They're sequestered and we're interviewing them. Hopefully someone heard or saw something."

"I don't know how much security this lot has, but I find it curious that a firearm could have gotten onto the premises."

"I tend to agree with you. This is a new facility, and it's obvious they haven't gotten all the wrinkles ironed out yet, with respect to security. I've been told they're suspending the tours for the time being. That'll help." He jotted something in his notebook. "Do you know Miss Maxwell at all?"

"I just met her for the first time a few days ago. We were both called at the same time for a wardrobe fitting."

"So you don't know if she would have anyone carrying a grudge for her? Any reason for her being a target?"

I thought for a moment and remembered the moment outside the wardrobe department. "I don't know if this is relevant or not, but the other day when we were done with the fitting, I saw a guy arguing with her as she was getting into her car."

"Do you know who it was?"

"No."

"Can you describe the person?"

"He was probably a foot taller than her. Wore a denim jacket and baseball cap. He had a mustache and goatee. At one point, he shoved her against her car. I then asked her if she was okay, and she replied that she was, so I drove off. Their conversation seemed to me to be pretty heated."

"Did Miss Maxwell say anything subsequently about the incident?"

"Not specifically. But during the table read—"

"Table read?" Ramirez said.

"That's where the company gets together and reads the screenplay. She at one point got a text. It seemed to bother her, but when I asked, she just shrugged it off and said it was somebody bugging her. She didn't get any more specific than that."

"So she didn't give you a name?"

"No. After the table read, we had lunch and I asked her if someone was harassing her. She made light of it, and said it was no big deal. Just someone from her past, as she put it."

Ramirez made a few notes and said, "Anything else you can think of, Mr. Collins?"

"No, that's it."

"Thanks for your time. You've been very helpful." He handed me a card. "If you think of anything else, give me a buzz."

"Will do," I said, and cracked open the SUV's door.

"Oh, one more thing, Mr. Collins. This has been bugging me since you gave me your name. Putting aside the baseball reference, your name sounds familiar. Have you had anything to do with the sheriff's department recently?"

There I was. Busted. Los Angeles County covers a lot of acreage and the Sheriff's Department is supposedly the largest in the country. But even with that vast coverage, I had no doubt that information flowed freely among its personnel.

"You got me, Deputy," I said, and closed the door. "I'm a licensed PI. A few months ago I was on a case and got caught up with four creeps over in Piru. Deputies from Ventura made an arrest."

"That's it," Ramirez said. "They'd been making snuff films or some damn thing like that."

"You got it. Real disgusting stuff."

"What happened to them?"

"They were indicted and are out on parole. The trial is sometime this summer."

"I'm surprised a judge granted parole for stuff like that."

"Me too. And, truth be told, I don't think I've seen the last of them."

"Why do you say that?"

"I'm probably being paranoid, but just this Saturday night someone took a shot at me and my girlfriend in Hollywood. A drive-by."

"You think it was one of them?"

"They're all wearing ankle bracelets, and I'm told none of them were in the vicinity at the time of the shooting. But…" I left the sentence hanging and watched Hugh and Lou leave the soundstage, headed for their trailers.

Ramirez finished my thought. "But you think there's a possibility they hired someone?"

"To be honest, yes. Me and an associate of mine are the DA's prime witnesses. Without us, they've got no case."

There was silence in the vehicle as Ramirez scribbled notes in his book. His radio crackled. He answered it and replaced the mic on a hook next to the transmitter, then looked at me. "LAPD is investigating, I assume?"

"Yeah, they've got a partial license plate of the shooter's vehicle. Hopefully they'll come up with something."

"Yeah," he said, as he stowed his notebook in his jacket's vest pocket. "But let me ask you this, Mr. Collins. What if Miss Maxwell wasn't the target?"

"Meaning me instead?"

"Right."

"I'd be lying if I said the thought hasn't crossed my mind. The guy's a lousy shot, whoever it is. He missed me on Hollywood Boulevard, and he missed again this morning."

"Let's hope there isn't a third try. Who in the LAPD can we contact?"

"Lieutenant Charlie Rivers. Hollywood Division."

"Thanks." He pulled his notebook out again and jotted down the name.

I opened the door and swung one leg out. "Anything else you need, let me know."

"Will do. Thanks for your help. We'll reach out to LAPD and compare notes."

We shook hands and I headed for my trailer as he drove his SUV across the street and parked it next to two other sheriff's vehicles. Back in my sanctuary, I turned on my phone to see a text from Carla. I responded with an update on the goings-on in *Burnt Hills*.

As I started to put Chet Cassidy's duds back on the clothes rack, the cell rang. It was Carla. Even though the phone was on the other side of the room I knew it was her because of the ring tone. A while back, I'd left it at her place when I went out on an errand. While I was gone, she configured a ring tone on the damn thing that was *The Stripper*, that bawdy tune associated with every bump-and-grind scene known to mankind. I asked her to change it, but so far she has ignored my plea, explaining that it was a wistful reminder of her days as an exotic dancer. A rather lame excuse, I thought, but I must admit that the ditty has grown on me. I may change my mind when it goes off in the middle of a meeting with somebody important, but so far that hasn't happened.

I answered before the ring tone repeated itself.

"Eddie? Are you all right?"

"I'm fine."

"What the heck is going on with you?"

"What do you mean?"

"First Saturday night, now today?"

"Whoa, whoa. I'm not sure the two are related."

"Not related? Explain, please."

"After I met Lois Maxwell at the wardrobe fitting, she was arguing with a guy. The argument looked pretty serious. He could be carrying a grudge."

"Enough to shoot her?"

"I don't know. LA County sheriffs are on it."

There was silence for a moment, after which she said, "I don't like this, Eddie."

"Believe me, honey, I don't either."

"Are you still filming?"

"No, they wrapped for the day. I imagine they've got some rescheduling to do."

"Well, you'll probably be home before me. Drive carefully."

"Will do," I said, and hung up.

I sat down and pulled off my boots. Carla's concern was understandable, and I wished I could have been more comforting to her, but today's event had also put me on edge. Granted, the two separate incidents had coincidence written all over them, but even so, they didn't lend themselves to much peace of mind on my part.

I was just finishing buttoning up my shirt when there was a knock on the door. It opened a crack and Preston Bridges stuck his head in.

"Hi, Eddie, glad I caught you. You got a minute?"

"Sure. What's up?"

He climbed up into the trailer and pulled the door closed behind him. "I just wanted to offer my apologies for the mess that went down today."

"Hey, no worries. Nothing you could have done about it."

"Just glad it wasn't any more serious than it was."

"Me too. Any word on Lois?" I said, as I pulled out a chair from the small table by the door and sat down. I gestured for him to do the same.

He sat and said, "I spoke to a nurse, who was a bit reluctant to give me any information, but when I told her who I was, she said that Lois was in no danger. The bullet basically grazed her and didn't do much damage. They're going to keep her overnight and she should be released tomorrow."

"Aw, that's great news," I said. "So she'll be able to come back?"

"Yeah, after a couple of days."

"Terrific."

"That deputy, Ramirez, said he talked to you, right?"

"He did. I told him I thought the shot came from that group of onlookers across the street."

"That's what he said, yeah. I was against having onlookers that close to a set, but the studio talked me out of it."

"Not a good idea," I said. "At least that's been my experience."

"Mine also. Well, anyway, they interviewed a couple of people who thought they'd seen someone running away from the crowd."

"So they've got somebody in custody?"

"Unfortunately, no. Whoever it was got away."

"Damn, that's no good."

"Absolutely. Obviously, I'm not very happy about the security situation here. I know it's a new setup, but there's no damn reason for somebody to get on the lot with a gun."

"I couldn't agree more."

"Fortunately, they've suspended the tours."

"So Ramirez told me."

"We've got enough to worry about without having looky-loos watching us every minute." He paused for a moment and then said, "Ramirez also told me that on Saturday night you had the same thing happen to you?"

"Yeah. Fortunately, the guy missed."

"Right. Do you think today is related?"

"Well, I've been rolling it around in my head and I'm not sure. For two reasons. First, the shooter on Saturday took off immediately, so he's got no idea whether or not he was successful. It'd be a stretch to think that he knew I was going to be here today."

"But it's possible, don't you think?"

"Yeah, I guess so."

"Any idea who the shooter might have been?"

I hesitated a moment before telling Bridges my other life. "I don't know if you know this, Preston, but I'm a private investigator."

"I do know. Does that figure in?"

"It might. A few months ago me and an associate of mine got involved in a case over in Piru. Four disgusting creeps were arrested for making snuff films. They're under indictment and awaiting trial. We're the DA's prime witnesses."

"And you think they're after you?"

"Well, they're all wearing ankle bracelets and I was told none of them were in the vicinity Saturday night. But…" I left the sentence hang there as Bridges took it in.

"But they could have hired somebody," he said.

"Speculation, but yeah, that's a possibility. I still think it's a stretch, though, for someone to know that I'm up here working on this film."

Preston drummed his fingers on the table and thought for a moment. "Well, you may be right, but the sheriff will probably take it under consideration. You said there was a second reason you thought there's not a connection to today's shooting."

"Right. As I told Ramirez, I saw a guy arguing with Lois at the wardrobe fitting. She told me it was somebody from her past, and that it was no big deal. Maybe so, but that tells me somebody's got an axe to grind with her."

"Yeah, could be," Bridges said. He stood up and pushed his chair back under the table. "Well, look, Eddie, again my apologies about what happened. We're going to beef up our security and hopefully it won't happen again."

"Let's hope so."

He stuck out his hand and we shook. "We're glad to have you on *Burnt Hills*. I hope this thing today is a total one-off."

"Me too," I replied, as he opened the door and stepped out of the trailer.

"Okay. Try and shake it off if you can."

"Will do," I said, and closed the door.

His concern over today's incident happening again was comforting. I got my personal effects together, left my dressing room and walked back to my car. I was fairly confident that safety on the *Burnt Hills* shoot was a high priority. However, there still loomed the matter of a renegade shooter in a dark SUV. My confidence with respect to that event wasn't as high.

15

I don't know this for a fact, but I would assume the bail bond business is thriving. Of course, it helps when you locate your enterprise across the street from a police station. I marveled at this ingenuity as I parked on Wilcox, strolled past Potter Bail Bonds, then jaywalked up to the front door of LAPD's Hollywood Station. A sign was bolted to the wall that proclaimed the location of a 24-hour ATM inside. I didn't know if Potter had anything to do with its placement, but it seemed to be awfully handy; if your shyster lawyer needed a retainer to handle your case, you could hit the ATM and tell him to walk across the street to arrange for bail.

An attractive Black woman with "Hawkins" on her name tag sat behind a counter. I told her I was here to see Lieutenant Rivers. She picked up her phone, hit a couple of keys, announced my presence and told me he'd be out in a couple of moments. I'd called him earlier and told him I was ready to drop by and submit the statement he'd requested yesterday. Just as I sat down and opened a magazine, he pushed his way through a door and told me to come on back. He had a folder under one arm, and his shirt looked like he might have slept in it.

He stopped at a vending machine and reached into his pocket for coins. "Coffee?"

"Sure," I said.

"Somebody burned the pot in the squad room so we're stuck with this. The department keeps telling us we'll get a new one, but so far, no dice."

He stuck some change into the slot. The machine began to gurgle as a cup dropped down and started to fill. "They call this coffee," he said. "I'm not sure I agree." The cup filled, he handed it to me and dropped more money into the machine. The brew was hot and black, but after a sip, I wasn't sure either. Charlie picked up the second cup and headed toward an interrogation room. "Follow me."

Satisfied the room was empty, he gestured for me to take a chair and put the statement form in front of me.

"Okay," he said, "describe the events of Saturday night. Everything you can remember."

"Where should I start?"

"How about right after you came out of the movie?"

"Got it."

"I'll give you a few minutes and check back in on you."

I nodded and he left the room. After another sip of the ersatz coffee, I picked up the pen he provided and set it to paper. My handwriting usually presents a challenge to anyone looking for clarity, so I carefully set about relating the incidents surrounding the drive-by shooting and its aftermath. Fifteen minutes elapsed and Charlie came back into the room.

"How you doin'?" he said, as he set down his coffee, pulled out a chair and sat across from me.

"I think I've got everything. I should sign it, right?"

"Read it back to me before you do. That way, I can hear if you've missed something."

I did so. He asked me if the statement was complete. I said it was, added my signature and pushed the form back to him.

"Now, tell me what the hell went down yesterday. You said an actress got shot?"

"Yeah," I replied, and went on to describe what had happened to Lois Maxwell.

He shook his head and said, "You sure you haven't been wearing a shirt with a target on the back of it?"

"Looks that way, doesn't it?"

"Despite your presence at both incidents, I can't help but think the two of them are random. Are you going to tell me otherwise?"

"Truth be told, Charlie, at first I thought they were related, but after I wrestled with the idea, I can't go there."

"Enlighten me."

"Well, Saturday night that SUV took off like a bat out of hell. The shooter didn't stick around to admire his handiwork. So how the hell would he assume I'd be at Sunset Ranch on Monday morning?"

"Good point, unless you've got somebody tailing you. However, that still doesn't explain the shooting of the actress."

"You're right, but when I first met her, she was arguing with a man, who she told me later was someone from her past that was bugging her. I think somebody had a grudge against her."

"Enough to risk taking a shot at her out in the open?"

"Maybe. A couple of people saw someone fleeing the scene, but whoever it was got away."

"They find a gun?"

"Not that I know of."

"Then they've got nothing."

"So far, yeah. A sheriff's deputy by the name of Ramirez will probably get in touch with you."

"What for?"

"I don't know. Compare notes, I guess."

He sipped from his coffee and put my statement in the folder he'd carried into the room. "He's probably grasping at straws, but nothing ventured, nothing gained, I guess. Here's the latest on that SUV." He jotted something down on a page from his notebook and slid it across the table. On it were the digits S2K6. "From what the witness said, those are the first four digits of the plate. A computer search has narrowed that down to a hundred and eighty-seven possibles. Right now, they're matching the digits to the DMV's descriptions of the vehicles in question. Hopefully, that'll narrow it down even further. Now the question is whether or not we've got enough manpower to start knocking on doors."

His comment put a sour taste in my mouth. "I could have been killed, Charlie."

"I know that, but the fact remains that you weren't."

"And that drops it off your radar?"

"Aw, Christ, Eddie, don't start busting my chops here. I can only work with what the department gives me. There are priorities. Some wheels get more grease than others."

"Yeah," I muttered. I thought about asking him how that pertained to "protect and serve," but thought better of it. "Well, keep me posted, okay?"

"You know I will."

"Any word on the Asian woman that was hit?"

"Her condition is serious," he said, "but she'll recover."

"Good to hear."

"And the actress?"

"Bullet just grazed her. She'll probably be released today."

He nodded and finished off his coffee. "Okay, thanks for coming in. And listen, I know you want more definitive information on the incident, but we're doing what we can, Eddie."

"Yeah, I know," I replied, as I stood and shoved my chair under the table. I stuck out my hand and he took it. "I'll let you know if Ramirez hears anything else."

"Good. In the meantime, watch your back. Okay?"

"I intend to. Even oiled up my piece."

"Smart move."

He opened the door and ushered me to the lobby. I stepped outside and looked up at the cotton-ball clouds overhead. I had no doubt that LAPD would work the case, but even so, I couldn't shake the nagging feeling of disappointment, making we wonder if there wasn't some way I could act on my own. When I got back to my car, I leaned over the top, pulled out my cell phone and made a call.

"Hello, this is Reggie."

"It's Eddie."

"Hey, how you doin', man?"

"Good. Say listen, when's the last time you had a hot dog?"

Silence for a moment, then, "Ah….I don't know. Since the last time we were at Pink's?"

"About time for another visit. You busy?"

"I'll meet you there."

I've got to hand it to Reggie Benson. He has one hell of an appetite, demonstrated by how he attacked his Chicago Polish hot dog. Mustard dripped down his wrist as he took a bite of the dog, then swiped up the yellow trail. He chewed and looked at me, nodding in delight. He had to wait for his mouth to empty before he could talk.

"Twice?" he said. "You've been shot at twice?"

"Once for sure. I'm skeptical about the second time."

I'd briefed him on the two incidents while we stood in line at the Hollywood landmark on the northwest corner of La Brea and Melrose. Burgers and dogs have been dished out there since 1939, and judging by the line of hungry customers, it didn't look like business was in any danger of falling off.

"What about the two women who got shot?" he said.

"The Asian lady from Saturday night is in the hospital but is going to make it. The actress was only grazed. Apparently, they're going to spring her today."

"Man, that is wild. Who the heck do you think did it?"

"I think there's somebody who's got a grudge against Lois Maxwell. And as far as the other one is concerned…well, I don't know."

I took a bite of my Polish Pastrami and chewed thoughtfully as I looked at Reggie. I don't know what it is between the two of us, but I could see in his eyes that he knew where my mind was going.

He set his dog on the paper wrapping, picked up his soda and took a huge slurp through the straw. "Wait a minute. Those four guys we ran into up in Piru are on ankle bracelets, aren't they?"

"They are. And the Ventura County DA says they were nowhere near Hollywood and Highland."

"So that could mean…" He trailed off and took a sip of soda. "Damn, Eddie, you think they hired somebody?"

"I haven't ruled it out."

"What's LAPD doing about it?"

"I just talked to Charlie Rivers. A witness at the scene got a partial plate number of the shooter's vehicle. They've narrowed it down to one hundred and eighty-seven possibilities. It's a dark SUV of some kind." I showed him the piece of paper Charlie had given me. "These are the digits a witness remembers seeing."

We shared a moment of silence as we sampled more of our respective hot dogs.

I swallowed, sipped some soda and said, "Does Bernie keep you busy during the days?" Bernie was Bernie Feldman, an undertaker friend of mine who'd given Reggie an apartment in exchange for his services as a sort-of security guard at his funeral parlor. He'd basically wanted someone to be on the premises during the night and Reggie filled the bill.

"Not really," Reggie said. "Maybe an errand here and there. Why?"

"You remember Ken Thompson? The guy we followed up to Piru? The one who lives at that place where I eavesdropped on the four of them?"

"Yeah."

"Can you stake out his place for a few hours a day? In case that SUV shows up? Thompson was the ringleader. If they did hire somebody, he'd be the one who arranged it."

"Is he gonna recognize my car?"

I thought for a moment and recalled events of a few months ago. "I doubt it. Benedetti was the one that came up on us when you pretended to be the bird watcher. To the best of my recollection, Thompson never saw your car."

"Okay. I can do that. When do want me to start?"

"This afternoon, if you can."

"No problem."

"Take pictures if you're close enough."

"Right."

"And Reggie, remember, we're both witnesses in their trial, so be careful. You hear? If they're dumb enough to come after me, they'll do the same to you."

"Got it, Eddie."

I wrote down the license plate digits on a page from my notebook, along with Thompson's address and gave it to him. We finished our dogs and walked to our cars. A part of me harbored some reluctance to involve Reggie in this fight. But on the other hand, as I told him, he was also going to be in the witness box, so it was his fight as well.

I never know what Mavis, my right-hand gal and purveyor of doodads and all things trivial, has in store for me when I open the door to Collins Investigations. Today was no exception. Stan Laurel and Oliver Hardy sat in the middle of her desk. Not literally, of course, but in the form of six-inch high porcelain dolls.

"Hey, Eddie."

"Howdy."

"No filming for you today?"

"Nope." I sat in one of the chairs in front of her desk and picked up Stan Laurel.

"Careful. These two have a pretty good price on their heads."

I gingerly set Mr. Laurel back where I found him. "Who's the lucky buyer?"

"A lady out in Tarzana. She's got a whole collection of stars from back in that era."

"While we're on the subject of collectibles, have you heard any more from Akeem Farouq?"

"Yeah, I stopped in there this morning on the way to the office. He's had his front window replaced. He said it's not the first time he's had to do that. And he wanted to know about that Asian lady that was shot. Have you heard anything?"

"Matter of fact, Charlie Rivers told me she's in serious condition, but she's going to be okay." My mention of the lady reminded me that I hadn't as yet told Mavis about the events of yesterday. As I launched into the story, she stopped fiddling with Laurel and Hardy and sat back in her chair. Her face registered a profound look of disbelief.

"You have got to be kidding me! Twice in the space of two days?"

"Afraid so, kiddo."

"How's that going to impact the film?"

"I'm not sure. That's why I'm on hold. They're trying to figure out how to proceed in the wake of the shooting."

"Was she badly hurt?"

"Fortunately, the bullet just grazed her. She's supposed to be released from the hospital today."

She ran a strip of packing tape along the seam of the Laurel and Hardy box. "Are you sure you weren't the target?"

"Pretty much. I think someone's got a grudge against her, based on what I saw after our wardrobe fitting."

"Let's hope so," she said, as she laid Stan and Ollie in their padded package.

At that point my cell rang. Speak of the devil. The display showed the call was from Lois Maxwell.

"Hi, Lois, are you all right?"

"I'm fine. They let me go a couple of hours ago. I just got home." I listened to her call and caught Mavis's attention. She stopped what she was doing and focused on me.

Lois finished her call and I put the phone back in my pocket.

"Was that Lois Maxwell?" Mavis said.

"Yeah."

"Is she okay?"

"She's fine, and guess what?"

"What?"

"She's got a job for me."

"You've got a job."

"A job on the other side of the fence. She wants to meet. And talk about hiring me to find this guy that's been harassing her."

16

Lois Maxwell lived on the northern edge of Glendale, almost in the small community of Montrose. The area is generally thought of as being the "Foothills," far away from the hustle and bustle of Hollywood and the San Fernando Valley. Her street was wide, with tall trees on both sides and no sign of apartment buildings. Neatly trimmed lawns and hedges fronted modest, single-story houses. I half expected to see Ward and June Cleaver standing on their front stoop yelling for Wally and the Beaver to come in and wash up for dinner.

Her house was on my left, halfway down the block. It was smaller than most of the neighboring structures. I parked, walked up a narrow sidewalk and rang the doorbell. Potted plants sat along the edges of a small porch stretching off to my right. Two chairs flanked a small table that sat under the front window.

After a moment the door opened and Lois appeared. A sling encased her right arm. She had a long scarf around her neck, complimenting a leather vest over a denim shirt. She wore jeans and had sandals on her feet.

"Hi Eddie. Come on in."

She pushed the screen door open and I stepped inside and immediately detected a faint trace of some kind of incense. A puffy sofa faced the front window and across a coffee table sat two upholstered chairs, one black, one dark red. A television set took up most of the right side of the room, a cable box and DVD player under it.

"How about a beer?" she said.

"I wouldn't say no," I said, and she headed for the kitchen beyond the front room. "You need some help?"

"Fortunately I'm a southpaw, so unless you want a glass, I've got it."

"Nope, don't need one."

"Okay. Have a seat."

I sank down into one of the upholstered chairs and she reappeared with two bottles of beer clasped in the fingers of her left hand.

"I like your house."

"Thanks. I landed a recurring part on a TV show a few years back. Gave me enough to buy it. Do you own a place?"

"Nope. I've got an apartment behind my office. But I spend a lot of time at my girlfriend's condo. I probably should just move in with her."

She set the bottles on the coffee table, then sat down on the sofa and propped her right arm on a pillow.

"How's the arm?"

"It's okay. They gave me some pain pills, which helped. Boy, howdy, did they ever help. I don't think I've been that high since the sixties."

"You sure you should be having a beer?"

"Oh, hell, it's okay. I haven't taken one in a few hours, so drink up, doctor Collins." I chuckled, picked up my beer and we toasted each other.

"Did you get clearance to go back to work?"

"Yes. All the doc told me was to keep the arm immobile as much as possible and make sure the wound is kept clean. They'll see me again week after next. There'll probably be some rehab tacked on."

"Good."

She took a sip from the bottle of beer, then set it down. "Pete O'Brien called and asked how I was. He said the company was on hold. What's with that?"

"I don't know. I think they're figuring out how to adjust their shooting schedule."

"Well, hell, I'm sorry I threw a monkey wrench into the works."

"Not your fault, Lois."

"Maybe, maybe not. I've got somebody harassing me, but I sure as hell didn't think he'd go this far. Which brings me to my phone call. I bet you were surprised to get it, huh?"

"I was."

"How long are you booked on *Burnt Hills*?"

"Through next week. Maybe longer, what with any rescheduling they're going to do. Why? What have you got in mind?"

"Well, I think I know who took the potshot at me."

"You mean the guy who's been harassing you?"

"Yup."

"The one who was arguing with you after the wardrobe call?"

"That's the one." She took a swig from her beer and set the bottle back on the coffee table. "For a while I was just going to let it go, but it looks like the son of a bitch has upped the ante, so I want to hire you to find him."

"Why don't you go to the cops?"

"Aw, hell, they ain't gonna do a damn thing."

"How do you know?"

She looked at me a moment before saying, "So, you don't want the job?"

"I'm not saying that. I'm just wondering why me and not them?"

"Well, first of all I'm not absolutely sure it's him. Secondly, I don't know where the hell to find him."

"Just so you know. I've already talked to an LA County Sheriff's deputy. Guy by the name of Luis Ramirez."

"And what did you tell him?"

"That I thought the shot may have come from that group of onlookers across the street."

"Anything else?"

"Well, I figured it was important, so I told him about your argument with the guy at the wardrobe call and that you'd told me he'd been harassing you."

"Damn," she said. "I suppose that means he's going to want to talk to me too."

"I'm sure he will."

She fished a handkerchief from a pocket and blew her nose, then stuffed the cloth inside her sling. "Here's the deal, Eddie. I don't want the cops involved, so I'm going to tell them it was just a dispute over a car accident. An insurance problem."

"You don't think you'll be withholding evidence?"

"What evidence? A guy with an insurance beef sure as hell isn't going to shoot me."

"What if they want a name?"

"I'll give them a fake one." After a minute she continued. "Is this going to be a problem for you?"

I looked at her for a long moment. Technically, Lois would be withholding evidence if she didn't level with Ramirez. On the other hand, I hadn't told the deputy what the disagreement was about between Lois and her harasser. If she told him their spat was over a minor insurance beef, what I told Ramirez wouldn't have any bearing on the shooting at Sunset Ranch. Maybe my reasoning wouldn't pass muster in some quarters, but once in a while you gotta do what you gotta do. Sometimes there's a soft spot in me when it comes to survivors of the Hollywood hustle and the crazy business I occasionally find myself in. People who've had to cope with constant rejection over the years, many times not knowing when the next paycheck will arrive. Lois Maxwell was one of those survivors, and it didn't set right with me that she was being treated unfairly by someone, regardless of who the person was.

"Okay, Lois, here's my deal. My license prevents me from getting involved in official police business, so the LA County Sheriff's Department doesn't have to know that I'm working a case, or even on whose behalf. That's between you and me. Make sense?"

"Perfectly."

"I'll send you a bill for a retainer. Given that I don't have a lot to go on up front, I'll only charge you if I get results. Fair enough?"

"Fair enough."

"Okay. Brass tacks. Who the hell is this guy?"

"His name is Burt Jacobson."

I took out my notebook and jotted the name down. "Any idea why he's been after you?"

"We worked together a while back and had a falling out."

"Worked together on a film?"

"No. We had a business deal together."

"So he's not an actor?"

"He was at one time. That's how we met. On a TV show a few years ago. But he got out of the business."

I jotted down some more notes. "What kind of deal were the two of you involved in?"

She picked up her bottle of beer, took a healthy swallow and said, "How many questions are you going to ask me?"

"Look, Lois, if you want me to find this guy, it would help to know what his motive is."

"Okay, okay. We had a real estate thing we were trying to put together. I backed out and he seems to think I took some money with me."

"Did you?"

She glared at me, eyes narrowed in displeasure.

"Just asking," I said. "Full disclosure, right?

"Right. And no, I did not take any money from him."

"And you don't know where he lives?"

"Last I knew he was in North Hollywood." She gave me an address and I wrote it down. "He's obviously moved, though. I went by his apartment building and the super told me he'd left."

"How long ago?"

"He couldn't remember. Not much to go on, huh?"

"Yeah, but I've gotten used to it. That day you were arguing with him after the wardrobe call. What kind of car did he have?"

"I don't know. I drove off and left him standing in the parking lot."

Now it was my turn to take a pull off my beer bottle. "He reached out to you by phone and text, right?"

"Yeah," she said, and dug into a vest pocket and pulled out her cell phone. "But I think he might have a burner. I called the number and got no answer." She poked at some keys and handed the phone to me. "There's the number.'"

I jotted down the number, handed the phone back to her and said, "Did you reply to his texts?"

"I did, but I got no indication that they were delivered."

"Is, or was he a member of SAG?"

She thought for moment and said, "I suppose. The show we worked on was under a SAG contract."

I made some more notes and stuck the book back in my pocket. "I don't imagine you have a picture of this guy?"

"Oh, my god, let me think." She looked off to her right as I finished my beer and set the bottle on the coffee table. "I don't, but he should be on IMDB." She held her phone in her right hand, but when she began to enter the website, it slipped out of her hand and landed in her lap. "Dammit."

"I've got the app on my phone. Let me do it," I said, as I pulled out my cell and accessed the app for the Internet Movie Database, the go-to source for all things relating to movie and television. Even if you're billed as "Florid Man Behind the Fern" you're going to wind up on IMDB. I typed in Burt Jacobson and his picture popped up. The photo wasn't a headshot per se, but depicted him as a character in some project. "Is this him?" I said, as I stretched out my arm across the coffee table.

She leaned forward and said, "That's him. The bastard."

"It's not the best photo of the guy, but it's better than nothing. I'll print it out when I get back to my office."

"So, you've got an office and the whole bit, huh? Secretary, too? Your own Effie Perrine?"

"Who's Effie Perrine?"

"Aw, come on, Eddie. She's Sam Spade's secretary."

"Oh," I said. Of course, I knew who Effie Perrine was, but I figured I'd play dumb and have some fun with her. "I thought Della Street was his secretary."

"No, no, she was Perry Mason's secretary. She…" Lois stopped and cocked her head, then glared at me, her eyes once again narrowing in displeasure. The slight grin on my face gave me away.

"You're being a smart-ass now, aren't you?"

"You got me." I chuckled and she tossed her pillow at me. "So who played her?"

"Barbara Hale, who, it so happens, I worked with."

"On a *Perry Mason*?"

"Yes. I've been around the track a few laps, mister private eye, so don't think you're going to crack wise with me and get away with it." I held up my hands in surrender and she laughed. "So, who's your Effie Perrine or Della Street, as the case may be?"

"Mavis Werner. And she's a whiz with her computer. If Burt Jacobson hangs his hat somewhere, chances are she'll smoke him out."

"Well, I hope so." She upended her bottle of beer, then stood. "Thanks for taking this on, Eddie. I know it's not much to go on, but the creep is out there somewhere. I just need to get face to face with him and try and settle this beef he's got with me."

"I'll do what I can."

"How do you want to handle the retainer business?"

"Mavis will send you an invoice."

"Okay. I'd shake hands with you, but I'm at a bit of a disadvantage here." She chuckled and stuck out her left hand. I did likewise, and we did a backwards shake.

We said we'd see each other on the set, whenever that was going to be, and I told her I'd keep her up to date on the search.

I walked back to my car, did a K-turn and drove back up the street. The image of Wally Cleaver and the Beaver was gone; it had been replaced by someone called Burt Jacobson.

Now, the question was: where was he?

17

I started up the on-ramp to the Glendale Freeway south. The long, gradual downward slope of the highway provided a panorama of downtown Los Angeles and its skyscrapers. The proverbial layer of smog shrouded them, and light from the sun gave the city center a dystopian look, almost like the backdrop of a science fiction movie.

Somewhere in that panorama was one Burt Jacobson. Who was he? And why was he after Lois Maxwell? If, indeed, he was. As I reached the bottom of the slope and segued onto the Ventura heading west, I mulled over my meeting with Lois. If, or when Luis Ramirez talked to her regarding the shooter, her decision to tell him that a guy had an insurance beef against her raised some doubt in my mind. Would a simple argument like that be motive enough for someone to open fire on her? I wasn't sure, but her decision was out of my bailiwick. She'd hired me to find Burt Jacobson, and that had to be my main focus.

As I swung onto the I-5 southbound I glanced at my watch. Three o'clock. Mavis should still be in the office. I was confident she could come up with the name Burt Jacobson. The only problem was how many of them would there be. But I was heartened by the fact that he had appeared in some film and television projects. That could serve as my starting point.

I exited the freeway at Los Feliz and made my way into Hollywood and Collins Investigations. When I stepped off the elevator I almost collided with Lenny Daye, one of my neighbors and the editor/publisher of *Pecs 'n Abs*, a men's magazine devoted to generous helpings of the male physique.

"Eddie Collins, my favorite private dick!" he bellowed, and doubled over in laughter.

I shook my head as I waited for him to compose himself. "How long have you been saving that one, Lenny?"

"I swear to God, Eddie, it just came to me."

"Yeah, right," I said, as I playfully punched him on the shoulder.

"Are you working?" he said.

"You ready for this? I'm cast in a western. An honest to God oater."

"Be still my heart. Guns and everything?"

"You got it, pardner."

"Oh, honey, I can't wait to see you on a horse."

"I think I've escaped that. I'm a bartender."

"Ah, well, that's more your style." I held the elevator door for him as he stepped into the car. "Gotta scoot. I'm interviewing a possible centerfold. Wish me luck."

"Try and keep the interview vertical."

"Yes, Mother," he replied, while the door closed on his laugh.

Always a treat running into Lenny, I thought, as I pushed open the door to my office. Mavis poked her head out of her off-limits-to-me cubicle.

"Hey, boss man. Have you got a new client?"

"I do," I said, and took a chair in front of her desk. "Are you in the middle of something?"

"Nope. What's up?" She walked over to her desk and stood behind her chair.

"Couple things." I retrieved Lois's address from my phone and handed it to her. "Send her a retainer invoice. This is her address." I pulled out my notebook and showed her the telephone number Lois had provided me.

She sat and wrote the address and the number on a pad of paper in front of her, then handed the phone back to me.

"Also, I need you to try and find somebody. Burt Jacobson."

"Burt, with a 'u'?"

"Right. Jacobson, spelled with 'on,' not 'en'."

"Got it."

"Also, go to the Internet Movie Database and look him up."

"Actor, I assume?"

"Yes."

She clicked some computer keys and looked at the screen. "Found him. Standing next to a cop?"

I leaned over her desk and looked at her computer. "That's him. Can you print out that photo and maybe crop it so the cop disappears?"

"I'll give it a whirl."

I left her to it, walked into my office and hung the day's porkpie on its peg. Mother Nature called; I answered and came back to my desk. Some mail lay in the middle of my desk, most of it worthy of the circular file behind my chair. In the midst of paying a bill, my cell burped with an unfamiliar number.

"This is Eddie Collins."

"Eddie, it's Debbie from *Burnt Hills*. Just wanted to give you a heads up. You're still on hold. We're working on some problems with the lot."

"What's going on?"

"I'm not sure. They're not telling much of anything. Stay in touch with your agent and keep your phone handy. We'll let you know when they've worked out the bugs."

"Okay. Thanks Debbie."

She hung up and I finished writing a check. I was glad to hear the news about still being on hold. That would give me an opportunity to get a jump on the search for Burt Jacobson. Before wading through more bills, I got up and stood in the door to Mavis's office.

"You got any fresh coffee in that sanctum sanctorum of yours?"

"Yeah, but it's decaf."

I put on my best frown, and she said, "Beggars can't be choosy."

"Permission to enter?"

"Permission granted."

I flipped her a salute and walked into the cubicle. The space contained a bathroom, about as big as one you'd find on an airplane. There was a tiny sink, and shelves that were crammed with her office supplies—reams of paper and packing supplies for her ongoing collectibles enterprise, rolls of bubble wrap and an array of flattened cardboard boxes of various sizes. I found a cup on a shelf above the coffee maker and poured myself some of the dreaded decaf. After a sip, I avoided making a face and stepped back into her office.

"Good stuff, huh?" she said.

"If you say so. You know, that room in there is awfully crowded."

"I know. Have you got a solution?"

"Not off-hand. You?"

She leaned back in her chair and swiveled it to face me. "Well, you know, you seem to be spending more and more time at Carla's place, so…"

She left the sentence hanging.

"So…what?" I said.

"Have the two of you ever thought of moving in together?"

I took another slurp of coffee and sat down in front of her. "To be honest, the thought has crossed my mind."

"Has it crossed hers?"

"I don't know for sure, but I'd wager it has. Matter of fact, the other day she started talking about the possibility of maybe jointly buying something."

"Just saying, but I could put a lot of stuff in that apartment of yours."

I had to agree with her. Mavis had been with me for quite a while and was an invaluable part of Collins Investigations. I would hate to lose her. This little collectible business of hers seemed to be flourishing. Giving her more space could be an incentive for her to continue being my gal Friday. Food for thought, I decided, and stood when I heard my cell ring in my office.

"Something to think about, kiddo," I said, as I walked to my desk. The screen indicated the was call from Reggie.

"Hey, what's going on?"

"I've been camped out on Thompson's street for a couple of hours. No sign of a dark SUV. But get this, Eddie. About a half hour ago a green Kia pulled up and parked. That's what that Roger Iverson dude drives, right?"

"Right. Did he have dreadlocks?"

"Yup, yup, serious dreads."

"That's him. What did he do?"

"He went into Thompson's house. Fifteen minutes later they came out, got in Thompson's car and drove off. I thought about tailing them, but wasn't sure you wanted me to do that."

"Probably not a good idea, at least at this point."

"I'll call it a day and come back tomorrow."

"Great, Reggie. Keep me posted. And be careful, okay?"

"Roger that. Check with you later," he said, and hung up.

Curious, I wondered what Thompson and Iverson were doing, hanging around with each other. Comparing ankle bracelets? Since they were both under indictment, I suppose they shared some commonality…birds of a feather, so to speak.

Mavis appeared in the doorway with a piece of photo paper in her hand. "Were you talking to Reggie?"

"Yeah."

"What's he up to?"

"I've got him shadowing that creep Ken Thompson. I'm still not fully convinced they didn't have anything to do with that drive-by the other night." I pointed to what she had in her hand. "That the photo of Jacobson?"

"Yeah, I don't know how much good it's going to do you," she said, as she handed it to me. "It's not that clean, but it's the best I could do."

"It'll work." She'd blown it up to a 4x6 size.

She sat down in a chair in front of my desk. "You know, I was thinking. If you ever did decide to move in with Carla, I'd be willing to contribute to the rent for this office. I mean, that's considering I'd move all my stuff back into your apartment. What do you think?"

"Yeah, we could probably work something out."

"Good. Well, anyway, think about it." She got up and headed for her desk.

I stood, grabbed the empty coffee cup and my hat and followed her. "I'm going to run up into the Valley and check out this address Lois gave me. Jacobson apparently lived there. Maybe the super can give me some idea where he moved to."

"Let me make a copy of that picture."

I handed it to her and took the empty cup into the sanctuary, rinsed it out and set it back on the shelf. Another quick glance at the contents of the room reinforced the possibility of turning my apartment into her new workspace.

"I'll do some more poking around," Mavis said, as she handed the photo back to me. "Maybe I can get a better handle on where this guy is."

"Great. I'll check in with you in the morning." I opened the door and turned back to her. "And listen, what we talked about earlier? I'll run it by Carla and see what she says."

"Okie dokie, boss man. See you tomorrow."

The address for Burt Jacobson that Lois had provided me was on Aqua Vista in Studio City. The apartment complex was two-storied. I found a parking space across the street next to an eight-foot high hedge that ran the length of the street. Good hedges make good neighbors, I guess.

I locked my car, waited for a pickup to pass in front of me and walked across the street. To the left of the apartments was a carport with stalls for a dozen tenants. All but three of them were empty. Entry to the complex was an unlocked wrought iron gate. I pushed it open and saw a deadbolt on the inside, obviously not in use during daylight hours. My eye immediately spotted a three-sided structure to the right. Under its ceiling were two washing machines and two dryers. On a shelf above them sat several bottles and cartons of laundry soap. The appliances were silent.

Directly in front of me a sidewalk ran along one building, two apartments on the ground level and two above them. Between the units a stairway connected the two levels. Four more units with the identical configuration were on the opposite side of an open courtyard. An additional four-unit building formed the third side of a triangle that surrounded the central courtyard that was dotted with small palm trees and various shrubs. In the middle of the courtyard a fountain gurgled. The water filled a top basin and then overflowed to the ones below it.

Next to the wall of the closest building was a bank of mailboxes. A quick glance at them didn't reveal the name Burt Jacobson, but did designate apartment number one as being that of the manager, Richard Halverson. I walked around the corner of the building and saw that number one was the first door.

I knocked and after a few moments the door swung open to reveal a short, balding man with heavy jowls and what looked to be a ten o'clock shadow on his face. He wore a blue flannel shirt over baggy jeans and stepped into the doorway.

"Sorry, but there ain't no vacancies," he said, in a voice that sounded like he'd been chewing on a Brillo pad. He turned to his left as an attractive young Hispanic woman came down the stairs carrying a plastic clothes basket, headed for the laundry machines.

"I'm not looking for an apartment," I said. "I just need to ask you a couple of questions about a former tenant of yours."

"Oh, yeah, who's that?" he replied, as I stepped out of the way of the woman.

"Burt Jacobson," I said.

The woman passed behind me and Halverson said, "Hi, Rachel. How ya doin'?"

"Okay, Rich," she said, and gave me a long look as she walked by. She wore a tight-fitting pair of jeans and a red sweatshirt. Her black hair was done up in a ponytail that reached the middle of her back.

Halverson leaned against the door jamb and looked at her as she walked away. He slowly shook his head and softly whistled, then looked at me with a lopsided grin. "Man, am I gettin' old, or what?" He chuckled and continued, "Sorry, what was the name?"

"Burt Jacobson. A former tenant of yours?"

"Right. Hey, what's he done?"

"Why do you say that?"

"There was a woman came by here a few weeks back, asking after the same guy. I figure he must have done something wrong."

"Not that I know of."

"So, who are you?"

"The name's Eddie Collins."

"Why you lookin' for him?"

"A family member is sick. They're trying to locate him."

"Well, he ain't here no more. Moved out about eight months ago."

"Did he leave a forwarding address?"

"Nope. I got two new tenants in there. They keep getting mail addressed to the guy and they keep stuffin' it back in the outgoing slot. He must not have filed a change of address. Nothin' I can do about it."

I pulled the picture of Jacobson from my pocket and showed it to him. "Just so we're clear. Is this the guy?"

Halverson slid a pair of readers out of a shirt pocket and looked at the photo. "Yeah, that's him. Come to think of it, he told me he did some acting work. This from something he was in?" he asked, as he handed the photo back.

"I guess so. Well, look, thanks anyway."

I put the photo back in my pocket as he closed the door. I started for the front gate. Rachel, the young Hispanic woman, called out to me as I reached the entrance.

"Hey, mister, wait a minute."

I stopped. She closed the top of one of the washers, pushed the coin slot in, then turned and walked over to me.

"You a cop or something?" she said.

"No. What makes you think that?"

"You've got it written all over you. Especially the hat."

"Good catch. I'm a private investigator. Trying to find a man by the name of Burt Jacobson." I again pulled out the photo. "Is this him?"

She looked at the photo and said, "Yeah, but his name isn't Burt Jacobson."

"What do you mean?"

"We went out a few times. He told me his name was Bryce Jesperson."

I asked her how to spell it and wrote the name in my notebook. "Do you know why he called himself Burt Jacobson?"

"Nope, but if you find him, tell the asshole he still owes me fifty bucks."

"Bad date, huh?" I grinned and put the notebook back in my pocket.

She shrugged and said, "Yeah, my sister keeps telling me I really know how to pick 'em."

18

Bryce Jesperson, not Burt Jacobson. I sat in my car and thought about what the young woman had just told me. Same initials—BJ—but two different names. I wondered why, and could only come up with one possibility. If the Screen Actors Guild determines that your name is already taken, or similar to an already established actor, you're required to change yours. You don't want anyone else getting your residuals or pension payouts. Reason enough, I suppose, why William Macy, the star of the Showtime series *Shameless,* couldn't be confused with Bill Macy, Bea Arthur's husband Walter on the sitcom *Maude.*

Good thing Eddie Collins, the baseball player, never became an actor, I thought, as I pulled out my cell and called up the IMDB website. And that's when an oddity popped up. I typed in "Bryce Jesperson" and got no hits. Then I entered "Burt Jacobson" and only got the one I'd already encountered…hmmm. So if there was no Bryce Jesperson on SAG's membership rolls, why did he feel the need to change his name to Burt Jacobson? Had Bryce Jesperson been involved in something nefarious, enough to warrant a change of identity? I didn't have an answer, but I knew somebody who might. The number I dialed went straight to voice mail.

"Hi Lois, this is Eddie. Give me a call when you can. Thanks."

A glance at my watch indicated it was closing in on five o'clock. That didn't leave any time today to proceed with this hunt for Burt Jacobson, aka Bryce Jesperson. Mavis would have to start a new computer search in the morning. I sat and looked at the eight-foot hedge for several minutes, still wondering why the need for two names on this guy. There could be a logical reason, but for the life of me I couldn't think of one without another conversation with Lois.

My introspection was interrupted by the realization that I hadn't had anything to eat since the hotdog at Pink's. It provoked another phone call and Carla picked up after two rings.

"Hey, Shamus, where are you?"

"I'm up in the Valley and am suddenly weak with hunger."

"Oh, you poor thing. What can we do to relieve you of your misery?"

"I thought I'd pick up some El Pollo Loco and then knock on your door. Are you home?"

"Good idea, and, yes, I am home."

"See you in a few," I said, and ended the call.

The El Pollo Loco franchise I opted for was on Vine and had drive-thru service, but when I pulled in, the line was long, so I parked and decided to go inside. The aroma that greeted me as I stepped through the door made me glad I did. Several tables were occupied by couples, two of them elderly. An Hispanic family of six took up a long table, and in a far corner a boisterous group of teenagers did what teenagers are wont to do, and enjoyed every minute of it. The Mexican chicken chain with outlets all over LA had become a particular favorite of mine over the years, an opinion shared by Carla. I placed my order and waited while a young Hispanic girl filled two Styrofoam containers with chicken, beans and rice. She placed them in a plastic bag, along with tortillas, and told me to enjoy. I assured her I would, added several plastic containers of salsa to the bag, then pushed the door open and started for my car.

Twilight had begun to descend. The parking lot contained a half dozen vehicles. One of them was a dark blue SUV that had backed into a space. It hadn't been there when I went in to place my order. My antenna immediately went up. As I pulled out my keys I glanced at the license plate and my pulse started to pound. The digits were clearly visible. Four of them looked familiar: S2K6. I opened the car and crawled in, heart racing. I quickly pulled out my notebook and found the page where I'd jotted down the digits Charlie Rivers had given me.

S2K6.

Panic welled up inside me. I looked over at the SUV. The windows were deeply tinted. I could discern a figure behind the steering wheel but the windows were too dark to provide any sort of identification. My eyes focused on the license plate of the vehicle. The rest of the digits were J55. I jotted them down next to the ones I already had.

For a fleeting moment I thought about approaching the vehicle, but decided against it. In today's climate, approaching a vehicle without knowing who was in it spelled nothing but trouble. Besides, the witness at Highland and Hollywood had provided only four digits, not enough to confirm that this was the vehicle that contained the shooter from the other night.

I started the car, backed out and made my way toward the parking lot's exit. A glance in the rear view mirror pushed my panic button up a few notches. The SUV's running lights came on and the vehicle pulled in behind me.

I turned right out of the parking lot and waited for the light at Fountain. The SUV slid in behind me. The light changed and I headed north on Vine. The SUV stayed right behind me. Granted, Vine was a traffic-heavy street, so it's possible the car behind me was headed in the same direction as me, but at the moment I wasn't convinced.

As I approached Sunset there were no cars in front of me. The green light gave way to amber. I ignored it and stepped on the gas. Horns blared as I barreled through the red light, but I accomplished what I had intended. The SUV was caught by the red light. I sped north on Vine, made a right at Selma, then an immediate left on Argyle into the parking lot of the Le Bon Hotel. I squealed into a parking space and doused the lights, then shut off the car.

Sweat had broken out on my face and my heart continued to pound as I caught my breath and looked behind me to see if an SUV had followed me. The street was quiet. I waited for five minutes, then restarted the car and made my way to Carla's apartment building, eyes glued to the rear view mirror.

I knocked on the door and after a moment she pulled it open. "What took you so long?'"

"You aren't gonna believe it," I said, as I pushed past her and set the chicken on the kitchen table.

I'm not sure I believed it myself.

"Eddie, your face is as white as this Styrofoam," Carla said, as she held up the empty container her El Pollo Loco chicken had come in. "You have to call Charlie and tell him what you saw." She set the to-go box down on the table, picked up a chicken breast off the plate in front of her and took a huge bite, then accompanied her chewing with a glare that could melt the cubes in her iced tea. I had to admit that seeing the SUV in the El Pollo Loco parking lot had unnerved me, but I didn't think I'd displayed it as much as Carla's hyperbole would suggest.

"I'll call him, but he's not going to be on duty this time of night."

"He has a cell phone, for crying out loud. Trust me. He'll answer it."

"All right, all right, I'll call him. Right after I finish my supper."

Her glare subsided and we polished off our servings of chicken. I took a hit from my bottle of beer and dialed Charlie's number. He answered after the second ring.

"Is this call going to spoil my dinner?"

"The exact opposite. That witness at Highland and Hollywood the other night thought the shooter was in a dark SUV, right?"

"Yeah, what of it?"

"I was followed about an hour ago by one fitting that description. The wit said the first four digits on the plate were Sierra-two-Kilo-six. That's the four you gave me, right?"

"Right."

"This SUV had those four, plus Juliet-five-five." There was silence on the other end of the line. "You got them?"

"I got 'em. That's seven digits. Standard DMV issue." After a beat, he continued. "Look, I haven't got the printouts in front of me. Let me run over to the office and get on the computer. See if we've pinpointed that plate, okay? I'll call you back."

"Great. Thanks, Charlie."

I hung up and looked at Carla across the table. "He's going to go over to the station and check it out."

"Good." She carried the plates into the kitchen and I followed with the Styrofoam containers. "Any idea where that SUV came from?"

"Nope."

"Where were you when you called me?"

"In Studio City, at that address for Burt Jacobson that Lois gave me."

"Did you get on the freeway?"

"No. I used Ventura Boulevard and came through the Cahuenga Pass and down Highland. Didn't pay attention to what was behind me." I dropped the Styrofoam in a recycling bin next to the refrigerator and slammed the lid down. "For crissakes, does this mean I've gotta drive with one eye on the rearview mirror for the rest of my life?"

"Hey, hey," she said, as she put her arms around me. "You've now got a license plate. Wait to hear from Charlie and see where it takes them." She put her hands on the sides of my face and pulled it down for a kiss. "I know how you feel, honey, but maybe it's registered to a little old lady."

"A little old lady who drives a small tank?"

"So maybe she's got a chauffeur. Like *Driving Miss Daisy*."

I laughed and kissed her. "That's what I like about you, kiddo. Optimism springs eternal." Except for the chicken bones, she scraped the remnants of our meal into the garbage disposal and hit the switch. While its noise filled the kitchen, she handed me the plates and I racked them in the dishwasher. "Oh, and get this," I said. "Burt Jacobson isn't Burt Jacobson."

"What do you mean?"

"I ran into a young woman who dated him a few times. She said she knew him as Bryce Jesperson."

"What does Lois say about that?"

"I don't know. I'm waiting for her to return my call."

"Sounds to me like you've got your work cut out for you, Shamus." She patted me on the butt and pulled another beer from the refrigerator and handed it to me. "Come on, let's see what's on the boob tube."

There wasn't much. Carla surfed for a couple of minutes and finally landed on a rerun of a Clint Eastwood movie. It was typical Clint: squinty eyes, thin cigarillo clenched at the corner of his mouth, and monosyllabic dialogue. While he dispatched a trio of bad guys with his usual impeccable aim, my cell rang and the display said the call was from Lois Maxwell.

"It's Lois," I said. Carla muted the television and tucked her legs underneath her.

"Hi Lois."

"Sorry it took me so long to get back to you. What's up?"

"I dropped by that Studio City address for Jacobson you gave me and ran into a young woman who went out with him a few times. She brought up a problem."

"What kind of problem?"

"She knew him as Bryce Jesperson, not Burt Jacobson."

There was a beat and then, "What?"

"That's what she said. He ever tell you he used an alias?"

"It's news to me. Never heard him refer to himself as anything other than Burt Jacobson."

"IMDB doesn't show any results for a Bryce Jesperson. So, the question is, why he would use two names?"

There was silence for a moment and she said, "I haven't the foggiest. But it doesn't really surprise me. I've always thought there was something hinky about him."

"'Hinky'? How do you mean 'hinky'?"

"Odd. Spooky. Like he was a float short of a parade."

Her assessments of him caught me by surprise. "Then why the hell did you get involved with him in the first place?"

"I keep asking myself that. It seemed like a good idea at the time. At least, that's what he told me. But that's a story for another day. What does this do to your search for him?"

"I don't know. I'll have my secretary switch gears and see what we come up with."

"I'm sorry this is turning into such a pain in the butt, Eddie. But if it turns out he's the one who took a shot at me, I'd like to know what the hell his beef is. Are you still on board?"

"Yeah, I'll keep poking around. I'm still on hold for *Burnt Hills*. Did they call you?"

"They did. Same for me. Said there was some problem with the studio."

"That's what they told me."

"What do you suppose is going on?"

"I don't know," I said. "Sounds like that shooting may have thrown a monkey wrench into things."

"Dammit! If Jacobson, or Jesperson, or whatever the hell his name is responsible for mucking things up, he's gonna have hell to pay."

"It's not your fault, Lois."

"Yeah, I suppose. Makes me feel a little guilty, though."

"If there's any blame to be dished out, it has to land on the lot for allowing someone to get on the premises with a gun." There was silence on the other end of the line. "How's the arm?"

"Pretty good. I'll have to lay off arm wrestling for a while, but it's okay."

"Good. I'll touch base with you and let you know if I've found anything."

We ended the call and I laid the phone on the coffee table.

"What did she say?"

"She's never heard of Bryce Jesperson." I took a sip from my bottle and peeled off a bit of the label as I stared at the muted Clint. Silence filled the room for several moments.

"What's the matter?" Carla finally said.

"I don't know. I can't put my finger on it, but somehow I don't think she's leveling with me."

"Not knowing her, I'll take your word for it." She reached for her glass of iced tea. "But, I mean, 'hinky?' I haven't heard that in a long time."

"Well, she does have a colorful way of expressing herself, I'll give her that. She also said this guy, whatever the hell his name is, may be 'a float short of a parade'."

She giggled and said, "I kinda like that one." I nodded in agreement, and she unmuted the TV. "So, where do you go from here? You going to tell her to forget it?"

"No, I already billed her for a retainer. Mavis can start over with a new name." Carla got up and went into the kitchen for more iced tea. She returned with a full glass and plopped back down on the sofa. "Speaking of Mavis," I said. "We had an interesting conversation today."

"Oh?"

"You know that little room where she keeps her office supplies?"

"Yeah. What about it?"

"Well, she actually allowed me to go in there today and get a cup of coffee. The place is a mess. Crowded beyond belief. I don't know how the hell she can find anything."

"So?"

I swallowed a sip of beer and said, "So, she asked me if you and I had ever given any thought of moving in together." I glanced at her to see what her reaction was. A trace of a smile had appeared.

"And what was your answer?"

"I said I'd discuss it with you."

"And here we are," she said, then sipped some tea. "That would require you to move."

"I know. Not my idea of a day at the beach."

"Well, let's face it, Eddie. It's not like you've got a lot of personal belongings. I mean, I've seen that closet of yours. I wouldn't consider your wardrobe to be extensive by any means."

"True that, but there is my trench coat. Every private eye has gotta have a trench coat."

"When's the last time you wore it?"

"I can't remember."

"Somehow that kind of proves my point."

I nodded and took a pull off my beer bottle. "The idea behind our conversation was that she could use my apartment to give her more room for all the material she uses in that tchotchke business of hers."

"That makes sense. Do you think you can forego your Murphy bed?"

"Might be tough," I said. "On the other hand, that second bedroom of yours is pretty comfortable."

A pregnant pause ensued as she set her glass on the coffee table. "What's the matter with the first one? You don't like the company?"

"No, I do. Don't get me wrong. It's just that when…how shall I say this? When the nocturnal noises start, I have someplace to seek sanctuary." I dropped the comment, knowing I would get a rise out of her, and I wasn't disappointed.

After a moment and her eyes had narrowed she said, "I suppose by that crack you're once again implying that I snore?" She got on her hands and knees and stuck her face in front of mine. "I do *not* snore!"

I grinned and took a swallow of beer to keep myself from laughing.

"Listen up, Shamus. I'm going to get a tape recorder and record you the next time you start sounding like a chainsaw at sunup."

That did it. I choked back a spit take, set the beer bottle on the table and burst into laughter, then picked up a napkin and wiped my mouth. She jumped on me and grabbed my nose with one of her patented grips. We tussled for a moment or two until I grabbed her hands and kissed her. She returned it and we lost ourselves in each other for a couple of minutes. Finally, we stopped and looked into each other's eyes. She ran one finger down the length of my nose and then across my lips.

"Okay," I said. "Seriously? What do you think? You know, don't you, that I'll kick in half your mortgage?"

"What about your place? You'll still have the office rent."

"Well, Mavis said she'd split it with me."

"Even so, that leaves you with two monthly payments."

"I'll manage." I glanced at her after watching Clint light another cigarillo and flick the match into the bearded face of a bad guy. She ran her fingers through my hair and looked lost in thought. "What?" I said. "That doesn't work for you?"

"That's not uppermost in my mind."

"Okay, so what's bothering you?"

She righted herself and sat back on her haunches, then reached over, picked up the remote and muted Clint again.

"What is it, Carla?"

After a moment she said, "You and I both know that we tend to have streaks of independence in us. There's a 'lone wolf' side to both of us, right?"

"Yeah, I suppose, but that doesn't mean we can't adapt." I sat up and put my feet on the floor. "I blew up that relationship I had with Elaine, but I'd like to think I've learned from my mistakes."

"You have," she said. "But I'm also thinking of myself. It's no secret that sometimes I'm not the best person to be around."

"Granted. So let's agree that there are times when we both need some space, and try and figure out how we can accomplish that. I'll still have my office, provided they don't tear down the damn building."

"Are you serious? Do you think that's going to happen?"

"I don't know. It's pretty old, and the way the gentrification of the Boulevard is going, it's anybody's guess." I reached over, picked up my beer bottle and took a hit. "But I'll cross that bridge when I get to it. What should I tell Mavis? Decision time."

"I like it, despite some adjustments we'll both have to make. When do you want to do this?"

"After I'm done with *Burnt Hills* and I find this Jesperson character. How does that sound?"

"Great." She picked up her glass and sipped, then set it back on the coffee table and curled herself next to me.

I put my arm around her and we watched Clint for a few moments. As bizarre as the thought of both of us having PTSD counselors was, it was probably a good idea. My doctor had been telling me to refrain from bottling up the feelings of angst and fear. To bring them out in the open and confront them. Having someone else with the same problems to share and compare notes could only be a positive way to deal with them.

Consequently, I found myself feeling a closeness with Carla that I hadn't experienced in a while. It's true that we've spent many nights together, but I've always had the option of my little hole-in-the-wall studio apartment with its Murphy bed, mini fridge and Juliet balcony that gives me a bird's-eye view of Hollywood Boulevard. True, ceding the place to Mavis wouldn't completely deprive me of those surroundings, but it would mean an adjustment, something I haven't always been receptive to. Change is good, I thought. Man up, Collins.

Our mutual reverie with Eastwood as company was interrupted by my cell phone on the coffee table. Carla unfurled herself and I picked up the phone and looked at the display. "It's Charlie."

She muted the TV as I took the call.

"Hey, Charlie. Any news?"

"Yeah, the computer kicked out the plate. Registered to a Langston Beaumont. I'm not going to give you an address, Collins, because knowing you, you'll be knocking on the guy's door tomorrow. And that I don't want. Let us talk to the guy."

"Understood," I said.

"Besides, also knowing you, you'll put your secretary on it and you'll find the address anyway. But hear me on this. It's not your fight. You got me?"

"Gotcha."

"Okay. I'll keep you up to date," he said, and ended the call.

I put the phone back on the coffee table and turned to Carla. "It's registered to a Langston Beaumont. He didn't give me an address."

"Well, good, that's a start."

"Yeah. Let's hope so."

19

Over the years that Mavis has worked for me I've generally been in the office when she arrives in the morning, having already made up the Murphy bed and stowed it in its hole in the wall. However, since Carla and I have been more frequently spending our nights together, of late I've arrived to see Mavis at her desk, pecking away at her computer or tending to the latest doodad, doohickey, or gewgaw that is about to find its way to an eager collector with money to burn on such trivial trinkets.

This morning was an exception. Carla had scurried off to her television show almost at the crack of dawn, leaving me with an opportunity to drop by my favorite bakery and pick up an assortment of pastries. I left the box on Mavis's desk, after selecting one for myself. With a fresh cup of coffee in one hand and a bear claw balanced on the cup, I slid open the door and stepped onto my Juliet balcony to survey the Boulevard, or my front yard, as I sometimes call it.

Traffic was light this early in the morning. A bus lumbered westward and sounds of metal doors and awnings being opened drifted up to me. Since Carla and I had made the decision to move in together, interludes like this would be less frequent. I was still trying to wrap my head around that fact, but in the end, the thought of waking up next to her outweighed honking horns and screaming sirens.

As I took a bite of the bear claw, I heard Mavis enter the office and then, "Eddie, are you here?"

"Yeah, be right there." I slid the door closed then pawed my way through the beaded curtain into my office. "Good morning. Help yourself to some carbs." I entered her office to see her examining the box of pastries.

"What's the occasion?" she said.

"Nothing. Carla had an early call. The bakery was on the way."

"Thanks," she said, as she picked up a sugared donut and laid it on a napkin the bakery had provided. "You're ruining my diet, you know."

"Life's a diet, kiddo."

"Says the man who could stand to lose a couple of pounds."

"Yes, Mom," I said, as I settled into one of the chairs in front of her desk.

"So, you spent the night with Carla?"

"Yup. Which brings me to the conversation we had."

"Let me get a pot of coffee going first." She took a nibble of the donut and went into her sanctum sanctorum. I took a bite of the bear claw and heard the sound of running water. After a moment or two she came back to her desk, sat down and booted up her computer. "Did this conversation deal with what we discussed yesterday?"

"It did. Carla's on board."

"Really?"

"Yup. We're maybe going to have to deal with a hurdle or two, but we both agreed it's probably time to do it."

"That's terrific. And when will this happen?"

"After I finish with *Burnt Hills* and this search for Burt Jacobson. Speaking of which, Burt Jacobson is now also known as Bryce Jesperson."

She took another bite of the donut, shifted it to one side of her mouth and slowly chewed, then said, "I'm afraid to ask."

I filled her in on the young woman revealing the alias and the telephone call with Lois Maxwell.

"So forget about Burt Jacobson?" she said.

"For the time being. I've got another name to look for too."

"Hold on. Let me get some coffee."

She went back to her alcove, and I pulled out my notebook and jotted down the names of Bryce Jesperson and Langston Beaumont. When she reseated herself, I put the slip of paper in front of her.

"Why does this guy have two names?"

"That's a good question. Lois didn't seem to have an answer."

She took a sip of coffee and said, "Who the heck is Langston Beaumont?"

"He may be the owner of that SUV from the night Carla and I got shot at." I went on to relate my discovery of the SUV at El Pollo Loco and giving the plate number to Charlie Rivers.

Mavis held up the piece of paper in front of her. "Langston Beaumont? Sounds like he should be sitting on a plantation veranda in Georgia looking at his cotton and sipping on a mint julep."

"Does have that ring, doesn't it? But he lives out here, somewhere. With a name like that he shouldn't be too hard to find."

"Charlie didn't give you an address?"

"Nope. He told me to keep my nose out of it."

"Good advice. Knowing you as I do, boss man, if I find him, you'll do exactly the opposite."

"Funny, that's just what Charlie said."

She nodded and gave me a perfect eye roll as I stood and went back into my apartment. I took a quick shower, brushed my teeth, dressed, and then opened the closet and surveyed my wardrobe. Carla was right; it wasn't very extensive. A couple of suits, maybe a week's worth of shirts and several pairs of trousers pretty much summed up the inventory. And, of course, the trench coat. Presenting more of a challenge to the move was my collection of DVDs. I couldn't justify thinning out all those movies; I'd spent too much time and money collecting them. In anticipation of the eventual move, I made a mental note to get a cardboard box or two.

After grabbing the porkpie *du jour* from its peg, I walked into Mavis's office with the intention of leaving, but she stopped me with, "Get this. Langston Beaumont runs a security company. Take a look."

I pulled a chair around the desk and sat next to her. Her computer screen showed the website of a company by the name of "Edge Security," located out in Encino. Langston Beaumont was listed as one of the co-owners. There was a picture of him. He didn't look like his name would imply. No southern gentleman, he. His head was shaved. He had black caterpillar eyebrows, steely eyes, and a prominent handlebar mustache. If you were looking for security, this guy looked like he could provide it. I pulled out my notebook and jotted down the address of the company and its telephone number.

"What are you going to do with those?" she said.

"Charlie didn't say anything about checking out a place of business. I might need security."

Mavis grabbed my chin and turned my face toward her. "Look, Eddie, if you think this guy is behind that ambush the other night, he damn sure knows what you look like. You pop into his office and you're looking for trouble."

"Who said anything about popping into his office? If he's linked to that SUV it behooves me to at least know where the hell he hangs his hat." I picked up the chair and returned it to its place in front of her desk, then headed for the door.

"Hey!" she said.

The volume of her voice made me do an about face.

"Promise me you'll let LAPD handle this, Eddie. Charlie is right. This isn't your fight."

"Duly noted," I said, and left the office.

As I edged my car out of its parking space, I reflected on what Mavis had said and how it echoed Charlie's admonitions. They were right, of course, but gimme a break. It's not like there was a bobblehead of each of them on the dash, every bump in the road a constant reminder of their instructions. I saw no harm in driving by Edge Security and scoping out the place. But first, I had another angle to pursue with respect to Burt Jacobson, aka Bryce Jesperson.

I parked in the lot of a Ralph's grocery, made my way to the liquor aisle and pulled a fifth of Wild Turkey off the shelf. The young man at the checkout gave me a curious look, one that implied, "Awful early, isn't it, pal?"

"I've got a sick friend," I said. "He needs his medicine."

"Whatever," he replied. "Hope it works."

Judith Quinn is one of the more venerable casting agents in town. She's been in business for years and is generally well-liked throughout the biz. She'd done right by me a few times in the past, bringing me in for jobs and lobbying for me to get the part. And I've always been grateful. A few months ago, I'd asked her for a favor in trying to locate the four creeps Reggie and I had encountered up in Piru.

As I opened the door of Quinn Casting, I hoped I could prevail upon her again. She was bent over the desk of one of her assistants, both of them glued to the young girl's computer screen.

She straightened up and turned when the door opened. "Oh, my God, leave a door unlocked and look what wanders in." Judith will never be regarded as shy and unassuming. She was a tall redhead with a booming voice and an outgoing personality that could strike fear into directors who happened to disagree with her about a certain actor up for a part.

"Hey, Judith, how you doin'?"

"Fair to middling." I handed her the brown paper bag containing the Wild Turkey and she said, "What's this?"

"To be honest, it's a bribe," I said, and glanced at her assistant. "You didn't hear that, okay?"

Both women chuckled and Judith pulled the bottle from the bag. "Damn, Eddie, you've got good taste. 'Taste' being the operative word. Thanks. If it wasn't so damn early, I'd invite you to help me break the seal on this puppy."

"I'll settle for a rain check."

"Coffee in the meantime?"

"If you've got it made."

She said she did, and after giving her assistant an instruction, beckoned me to follow her into her office. I looked at the assistant and put my finger to my lips with the "shush" signal. She reciprocated with a big smile and then ran her fingers across her mouth, giving me the universal "my lips are sealed" sign. Judith shut the door behind us, put the Wild Turkey on a shelf underneath a coffee maker and told me to have a seat. I took one of the chairs in front of her desk.

"How's tricks?" she said.

"Not bad. I've got a part in something called *Burnt Hills*. You heard of it?"

"Yeah, as a matter of fact I have. I submitted one of my clients that resulted in bupkis. But that director, Pete O'Brien, is a nice guy."

She asked me how I took my coffee, and after I said just black, she handed me a mug and sat behind her desk.

"Let me think now," she said. "Last time you graced me with your presence you were looking for some actors, I seem to remember. Bring me up to speed."

I sipped some coffee and told her the whole sordid episode of Reggie's and my run-in with those four animals who came close to punching both of our tickets. The look on Judith's face was one of complete disgust.

"So, they were essentially doing snuff films?" she said.

"That pretty much characterizes it."

"Oh, my God, Eddie! Please tell me they're wearing orange jumpsuits."

"Well, they've been indicted and are awaiting trial. I'll probably have to testify against them."

"I hope they get the book thrown at them and they wind up in gen pop. Jailhouse justice couldn't happen to nicer guys. Yuck! Turns my stomach just to think about 'em."

"I agree. The evidence against them is pretty overwhelming."

"Okay, moving on. What's up?"

"I've got a client who's looking for somebody. An actor she worked with at one time and now has lost track of. Guy by the name of Burt Jacobson. Ring a bell?" Since I hadn't got a hit on IMDB for Bryce Jesperson, I didn't think it necessary to give Judith that name.

She took a sip of coffee and set her cup down. "Hmmm. Not off hand. He still in the business?"

"Not sure, but I did find him on IMDB." I handed her the picture of Jacobson and she looked at it for a moment.

"He looks kind of familiar." She turned to face her computer. "Let me try something here. There's an amazing new database I've subscribed to. If the guy has, or had a SAG card, I can probably find him." She clicked keys for a moment and landed on a website. "Well, lookee here." She turned to me. "You're still with Morrie Howard, right?"

"Yeah. Why?"

"You better drop in on him. He once had a client by the name of Burt Jacobson."

20

The thought never occurred to me that Burt Jacobson and I would share the same agent. I've been with Morrie Howard for quite a few years, but have never really gotten to know who his other clients are. It's not like we have Christmas parties, exchange gifts and raise a glass of eggnog.

His office was located on the third story of an old brick building a block and half south of Hollywood Boulevard. There was no elevator. As I started the climb I noticed how each step bowed in the middle from many years of young hopefuls trudging up the flights in pursuit of fame and fortune. At one time I was one of those climbers.

I opened the door and immediately noticed the distinct odor of cat piss and stale cigarette smoke. The latter, of course, was from Morrie, who I constantly pestered to quit, so far with no results. The other faint odor was due to the presence of Hitchcock, Morrie's solid black cat he'd adopted on the pretense that the office had mice. I'd never seen one of the varmints, and given Hitchcock's age, I doubted he could catch one even if he tried. I closed the door and saw the black bundle curled up in his favorite chair. I reached over, scratched his head, and was rewarded by a bounce of his tail and a huge yawn. So much for visitors.

Kevin Reynolds, Morrie's assistant, a young Black man, sat behind his desk, pecking away on a computer. He wore his typical black tee shirt and his hairstyle was more subdued than I'd seen it since my last visit. For a change, it didn't look like he'd stuck his finger in a light socket.

"Hi, Eddie. How's that *Burnt Hills* shoot going? Heard you had a little excitement the other day."

"Yeah, if you can call someone getting shot with a real bullet excitement."

"Lois Maxwell, right?"

"Right."

"Is she okay?"

"She was lucky. Whoever did it was a bad shot." I gestured to the cat on the chair. "How's Hitchcock holding up?"

"Day to day."

"How long has it been since his litter box was cleaned?"

"You noticed, huh?"

"From the minute I opened the door."

"Morrie's supposed to do that, but he forgets."

"Speaking of the devil, is he in?"

"He is. Do you wish to be announced?"

"I'll announce myself. You take care of the litter box."

He flashed me a scowl and I knocked on Morrie's door.

"Enter," I heard from behind the frosted glass.

I opened the door and saw him in a far corner feeding two yellow parakeets. A cigarette dangled from the corner of his mouth. He wore baggy pants and a shirt that looked like it was in need of a few minutes under a hot iron. His gray hair was mussed and longing for a trim.

"Eddie Collins! The best private eye I know."

"The only private eye you know, Morrie."

"That's true. Have a seat and let me finish feeding Thelma and Louise here."

"How do you know which one is which?"

"Louise has got a little splotch of blue on her hind end."

"And how do you know they're both females?"

He plucked the cigarette from his mouth and put it in an ashtray that sat on a shelf next to him and brushed the ashes off his shirt. "What, are you an ornithologist all of a sudden?"

"Just curious."

"The guy who sold them to me assured me they were."

"I see. Maybe you should get a male and put him in there with them. That way you'd know for sure. You could call him Brad."

He closed the cage door and looked at me. "Brad? Why Brad?"

"After Brad Pitt. He was in the movie *Thelma and Louise*."

"*Oy vey*. You're a font of useless information, *bubbeleh*." He picked up the cigarette, took a big drag and walked behind his desk. After exhaling, he stubbed it out and let loose with a deep, phlegmatic cough, then followed it with a swallow of Diet Coke from a plastic bottle. He plopped into his chair, folded his hands and looked at me. "Now, what can I do for you, my movie junkie friend. But first, tell me what the hell happened on that *Burnt Hills* job?"

I filled him in on what had gone down with regard to Lois Maxwell.

"For crissakes, don't they have security on that lot?"

"*Burnt Hills* is the first shoot. Apparently they haven't got their security ironed out yet."

"Is she okay?"

"Yeah, she's fine"

He picked up a pack of cigarettes and shook one out. "Now then, what brings you to my humble office?"

"The name Burt Jacobson ring a bell?"

He paused with his Zippo lighter about to be flicked and looked up at me. "Yeah, but not very loud." He lit the cigarette, pushed a cloud of smoke into the air and closed the lighter. "Why do you ask?"

"I just came from Judith Quinn's office. Thought she might know where he's at. She told me he used to be a client of yours."

"He was. Up until a few years ago. Why do you want to know about him?"

"Well, I've got a client who's looking for him. I was hoping you might know his whereabouts."

"Who's your client?"

"That's confidential, Morrie."

He glared at me as he puffed on his cigarette and exhaled another cloud. "Yeah, yeah, confidential. Some smart aleck PI sits in my office and talks to me about confidentiality. Gimme a break already. What if I told you the same thing about a former client? What about that?"

"Hey, I didn't mean to put a burr under your saddle." Morrie's attitude puzzled me and I decided I would do something I very rarely do, but my thought was interrupted by his intercom. He reached over and pushed a button. "Yeah?"

Kevin's voice came back with, "Randy Fitzgerald on line one."

"Tell him I'll call him back." He took his finger off the button and then inhaled another puff of the cigarette.

"All right, look," I said. "I don't mean to be a pain in the ass. Lois Maxwell thinks this Burt Jacobson character might be the person who took a shot at her. She was involved in some sort of business deal with him in the past, which blew up, and now she says he's harassing her. She's not sure why and she hired me to find the guy. That's it. Confidentially speaking, of course."

He chuckled and tapped the end of his cigarette into an ashtray in front of him. "Sorry. I got up on the wrong side this morning, and the wife damn sure didn't help. So, you can't find this Jacobson guy, huh?"

I handed him the IMDB photo. "This is him, right?"

He looked at the picture and said, "Yup. I got him that job. It was a TV movie. He did pretty good with it."

"Did he ever use the name Bryce Jesperson when he was with you?"

He took a hit off his cigarette and said, "Nope. That doesn't ring a bell. What is that? His real name?"

"Apparently. At least someone who dated him a couple of times thought so."

He put his cigarette in the ashtray and pushed his chair back, then swiveled it around and slid up to a filing cabinet. "I think I may still have a file on him. Just in case someone's looking at him for a role." He pulled a drawer open and pawed through several files, then pulled one out, slid the drawer closed and scooted back up to his desk. "Okay, I've got an address here for him on Aqua Vista in Studio City."

"Nope. I checked that out. He moved."

"Well, so much for that. You got a phone number?"

"I do, but Lois thinks it's a burner."

"What is it?" I found the number in my notebook and gave it to him.

"Nope. This one I've got here is marked as a cell phone." He took a drag off the cigarette and after a cough said, "Even if he moved, he wouldn't change his cell phone number, would he?"

"Not likely," I said. "What's the number?"

Morrie gave me the digits and I jotted them down in my notebook.

"So what good is the number if he doesn't want to be found? He probably won't answer. What does the PI do then?"

"Leave it up to my secretary. His cell phone account has to have an address linked to it. Mavis is a whiz when it comes to finding someone who doesn't want to be found. Trust me."

"Okay, if you say so."

I put my notebook back in my pocket and stood up. "Thanks, Morrie."

"Yeah, no problem. Let me know if you find out where he lives."

"You got it."

"Are you filming tomorrow?"

"No, I'm on hold. I think they've got some sort of problem with the studio in the wake of that shooting."

"Well, the good news is you're still getting paid. And look at this way," he continued, "if they have to extend your contract there'll be more bucks in the till."

"Keep that thought, Morrie. I'll check in with you later." I started for the door and said, "Give some thought to getting a male parakeet. Those two might be lonely."

"Oh, hell, they talk to each other all the time. They might tear the poor bastard to pieces."

I left his office and saw that Hitchcock had vacated his chair. I turned to Kevin. "Where did he go?"

He gestured to a small bathroom behind his desk. "Fresh litter. He had a pee and then figured he'd have a snack."

"Good man," I said, as I left the office.

While I sat in my car and let the air conditioning kick in, I dialed the phone number Morrie had given me. It rang four times and a recorded, generic voice said, "Your call has been forwarded to an automatic answering service. At the sound of the tone, please leave a message and your call will be returned as soon as possible." With all the robocalls and telemarketing intrusions in today's telephonic traffic, I wasn't surprised by the disembodied voice, even given the fact that it was a cell phone number. When I heard the tone, I left him my name, phone number and told him I was calling on behalf of Lois Maxwell. Hopefully Mavis could come up with an address for him, so either Lois or I could follow up the phone call with an in-person visit.

After I broke the connection, I dialed directory assistance and asked for a listing for Burt Jacobson. There was none. I then requested one for Bryce Jesperson. Same result. That told me one of two things: Either he had an unlisted number, or he didn't even have a landline, which was becoming more and more common these days.

Giving an agent your cell phone number, rather than a landline, made perfect sense. When I first arrived in this town in pursuit of the brass ring, I insured my availability with a pager, which then required a roll of quarters and a search for the nearest payphone. With the advent of the cell phone and texting, those glass-enclosed booths were becoming as extinct as manual typewriters.

After my calls to directory assistance, I checked in with Mavis. She picked up on the second ring.

"What's the news, boss man?"

"Would you believe Burt Jacobson was once a client of Morrie Howard?"

"You're kidding."

"Nope. Morrie has what is apparently a cell phone number for him." I gave it to her and continued. "See if you can find an address for him. Even though he's moved, he's probably kept the same cell number. Whoever his carrier is has got to know where to send the bill. Do your thing, kiddo."

"I'm on it," she said, and hung up.

Before heading to Encino, I got in the queue for an In-N-Out drive-thru and parked under a tree in their parking lot to savor what many consider to be the best burger in Los Angeles. I wouldn't disagree. As I unwrapped my double-double and took a bite, a debate swirled in my head as to how Burt Jacobson, aka Bryce Jesperson, should be approached. If indeed Mavis found an address for him, should I just cold call on him with a knock on his door, or should Lois be the one to make the overture? I decided to broach the subject with her the next time I saw her and let her decide how she wanted to proceed. After all, if I provided her with his phone number and hopefully an address, I'd fulfilled my obligation to her. She'd be on her own.

The address for Edge Security Mavis had provided me was in an industrial zone on the northern outskirts of Encino. I slowly drove down the street and spotted the address on my right. The building was a one-story concrete block structure, painted white with blue trim on the corners. On the roof over the front door a sign proclaimed the identity of the company. It, too, was blue with the word "Edge" sprawled across what appeared to be a cliff of some sort, with "Security" running parallel under the ledge.

There was no dark SUV in the small parking lot adjacent to the structure. Instead, a silver Mercedes that looked familiar sat in front of the building. I made a U-turn at the next intersection and parked half a block away behind a monster pickup. I then pulled a small pair of binoculars from the glove compartment and focused on the license plate of the Mercedes. I flipped some pages in my notebook until I found what I was looking for: the plate matched the one for Vic Benedetti, one of the four creeps from the Piru incident. I reached into the glove compartment again and pulled out my digital camera, then took a picture of the Edge Security building and zoomed in on Benedetti's Mercedes and took a picture of it as well, along with the license plate.

About ten minutes later an Edge van pulled into the parking lot next to the Mercedes and two men got out. I again zoomed in and caught both of them on camera. One had a blond head of hair and the other was dark. The blond opened a rear door, picked up a small duffel bag and the two men entered the building. Neither of them bore any resemblance to Langston Beaumont. I waited another ten minutes, but no dark SUV appeared. I stuck the binoculars back in the glove compartment and took a couple more shots of the license plate on the Mercedes and the Edge Security building. My hope of seeing the SUV with the license plate S2K6J55 sitting in the parking lot of Edge Security hadn't been realized. But that fact became insignificant given the presence of Vic Benedetti. What the hell was he doing there?

I didn't have an answer, but in the meantime, I told myself to keep my eyes focused on my rearview mirror.

That's exactly what I did all the way back to my office. The presence of Benedetti's Mercedes outside Edge Security told me three things. One: He—and probably the other three pornographers—had a connection to Langston Beaumont and a dark SUV with the license plate S2K6755. Two: The driver of said SUV more than likely attempted to kill me on Hollywood Boulevard. Three: It was becoming more and more clear that someone was trying to keep me and Reggie from testifying in that trial up in Ventura County.

Those three assumptions then led me to wonder about the gunshot that wounded Lois Maxwell. Was Burt Jacobson, aka Bryce Jesperson aiming for Lois, or was the shot meant for me? Whoever was in the SUV had missed me; whoever fired the shot that wounded her had also missed me. Would a third time be the charm?

As I left the Ventura Freeway and segued onto the Hollywood, those morbid thoughts hung over my head like a thunder cloud. Tomorrow I was scheduled to meet with my counselor. Given my mood, it promised to be an interesting session.

As it turned out, I had to reschedule the session with my doctor. I'd no sooner entered my office when Debbie Merton from *Burnt Hills* called saying that the company was called at ten o'clock in the morning. We were to report to where the table read had been held. Important news from Preston Bridges, the production manager. She didn't elaborate.

She didn't have to. Something was in the wind and headed toward *Burnt Hills*.

21

The room where the table read for *Burnt Hills* had taken place held no similarity to the one I walked into the following morning. Preston Bridges, the production manager, was sequestered in one corner talking to his director, Pete O'Brien. The assistant directors stood next to them. They all looked like they were auditioning for places on Mt. Rushmore. Their conversation consisted of nothing louder than whispers. As before, three tables had been set up in a triangular formation. Urns of coffee and plates of nibbles occupied another table next to one wall. The cast stood in groups of two or three, somber looks on their faces. I had the feeling I'd entered the viewing room of a funeral parlor.

I spotted Lois talking with one of the wardrobe people. When she saw me, she excused herself and walked up to me, a sling over the arm that had been shot. She had a cup of coffee in her left hand.

"Good morning," she said.

"Morning. If I didn't know any better, I'd ask who died."

"Yeah, I know. Why do you suppose they called us?"

"I'm not sure, but it doesn't look like they're ready to give all of us salary bumps. Let me get a cup of coffee. Why don't you lay claim to a couple of chairs?"

"Will do," she said. She sat down in one and plopped her shoulder bag down on the one next to it.

I filled a cup with coffee, picked up a muffin, then handed her the bag and took the chair next to her. The cluster of production heads broke up and they all found chairs at the bottom of the triangle.

"Good morning," Bridges said. "Let's all take a seat and we'll get underway." Everybody found a chair and he continued. "First of all, let me extend a hearty welcome back to Lois Maxwell." He led a round of light applause, which made Lois blush as she voiced her thanks to everyone. "I think I speak on behalf of all of us when I say we couldn't be more grateful than to see you're all right, Lois."

"Thanks, everyone," she said. "Next time I'll duck."

Chuckles rolled around the tables and Bridges continued. "It's often said that law-making in Congress is like making sausage. It's done away from the public eye. I'm beginning to think that movie-making is similar. Nobody knows the turmoil that goes on in trying to bring something to the screen. *Burnt Hills* seems to have fallen victim to that. So, having said that, I have some good news and some bad news.

He paused for effect and the people around the tables glanced at each other. My suspicion about something looming over the production looked to be fact.

"First, the bad news," Bridges went on. "In the wake of what happened to Lois, the owners of Sunset Ranch have shuttered the location. For how long, we don't know. The biggest issue was their liability for the incident. They obviously had some failings in their security protocols, and they felt it best to straighten out those problems before making the lot available for further shooting. So, in essence, we're left out in the cold."

He again paused and Lois filled the void by saying, "I'm not going to sue, Preston. I can't afford a lawyer." Her comment released some tension in the room and subdued laughter came from several people.

"I didn't think you would, Lois," Bridges said. "The less I see and hear from lawyers the better." He paused to swallow some coffee and then continued. "But amidst all this there is some good news as well. We've been on the phone, and it turns out that Rancho Deluxe is available to us. It's up in Santa Clarita, not far from Sunset Ranch. Maybe some of you have worked there before?"

A couple of hands went up.

"Fortunately," Bridges added, "we've got our saloon interior already in the can, which is a big relief. The number of interiors we still need can be done at the new location. And also the good news is that there's a western street on the lot which gives us the opportunity to reshoot the scene with Lois. That's going to be first up tomorrow when we get back in the saddle. We'll get directions to you before you leave this morning. We've had to juggle some of the scenes and tweak some others, but in the end I think we're going to be okay. Now, some would probably say to cancel the project, but I, along with Pete, believe in this film and we're going to do everything possible to see it come to fruition. We're going to see that the damn sausage gets made!"

A few hearty "hoo-rahs" and applause erupted around the tables. Obviously, *esprit de corps* was alive and well in *Burnt Hills.*

"Are there any questions?" Preston said.

Hugh Danton, the actor playing Bart Kincannon on the picture raised his hand and said, "How about our contracts, Preston? With the interruptions in the schedule, mine might lapse before you're done shooting."

"Good question. We'll be in touch with your agents and keep them in the loop. If extensions are necessary, they'll be made. Anybody else?" Nobody raised a hand and Bridges went on to say, "both Pete and I want to express our heartfelt thanks to all of you for rolling with us. The film is special to us and we hope it is to you as well."

With that the meeting ended and directions to the new location were passed around the tables. Lois and I checked in with Brad Foster, the 1ˢᵗ AD, and were given an eight o'clock call for tomorrow. We started to leave the room, but Lois got held up with some good wishes from several members of the company. I waited for her outside the building. Conversations with a few actors revealed that we were all glad the job would continue. Any port in a storm in this factory of unemployment known as the movie biz, or—to coin a phrase from Preston Bridges—the sausage business.

Lois appeared the doorway and slung her tote bag over her left shoulder.

"You're the most popular gal on the movie," I said.

"Well, somebody's got to tackle all the testosterone flying around the place."

I chuckled and said, "Buy you a cup of coffee?"

"You betcha," she replied, and pointed to Earl's across the street, where we'd previously had lunch. "Figure it's worth a repeat?"

"Why not? We'd better move our cars." She agreed we nudged our cars out of the parking lot and found spaces on the street in front of the deli.

Earl's coffee was better than the stuff we'd just had in the meeting. With two steaming mugs in front of us, I looked at the directions to Rancho Deluxe. "You ever been on this lot?" I said.

"Once," she said. "If memory serves me correctly, I think it was an episode of *Maverick*."

"Damn, you have been around," I said.

"I'm older than dirt," she replied, and followed her comment with a laugh. She sipped her coffee and set the cup back on the table. "You know, I felt a little awkward getting all that attention. Made me feel kind of funny."

"Yeah, I get that, but look at it this way. They're probably pretty tickled that you're not going to press charges against them."

"Oh, no way! It's not the company's problem. If anybody's to blame, it's the owners of the lot, and that would be a waste of time. They've probably got lawyers stacked a mile high."

"No doubt. But I know some actors who'd jump at the chance."

"Well, let 'em have at it. I'm just damn glad it wasn't worse." She raised her cup, took a sip and set it down. "So, any news from my private eye?"

"Matter of fact, there is. My agent is Morrie Howard and—"

"Morrie Howard?" she said, interrupting me. "Heck, I know Morrie Howard."

"Well, it turns out he had Burt Jacobson as a client a while back."

"You're kidding. How did you find that out?"

"Do you know Judith Quinn?"

"Sure. Have for years."

"Same here. Anyway, I asked her for a favor. She did an Internet search and found out Jacobson was with him at one time. So I dropped in on Morrie, which is something I don't do often enough, I suppose. I've never been very good at courting an agent, schmoozing, that sort of thing. In any case, the only address Morrie had for Jacobson was the one on Aqua Vista, but he had what he thought was a cell phone number for the guy. I called it but it went to voice mail. I left a message, explained who I was, and asked him to give me a call." I pulled out my notebook and showed her Jacobson's number Morrie had given me. She entered it into her phone as I took a sip from my cup of coffee.

"She looked at her watch and said, "In that message you left, did you tell him that I hired you to look for him?"

"No. I thought it better to leave that to you."

She swallowed a mouthful of coffee and thought about what I'd revealed to her. "You know what I can't figure out, though, is why he changed his name from. . . what the heck was it? Bryce something?"

"Jesperson. Yeah, I've thought about that too. I didn't get any hits on the Internet Movie Database site for Jesperson, so it's not like the Guild told him he had to make the change."

"Well, he's damn sure got some explaining to do," she said.

I nodded in agreement. We finished our coffee and walked to our cars. I told her I'd see her in the morning.

"That you will, my own private eye. And this time we'll get it right."

Rancho Deluxe wasn't too far from where we'd been shooting up to this point, so it didn't take me any extra time getting there. A security guard at the entrance to the lot directed me to company parking. The honey wagons had already arrived from the previous location. After locking my wallet in the car, I found my trailer and saw that Chet Cassidy's trappings had also successfully made the trip. The day's shooting schedule and sides were on the dressing table. After scanning them and seeing that no changes had been made in the dialogue between Lois and me, I stepped outside, found Cheryl, the PA, signed in with her and went in search of breakfast.

The roach coach—or chuck wagon, in keeping with our western theme—was parked up against a soundstage, in front of which sat tables and chairs. I spotted Lois and as I made my way to the chow line, I noticed a Los Angeles Sheriff's Department SUV parked nearby. Officer Ramirez leaned against the front end, engaged in conversation with Preston Bridges.

I poured a cup of coffee, picked up an orange juice container and carried the tray to where Lois sat. "Morning," I said, and gestured to Ramirez and Bridges. "I see John Law has followed us. Word gets around fast."

"Yeah, Bridges already cornered me," she said. "The deputy wants to interview me when we're through shooting our scene."

"He talked to me at the other location. I told him about your run-in with Jacobson. He probably wants some corroboration."

We dug into our breakfasts and as we sipped our coffees Bridges finished his conversation with Ramirez and walked up to our table, took a chair and sat down.

"Good morning, folks," he said. We responded and he pointed off to his right toward a western street that stretched out for a couple of blocks. "There's our new street. It's a bit shorter than the one we had, so we'll have to adjust the blocking a little, but it should work out fine."

"I see that Ramirez obviously found out that we moved," I said.

"Yeah," Bridges said. He gave me an update on the aftermath of the shooting."

"What do they know?" I said.

"This is what he told me. Apparently, there was a group of seventeen tourists watching us film. Despite my objections, by the way. Anyway, they were split into two groups, thirteen of them separated from the other four by a hitching post sort of deal running down an alley between two buildings."

"Real structures?" I said. "Or just facades?"

"No, working buildings. I don't think they've got anything but the real thing on that lot. When the looky-loos heard the shot, they ducked, thinking it came from where we were filming. That's when somebody in the group of four discovered that one of their quartet had gone inside the nearest building. It had a real window. This person saw the gun, but whoever it was took off, ran though the building and out a rear door."

"And he disappeared?" I said.

"That's what Ramirez tells me. The gunman was seen running down the alley and then jumping into the side door of a van that hightailed it out of the parking lot."

"Anybody get a description?" Lois said.

"The other three people who were with the shooter said he was blond, pretty well buffed, but other than that they didn't notice anything extraordinary about him."

The mention of the guy being blond sent up a little red flag in me, but it quickly disappeared when I realized how many people are fair-haired. Instead, I asked, "How did someone get on those premises with a gun?"

"Good question," Bridges said. "That lot hasn't been up and running for very long, so I imagine they were still trying to establish security protocols. Thus their reason for shutting it down. One of the onlookers said the guy who took off running was wearing some sort of denim jacket. He could have hidden the gun inside."

"They must have had a list of the people who were on the tour, right?" I said.

"I was told they did."

"Did they interview everyone?"

"I assume they did."

"So if they talked to sixteen people, the one left should be the shooter."

"Makes sense to me," Bridges said. He stood up and shoved his chair back under the table.

"No metal detectors or anything like that?" Lois said.

"Apparently not," Bridges said. "Hopefully they'll correct their mistakes. That obviously doesn't do anything to explain away what happened to you, though."

"Well, it could have been worse," Lois said.

"And thank goodness for that," Bridges said. "Once again, my apologies, Lois, and we're glad you're back with us."

"Thanks."

"When you guys are finished up here why don't you head to makeup and Cheryl will catch up with you, okay? Lois, we'll set you up with Ramirez after you and Eddie finish that scene."

"Gotcha," she said, and Bridges walked off.

Lois sipped some coffee and watched him. "Nice guy." She turned to me. "Have you worked with him before?"

"Nope. Judith Quinn also gave him a thumbs-up."

We were silent for a moment as we ate.

"Okay, back to Burt Jacobson," she said. "How are we going to find out where he lives?"

"My secretary is working on it. We've got access to several search engines. She's worked wonders in the past. I'm pretty confident she'll come up with a current address." I swallowed a forkful of scrambled eggs and sipped from my coffee cup. "What do you plan on telling him when you get him on the phone?"

She dabbed at the corner of her mouth with a napkin and said, "I'm going to extend an olive branch. Tell him to stop this nonsense and sit down and talk with me."

"You going to tell him you were shot and that you suspect him?"

"Hell yes."

"What if it turns out he didn't do it? From what Bridges just told us, he doesn't seem to fit the description that witness gave."

"Yeah, that's true, but he doesn't have to know that." She broke off a piece of muffin and popped it into her mouth, and after a moment said, "So if he didn't do it, what does that mean? That you were the target? What if it's the same guy that took a shot at you the other night?"

"Could be. I don't know how the hell he knew I'd be on that lot, though."

"You looking in your rear view mirror?"

"All the time." I finished my breakfast and put the plate back on the tray. "You ready to get powdered and pampered?"

"Let's do it," she said, and put her plate on my tray. I bussed it, and we headed for the makeup trailer.

22

Our new western street was considerably shorter than the one on which Lois had been wounded. O'Brien compensated by tightening the focus on the two of us as we strolled about a block down the wooden sidewalk. As before, Lois stopped to talk to a woman who poked her head out of a shop, after which we continued walking while saying the scripted dialogue. We ran it a couple of times until the Steadicam operator had his blocking down pat. When O'Brien was satisfied, the sound man wired us up and we did a take without a hitch. He did another one for safety's sake, and after he and his crew huddled, Brad Foster, the 1st AD, said that was a wrap on the scene and that we'd be moving on.

Lois turned to me and said, "How weird is this? I kept expecting to hear a gunshot."

"Yeah, I know," I replied. "Sense memory on something like that must be pretty damn strong."

O'Brien walked up and wrapped his headphones around his neck. "Perfect, guys. You haven't lost a step."

"I was just saying to Eddie," Lois said, "that I half expected to hear a gunshot."

O'Brien chuckled and said, "Well, let's hope we've heard the last of those."

Foster finished a cell phone conversation and turned to Lois. "That was Preston. He said when we wrapped this scene, the sheriff's deputy will meet you in your trailer." He turned to O'Brien. "She good to go, Pete?"

"Yup. That's a wrap for her," O'Brien said. "We'll see you tomorrow, Lois. I haven't got a call time yet but stay close to your phone."

"Roger that," she said, gave a mock salute, and turned to go. "I'll check in with you later, Eddie."

"Right," I said.

She signed out with Cheryl and headed for her trailer. O'Brien went on to outline the next scene for me. It took place in the sheriff's office and was between Bart Kincannon, Sheriff Haynes and me, Chet Cassidy. Also present was Buck Taylor, Haynes's deputy, a role being played by a young actor by the name of Wes Burns.

The scene followed the one which Lois and I had just completed. The idea was that after Lois stopped to talk to the lady who popped her head out of a store, she and I had a brief conversation outside the sheriff's office. She then went on her way, and I stepped through a door leading to the sheriff's office.

The wall was just a façade; the actual office had been constructed inside a nearby sound stage. When I walked onto the set Hugh Danton and Lou Anson were already there. Danton played Kincannon and Anson was Sheriff Haynes.

O'Brien called for a rehearsal, and we went to our marks. While the camera was being put in place, Wes Burns walked up to me and stuck out his hand. He looked to be in his twenties, had sandy blond hair and a handlebar mustache, which looked like it was fake.

"Hi, Mr. Collins. Wes Burns. I'm playing Buck Taylor, the deputy."

"Yeah, I know. How ya doin', Wes? Drop the 'mister' though. Just Eddie's fine."

"Good to be working with you. I've seen you in some things. I like your work."

"Thanks. Welcome aboard. A rough start, but it looks like we're back in the saddle." I pointed to his mustache. "Makeup put that cookie duster on you?"

"Yeah, I couldn't grow one fast enough."

"Watch out for that spirit gum. Vile stuff. I can't use it anymore. I wind up looking like a leper."

He chucked and I clapped him on the shoulder as Foster called for us to get into position. Wes walked to a desk in the corner of the room and sat down. Danton and Anson positioned themselves in the entrance to a hall leading to the cells in the rear of the set. I stood at the outside door, as if I was just coming into the office.

A woman with a large, three-ringed binder in her lap sat next to the camera. She was the script supervisor, charged with keeping track of every take of every shot. Continuity was her domain: she made sure every glass was filled the same from take to take. If a clock on the wall indicated it was noon, it was noon on every take.

Next to her the sound man, whose name I'd learned was Stan Erdman, set up his little portable table. Headphones covered his ears. He fiddled with the tape recorder and the table in front of him and gave a couple of instructions to the guy on the boom mic. There has to be a special place in Heaven for these guys, who, for hours on end, hold at arm's length a long pole with the microphone at the end of it. The camera operator told him when he had the mic out of the frame and we were ready to go.

"Open the door a tad, Eddie, and shut it on 'action'," O'Brien said.

"Got it," I replied.

The essence of the scene was that Kincannon and Sheriff Haynes carry on a conversation concerning what needs to be done about the looming dispute with several ranchers. At one point, Buck and my character are given instructions by the sheriff and the scene ends.

Brad Foster went through the litany and finally O'Brien called for action. The scene was only a page long and we made it through the rehearsal with no major goofs. O'Brien made some adjustments and told Foster he was ready to do a take. We all went back to our marks and the AD repeated his call for sound and camera. A grip clapped the sticks and we repeated the scene for real. Everything seemed to go as planned. O'Brien called, "cut," huddled with us, made a couple of suggestions, and said he'd like one more take.

We went back to our marks, settled, and again the countdown started. On "action" I shut the door behind me and walked into the interior of the office. Again, no mistakes, and O'Brien told the camera operator to cut and he'd do some closeups. Those completed, Foster said we were moving on. All of us started for the door but were stopped by Stan Erdman.

"Pete," he said. "I need sixty seconds of room tone."

"Hold it," Foster said.

We stopped in our tracks and froze. The guy with the boom stuck the business end of it into the middle of the room.

Erdman called the scene number and added, "Room tone. Sixty seconds. Rolling."

Our interior clocks started ticking, but, like the other day in the saloon, they were interrupted when Erdman said, "Cut it. I'm picking up something outside. Sounds like a motor."

We relaxed and I looked over to see O'Brien bending over, hands on his knees, shaking his head. "Goddammit, it! Is there anything else that can go wrong around here? Brad, find out what the hell's going on out there."

"On it," Foster said, and walked off the set, headed for the door of the sound stage.

"Sorry, guys," O'Brien said.

We offered a collective shrug and said it came with the territory. After a couple minutes, Foster returned. "A pickup hauling props. They've stopped. We should be clear."

Erdman listened intensely for a couple of moments and then confirmed Foster's report. He again called the scene number, asked for quiet, and sixty seconds elapsed with no further interference. Foster then announced we were moving on.

I left the makeshift sheriff's office and found a bench outside the sound stage. Taking advantage of the few minutes to set up the next scene, I pulled out my phone, turned it on, and checked for messages. There were none. As I powered it down and stuck it back in my pocket, Wes Burns walked up.

"Hey, Eddie, mind if I ask you a question?"

"Not at all," I said, as I scooted over to one end of the bench. "Have a seat."

"Thanks for the tip about the spirit gum, by the way."

"No problem. What's on your mind?"

"This is probably a silly question, but just what the heck is room tone anyway?"

I chuckled and said, "Not silly at all. There probably isn't an actor working that at one time or another hasn't asked that question. It's a little above my pay grade, but as far as I've been able to learn, room tone is used in post-production when the sound engineers are putting the sound track together. It's basically ambience. Let's say you're in a scene where you open a door and enter a room in complete silence. You walk to another part of the room and look up a staircase and think something is wrong, out of place. That ambience will vary from one part of the room to another, depending on where and how furniture and objects are placed. So the room tone will give the sound engineer different levels of ambience to layer into the sound track. I don't know how much of it they use, especially with music and sound effects added, but it just gives them more options."

"You ever see them do it in the editing room?" he said.

"Never have, but I'd like to sometime. Those guys are wizards."

"And the sound man wants it for every scene?"

"Pretty much, although sometimes they can get carried away. I was on a shoot one time where we were filming next to a highway, and the sound guy still wanted room tone after the director cut. Guess he never got the memo that there wasn't a room."

The sun had favored us with its presence and we sat and chatted for a few minutes. Wes told me he was from Oakland and had been in Hollywood for a little over four years. He'd done a commercial or two and expressed his hope that this gig would lead to bigger things. I wished him well and we turned to see Debbie Merton, one of O'Brien's 2nd ADs, walking toward us.

"Wes, they need you back on the set," she said. "A slight change in a piece of business."

"You bet," he said, as he jumped up from the bench and went into the stage.

"Eddie, you can relax for a bit," Debbie continued. "The two of you are up next."

"Roger that," I said, and watched her walk back into the sound stage.

My next scene was an exterior with Deputy Buck Taylor and me, Chet Cassidy, walking away from the sheriff's office as we digested the instructions we had just been given. Young Wes Burns obviously had some acting chops. He was letter-perfect with his dialogue and looked me right in the eye when he said it. A litmus test for me as to an actor's worth is the old Spencer Tracy rule of thumb: look the actor in the eye and tell the truth. Burns passed with flying colors. We did the scene a couple of times with no screw ups and O'Brien said he had what he needed and that they'd move on.

The AD told me I wouldn't be called until after lunch, and as I started to walk to my trailer Wes Burns caught up with me.

"Hey, Eddie, that was a nice little scene, but there was one thing missing."

"Yeah? What's that?"

"No room tone," he said, which provoked a laugh from both of us.

"I guess Erdman got the memo," I said.

We parted ways and I caught sight of Deputy Ramirez' vehicle. The driver's side door was open and he sat behind the wheel, jotting down notes.

He caught my eye and closed his notebook. "Howdy, Mr. Collins."

"Good morning," I said. "How goes your investigation?"

"Not worth a damn, to be honest."

"Yeah, Bridges talked to Lois and me over breakfast. Probably doesn't help that we got kicked off the Sunset Ranch lot."

"Well, it's a bit of a hassle going back and forth between the two, but I'm not paying for the gas, so I can roll with it."

We shook hands and I said, "You got a minute?"

"Sure. Hop in."

I walked around to the passenger side and opened the door.

He reached for a stack of files on the seat. "Let me get this stuff out of your way." He put the files in his lap and I folded my six foot plus into the vehicle.

"Not making any progress, huh?" I said.

"Not much."

"Bridges told us there were seventeen tourists watching the filming, and that the shooter was probably among them."

"That's right."

"And he hightailed it out the back door of a building?"

"Correct. Apparently piled into a van that was waiting for him."

I thought back to the day of my costume fitting when I saw Lois in a heated argument with whom I now assumed was Burt Jacobson, aka Bryce Jesperson. "Have you interviewed all of them?"

"Except for the one who took the shot."

"And you've got names for all of them?"

"Yeah."

"What name do you have for number seventeen?"

"You're gonna love this." He opened one of the files in his lap and pointed to a spot on the top page. "Would you believe number seventeen is Jack Jones?"

I chuckled and said, "Not very original."

"You think? Care to take a guess how many Jack Jones there are in this county?"

"I'll pass, but I'll lay odds it's a fake name."

"I'm afraid I agree with you," he said.

"Did you get a description of him?"

"Nothing outstanding. Witnesses said he was white, about six foot, one-sixty, seventy, thereabouts. A big guy. He wore a tan safari-like jacket and had sunglasses on."

"Any facial hair?" I asked.

"No." He looked up from the files in his lap. "Why? You got somebody in mind?"

"Remember I told you I saw Maxwell arguing with a guy outside the costume shop?"

"Right. I just got through talking with her. She confirmed that conversation."

"Well, he had a mustache and goatee."

He pulled out his notebook and flipped a couple of pages. "Yeah, that's what she told me." He flipped another page. "Witnesses said the shooter had blond hair, but nobody mentioned anything about facial hair."

"Then it looks like the shooter's not him," I said.

Ramirez pulled a bottle of water out of the cup holder and took a healthy swallow. "Maybe she wasn't the target."

I looked over at him. "So that leaves me."

He nodded. "Has LAPD uncovered anything about that drive-by you told me about?"

"They've matched a plate number with a dark SUV. I'm waiting to hear who it belongs to." I didn't want to put all my cards on the table, so I neglected to tell Ramirez about Langston Beaumont and Edge Security. Lois Maxwell was the one that got hit, not me. It seemed to me she was the subject of his investigation. My incident was LAPD's concern.

"Did Sunset keep records as to how those seventeen paid?" I said. "Cash? Credit cards?"

Again, he consulted the files in his lap. "Looks like the majority of them paid by card." He flipped up a page in the file he was looking at and chuckled. "And get this. Three of them were walk-ups. Guess who was one of them."

"Jack Jones."

"Bingo," he replied, and closed the file. After emitting a huge sigh, he took another swallow of water and continued, "Fortunately, the shooter was in a hurry, so we were able to find the brass. I don't know how successful we're going to be in tracing it to a gun, though, much less to an owner. If he had a false name, my guess is he got rid of the firearm."

I couldn't disagree with him. After a moment I decided to put some of my cards on the table. "Full disclosure, Deputy. Maxwell hired me to find the guy who's been harassing her. She thinks his name is Burt Jacobson, who also goes by the name of Bryce Jesperson. I've found a cell phone number for him, but so far no address. She's going to call him and see if the two of them can settle whatever the hell is between them. I'll fill you in on what she finds out."

"Thanks," he said. "So, if the description we have for the shooter doesn't match the guy you saw harassing Maxwell, is it safe to say you were the target?"

"Logic would say you're right," I said.

He nodded and swallowed more water. "Well, we'll keep poking around up here, but I need to get in touch your LAPD contact. Lieutenant Rivers, you said?"

"Correct." I pulled out my phone, found Charlie's number and gave it to him. He wrote it down in his notebook and put it and the pen back in his uniform shirt.

Thanks for the input, Mr. Collins. I guess I don't need to tell you to watch your back."

"Nope." I opened my door and stuck out a hand. "Keep in touch, Deputy. I'll do the same."

"Roger that," he replied.

I got out, shut the door and watched the SUV glide down the street, kicking up small wisps of dust as it moved. As I walked toward my trailer, the realization that I had a target on my back loomed even larger in my head. Unlike Sunset Ranch, security on this lot was not a problem. But whenever I left the safety of the *Burnt Hills* conclave, all bets were off.

Back in my trailer, I doffed the Stetson and powered up my phone. There was a message from Charlie Rivers telling me to return his call. After three rings he picked up.

"What's the word, Charlie?"

"We've found a match with that SUV plate. Guy by the name of Langston Beaumont. Does that name ring a bell with you?" I didn't reply immediately, and after a beat, Charlie said, "Look, Collins, your silence speaks volumes. I know you too well to think for one minute that you haven't scoped out who that plate belongs to. Am I right?"

"Yes, you're right. He runs a company called Edge Security."

"And next you're going to tell me you drove out to Encino and knocked on their front door."

"Nope. Just drove by. Gotta know where the enemy lurks, Charlie."

"Yeah, well, there's no proof yet that he's the enemy, so let him lurk. I've sent a team to find out where he and his vehicle were when the event happened."

"Doesn't that plate tell you he was at Hollywood and Highland?"

"Not necessarily. Those three digits you picked off that SUV when you were getting your chicken doesn't mean it's the vehicle that contained the shooter."

"But the odds are pretty good, aren't they?"

"I don't deal in odds, Eddie, only facts. The witness at the drive-by got four numbers, not the rest of them. You got three more, but that doesn't mean they correspond with the other four the witness saw. You've been around long enough to know that there's one hell of a lot of license plates in this town."

"Yeah, I hear you. So, where does that leave you?"

"Looking at a long computer printout and matching those seven digits with a dark SUV answering the description the witness gave us. We'll run down all the matches we come up with. It's time consuming, but we're on it. In the meantime, you still think someone's after you?"

"Absolutely."

"Because you and Benson are set to testify against those four that were arrested up in Ventura County?"

"That, and something's that happened up here on this film set."

"What?"

I propped my feet up on the table and related the whole scenario with Lois Maxwell, Burt Jacobson/Bryce Jesperson and the shooter that took a powder.

"If the shooter that got away is tied to the drive-by in any way, how the hell did he know you're working on this movie?" Charlie said. "And way out in the boondocks? Christ, somebody must have a hell of a tail on you."

"Yeah, and it's bugging the shit out of me," I said. There was a knock on the door. "Hang on, Charlie, someone's at the door." I took the phone away from my ear and called out, "Yeah?"

The door swung open and Cheryl, the PA, stuck her head in. "You're good to go to lunch, Eddie. I've got wheels here for you."

"Thanks, Cheryl, but I'll hoof it over there."

"Roger," she said, and closed the door.

"Charlie, I gotta run. Lunch time."

"Damn, must be nice. Free lunch. How's the chow?"

"Dynamite. I'd save you a doggie bag, but I don't think it'll stay hot."

"Yeah, well, thanks for thinking of me, but you keep checking your six. Got it? I'll be in touch."

With that, he hung up. I put my Stetson on and headed for the roach coach. Maybe some good movie grub would make me feel better.

The day's entrees included salmon, a ribeye, or fried chicken—all the major food groups covered. I went with the ribeye, mashed potatoes, and a dollop of creamed spinach. I dished up a small bowl of salad to complete the meal, and along with a bottle of Snapple on my tray I made my way into the soundstage where the tables were set up in one corner. I was surprised to see Lois sitting by herself. She noticed me and waved me over. I pulled out a chair and sat down across from her. She was working on a piece of salmon and some salad.

"I thought you were wrapped," I said.

"I am, but when that deputy got through with me, I looked at my watch and figured I might as well stay and get some free grub."

"Good plan."

She took a sip from a bottle of water and set it back on the table. "When the AD signed me out I was told that most of the company is going up into Kern County for three days. Exteriors."

"Really? First I heard of it."

"They going to put you on a horse?"

I froze with some mashed potatoes on its way to my mouth. "Are you kidding? They'll have to fork over hazard pay."

She stifled a laugh and put a hand over her mouth. "So I take it you're not one of those actors who put on their resume that they can ride a horse."

"Nope. Nor ride a motorcycle, play the banjo, speak French, or scuba dive."

She grinned and cut off a piece of salmon. "That means we're on hold, I guess. Perfect opportunity to get in touch with Burt and set up a meet with him."

"Have you called him?"

"Yeah, last night, but it went to voicemail."

I cut off a piece of ribeye, but before putting it in my mouth said, "How did your interview with Ramirez go?"

"Fine. Did he talk to you too?"

"Yeah. He told me there were seventeen of those looky-loos watching us that day. He said they interviewed sixteen of them. The one they didn't is the shooter, who got away. Turns out he doesn't fit the description of Jacobson. Besides, he gave his name as Jack Jones."

She sat back in her chair and looked at me. "Well, hell, that means Burt didn't do it, right?"

"Looks that way," I said, and put a piece of steak in my mouth. I watched her face and saw the realization wash over it.

"Then that means you were the target. Is that what you're telling me?"

"I have to assume so."

We were silent for a few moments as we ate. Finally she said, "Look, Eddie, I realize you've fulfilled your end of our bargain, but let me run something by you."

"Shoot." I paused in mid chew. "Wrong word. My bad."

She grinned and waved her hand. "Water under the bridge," she said, and continued. "Anyway, Burt has really been nasty to me over the course of a few weeks now."

"So I gather. I saw the two of you getting into it after our costume fittings."

"Exactly. He's got a hell of a temper. So, what I'm wondering is this. When I arrange to meet him, would you consider coming with me?"

I laid down my fork and took a sip of Snapple. "Why?"

"To act as a buffer in case he goes off on me."

I thought about her request for a moment as I chewed on some lettuce. She was correct in saying that I'd fulfilled my contract with her, but as I'd gotten to know Lois, I'd taken a shine to her because she was a survivor in this crazy business the two of us were in.

"Yeah, if you can get it set up while we're on hold," I said. "LA cops are working on that drive-by I was involved in, so *Burnt Hills* is the only thing on my plate."

"Great. You said you left your name when you called his number, right?"

"Right."

"Then he knows that I haven't made you up out of thin air. Otherwise, knowing him, he'd tell me to go to hell."

"Charming fellow. Can't wait to meet him."

"Yeah, he's a day at the beach." She reached across the table and squeezed my hand. "I appreciate it, Eddie."

"No problem," I said, and looked up to see Cheryl, the production assistant headed in our direction. Lois said she'd let me know if she heard from Jacobson. We bussed our trays and I followed the PA out of the stage. Time for more pampering and powder. Such is the life of the working actor. Even for one with a target on his back.

I was wrapped at five-thirty, and with eyes glued to my rearview mirror, I made it to Carla's place in just under an hour. I'd called her on the way and when I opened the door I was met with welcoming arms and the aroma of char-broiled steak and baked potatoes.

"I could get used to this," I said, as I laid down my knife and fork and raised my wine glass in a toast. "Here's to the chef."

"Don't get too comfortable," Carla said. "With the chef slaving away in front of a camera every day, this may not be the norm. I just happened to get off early."

"And I just happen to be on hold again for a couple of days."

"How come?"

"The company's moving up to Kern County for exteriors."

"Well, then, maybe you should call your doctor and see if he can fit you in tomorrow."

"Yeah, that's a good idea," I said. "There could be one wrinkle."

"What?"

"Lois talked to Burt Jacobson and he agreed to meet her. She asked me to go along with her and I told her I would."

"When's that going to happen?"

"Sometime this weekend hopefully." I could see the trace of a frown on her face.

"You have to keep seeing that doctor, Eddie."

"Yeah, I know. I will. This thing with Lois shouldn't be a big deal."

"Why does she need you to go with her?"

"I don't know. Moral support, I guess. This Jacobson character sounds like he's got a hell of a temper."

"Well, just be careful, okay?" she said.

"Always am," I replied.

We cleared the dishes, filled the washer, tidied up the kitchen and found a movie on Netflix we hadn't seen. About halfway through my cell went off. The display said it was Lois.

"Hi, Eddie, sorry to bother you, but Burt called me. He said he's willing to get together tomorrow afternoon. About one o'clock."

"Okay. Where?"

"Believe it or not he lives in an apartment above a stable, for cryin' out loud. I guess he's getting a break on the rent, helping with the horses. It's up in Sunland. How about I pick you up? Say twelve-thirty?"

"I could meet you there."

"No problem. I kinda know where it is."

"I'll be at my office," I said, and gave her the address. "Look for me at the curb."

"See you then." I hung up and looked over at Carla. "I know, I know," I said.

My comment was met with another frown.

23

As far as panhandlers go, the guy didn't fit the bill. His jeans were clean, sneakers white, and the orange hoodie he wore was spotless. I stood at the curb in front of my office building, leaned against a lamp post and eyed him as he scoped me out. Earlier, I'd been approached by another young man who said he needed help to get a flu shot. When I told him it wasn't flu season, he looked puzzled and wandered off, muttering to himself.

Finally, orange hoodie summoned up his courage and walked up to me. "Excuse me, sir, can you help me out? I'm trying to get through UCLA."

"Oh, yeah? What are you studying?"

"Economics."

"Really? So you're getting in on the ground floor here, huh?"

"Something like that."

I heard Lois Maxwell's car horn and pushed myself off the lamp post as she pulled up.

"Good luck," I said, and pulled open the car door. "But take my advice. Find a cheaper school." He flipped me off and I folded myself into the VW and closed the door.

"What was that all about?" Lois said, as she pulled into traffic on the Boulevard.

"Creative panhandling. He's working his way through UCLA."

She laughed and turned right at the intersection and headed toward Franklin Avenue. "Oh, man, only in Hollywood. And you're right in the middle of it."

189

"For the time being."

"Why do you say that?"

"The way gentrification is going, who knows. My building is old and the elevator is on life support. I'm not very optimistic."

"Gotcha," she said, and pointed to my scrunched-up knees. "Sorry about the leg room. My limo's in the shop."

"I'll manage." She caught a green light at Franklin and turned right. "So what did Jacobson say when you talked to him?"

"Well, first I told him that I'd been shot and thought it might have been him that did it, which prompted a huge laugh. He then went on to say that if it had been him, he wouldn't have missed."

"That's comforting."

"Yeah, no kidding."

"Are you sure you want to do this? This guy sounds kind of dangerous."

"I know, but I'm tired of his hassling me all the time. I figured the best thing to do is to try and reason with him. Put this thing behind us." She looked over at me. "If you're having second thoughts about coming along with me, just say the word."

"No, I'm good."

"If he starts to get nasty and threatens me I'll have a witness. In case I need to call the cops on his ass."

"Okay," I said, and thought about what she said as we pulled onto I-5 heading north. For a fleeting moment I'd considered whether or not I should have taken my gun but decided against it. Lois impressed me as being someone who had no trouble taking care of herself. Nevertheless, I confess I was a tad apprehensive about this whole situation, but at the same time I wanted to help her if she needed to get rid of this guy. Also, she was my client, so put your reservations aside, Collins, and help the lady out.

We talked shop about *Burnt Hills* as we cruised north with Burbank and Glendale on our right. Lois exited at Sunland Boulevard and we wound our way northeast into the Foothill section of Los Angeles.

She took a left off Sunland onto Johanna Avenue. "I'm looking for Shadow Hills Drive off to the left," she said.

On my right I saw a sign denoting the streets Mustang Way and Appaloosa Way. "We're definitely in horse country," I said, pointing to the sign.

"Yeah, he said he has a place above a stable."

"With horses and the whole nine yards?"

"I guess."

"And the smell of horse shit?"

She chuckled and said, "I suppose. He told me the place belongs to a friend of his. He does odd jobs in exchange for cheap rent."

"Let's hope that includes mucking out the stalls."

A little further along Johanna we came to Shadow Hills Drive. Lois took a left and we started searching for house numbers. The street had been paved at some point, but was now full of potholes. There were no curbs to paint addresses on, so we started to look at mailboxes. The neighborhood bore rural vestiges. Sprawling houses sat back from the street, many of them with stables visible, along with white fences. At one point I caught sight of a couple of horses behind one of the houses, grazing in a sizable lot.

We spotted the address on our right, pulled over and parked under a huge elm tree. The location in question was a double-wide. A carport was at the left end and a fenced-in enclosure on the right end, with a door into the trailer. An American flag hung by the front door. A small lawn was neatly mown and flower beds ran the length of the trailer. Along the fenced-in enclosure a driveway led to the rear of the property. The fence was about four feet high and had a sign on it that read "Dog On Premises." What appeared to be a stable sat at the end of the gravel driveway.

Lois pulled her phone out of a pocket and punched some keys. "We're here. Are you at the end of the driveway?" After a pause she said, "Okay, we're coming back." She put the phone away, opened her door, got out and slung her tote bag over her left shoulder. "He said to come on back and pay no attention to the dog."

"Said the homeowner to the mailman while his uniform was being shredded," I said, as I climbed out of the car, stretched to get the kinks out of my legs and followed her.

To prove my point, as we drew near to the fenced-in enclosure, the dog started to bark and growl. The entrance into the trailer must have had a pet door because the barking caught us both by surprise. We sidled over to the edge of the driveway and watched the animal's head pop over the edge of the fence as he tried to jump over.

We got to the end of the dog run and saw that the stable was a two-story structure. It didn't resemble the barns I remembered from growing up in the Midwest, but nevertheless it had a sliding door in the side facing the street and a door on the wall of the second story.

A shingled roof jutted out from above the main door, supported at its four corners by 2x6 posts, which were connected by 2x4 railings. Two saddles straddled the railings and pieces of tack hung from hooks on the posts. A weather-beaten picnic table occupied the space to the left of the sliding door

Against the left wall of the stable several bales of hay were stacked; a pitchfork protruded from one of them. A small fenced-in corral filled up rest of the trailer's back yard. A water trough sat next to the fence and a buckskin-colored horse drank from it. As we approached, the animal raised its head, looked at us, then went back to drinking. At the rear of the corral a gate led to a small pasture, in which another horse, this one black, grazed.

Our canine welcoming committee continued to bark until Burt Jacobson, aka Bryce Jesperson appeared in the door of the stable. He wore jeans with a black vest over a gray tee shirt and had western boots on his feet. A ball cap was pushed back up on his forehead. He was indeed the man I'd previously seen arguing with Lois outside the costume shop.

"Bullet, shut up!" he yelled. It worked; the growls and barking stopped.

"So much for not paying attention to the dog," Lois said.

"Yeah, well, he's pretty much harmless," Jacobson said. "Just not used to being around a lot of people."

He walked over to the end of the enclosure that had a gate in it. The dog—a Doberman, as far as I could tell—stood on its hind legs and draped his front paws over the top of the gate. Jacobson scratched him behind the ears and murmured what I suppose were sweet nothings to any dog owner. I, however, didn't share the sentiments.

He left the dog and walked up to us. "So," he said to Lois, "where'd you get shot?"

She pointed to her upper right arm. "Right here. Pretty much a flesh wound."

"I guess you must be Collins, the private dick," he said, as he turned to me. His face broke into a shit-eating grin as he emphasized the word "dick" in describing me. I'd heard it many times before from punks like this and didn't bother to offer one of my usual retorts.

"That's right."

"And she hired you to find me?" he said.

"Right again," I said.

"And how did you do that?"

"I also happen to be an actor," I said. "Turns out you used to be with my agent, Morrie Howard. He still had your cell number."

"Ol' Morrie, huh? I'll be damned. He still suckin' on those cancer sticks?"

"Every day."

"Eddie's working on the picture with me," Lois said. "Matter of fact, it looks like the shooter was aiming for him."

"Oh, yeah? What the hell did you do?"

"Long story," I said. "We private dicks get used to it."

He nodded and walked toward the stable. "Let's get out of the sun." He led us over to the weathered picnic table and straddled a bench with his back to the corral. Lois and I climbed over the opposite bench and sat down, she on my right.

"You live on the second story?" she said.

"Yup," he replied.

"What's it like waking up every morning to the smell of horses and what they leave behind?" I said.

Jacobson looked at me with contempt written all over him. "You get used to it. Sort of like you private dicks get used to being shot at."

"Touche," I said. "Let me ask you something else. Why the name change? Bryce Jesperson hasn't got any film credits, at least according to IMDB, so why did you feel you had to change it?"

He gestured to Lois and said, "She told you my real name?"

"No, I ran into a Latina by the name of Rachel," I said. "She told me she went out with you and knew you as Bryce Jesperson."

"Yeah, sweet little Rachel." He turned to Lois and said, "Why didn't you tell your private dick here my real name. Coulda saved him a lot of time."

She didn't respond and just glared at him. There was silence for a moment until I finally said, "Did you know his real name, Lois?"

"Yes," she said.

Her answer caught me completely by surprise. "Why didn't you tell me?"

"What does it matter?" she said. "Let's get to the reason we're here."

"No, hold on a minute," Jacobson said. "What exactly has she told you, Collins?"

"That the two of you were involved in some sort of business deal and that you accused her of walking out on it."

Jacobson looked at her and broke into a laugh. "Oh, man, that's rich! That is complete bullshit, Collins. First of all, she's my stepmother."

Another bombshell of surprise. I turned to look at Lois, but she avoided my glance. Instead, she stared at the tabletop in front of her, her hands clenched into fists.

"Yeah, that's right," he continued. "Complete bullshit. She was married to my father, Leland Jesperson. He ran a tech company. Very successfully, I might add. He died two years ago and named her executor of his will. Why he would do that beats the hell out of me. They didn't get along worth a damn."

"That's because he was a total asshole," she said. "Which you inherited from him, I might add."

"He wasn't exactly Father of the Year, I'll give you that," Jacobson said. "That's why I ditched the name. And by the way, Lois, the feeling is mutual."

The two of them glared at each other, and if looks could kill, I'd be sitting with two corpses. "Okay, so you two obviously don't like each other," I said. "But what's the business deal you alluded to, Lois?"

"There's no goddamn business deal," Jacobson said. "My asshole father left me a sizable trust. It became available to me when I turned thirty-five. But here's the problem, Collins. My thirty-fifth came and went eighteen months ago, and my sweet stepmother here won't release the money. That's the only business deal I know about."

"And I'm not going to," she said. She stuck her left hand into the tote bag that sat next to her and pulled out an automatic and aimed it at him. "You're not entitled to that money, and you damn well better stop harassing me about it."

Jacobson rose from the table, stuck his hands out in front of him and began to crawl over the bench. "Whoa, whoa! Put the goddamn gun down!" He backed up to the 2x4 railing. "Bullet!" he shouted. The dog immediately began barking.

Lois stood up from the bench and started to slide out from behind the table. I reached out and grabbed her left hand that held the gun. We grappled for a moment and the gun went off, firing a round into the air that caused the buckskin to bolt for the pasture behind the corral. She pushed her shoulder into me and caught me off balance. She wrestled loose and went around the end of the picnic table, following Jacobson, who had jumped over the railing.

I righted myself, climbed over the table's bench and started for her but didn't get far. The dog had somehow climbed over the fenced-in enclosure and bounded toward me. He latched onto my left leg and wouldn't let go. He didn't nip me. I felt his teeth sink into my left leg and hang on.

"Jacobson, call off the goddamn dog!" I yelled. Pain shot up my leg as I dragged the animal behind me, trying to catch up with Lois.

Defying her age, Lois climbed over the 2x4 railing and advanced on Jacobson, still pointing the gun at him. He pulled the pitchfork from a hay bale, lunged at her and drove the tines into her chest.

She staggered back, dropped the gun and collapsed to the ground.

"Jacobson, the dog!" I yelled.

He stared at Lois and what he had done, then looked up and shouted, "Bullet! Come!"

The dog let go of my leg and trotted over to him. I limped around the end of the picnic table, climbed over the railing and bent over Lois. The four tines of the fork had punctured her upper chest, one of them close to her heart. I pulled the fork from her body and hurled it in Jacobson's direction. He blocked it with his arms and made a move toward the gun.

"Stay right where you are!" I said, as I reached over her body and picked up the gun. I ejected the clip and the round in the chamber, then tossed the gun behind me toward the picnic table and leaned over Lois. Blood seeped from the punctures, and she gasped for breath.

"Shit, Eddie,…I…I…was only gonna scare him. It was loaded with blanks."

"Well, how the hell was he supposed to know that?" I said. "You scared the crap out of both of us. Now just lie still."

I pulled out my cell phone and dialed 911.

When I finished giving the dispatcher the information she needed, Jacobson took a step toward me. Bullet followed him.

"Keep that goddamn dog away from me," I said. I looked around for something to staunch the bleeding. A soiled towel hung from one of the 2x6 uprights supporting the roof. I grabbed it and pressed it against one of the punctures. She gasped for breath and fear filled her eyes.

Jacobson had grabbed Bullet by the collar and led him to the dog run, opened the gate and closed it. He then walked back to where I was kneeling over Lois.

"Christ, Collins, she was gonna shoot me. What the hell else was I supposed to do?"

"I don't know, man. You think about it, and when you come up with an answer, tell it to someone who gives a damn. The damage is done."

24

After calling 911, I kept pressure on two of the punctures from the pitchfork. Jacobson stood next to Lois, his face in shock. "Ditch that vest of yours and rip your tee shirt in half," I said. "I can't handle all four of these wounds. Do it now!"

He followed my instructions and dropped to his knees next to her. Blood flowed from two of the wounds at an alarming rate, soaking her shirt. She gasped for breath, and at one point her eyes landed on him. She raised one hand and tried to place it on Jacobson's cheek, but the effort was too much and the hand fell back to the ground.

I heard a siren and saw an ambulance start to pull into the driveway.

"Signal them to come back here," I said to Jacobson. "They're probably going to have to back in." He started down the driveway and I switched pressure points on Lois's chest. I shouted after him, "And put that goddamn dog in the house before it goes berserk again."

A female paramedic jumped out from the passenger side and Jacobson pointed to where I knelt next to Lois. The driver saw the narrowness of the driveway and backed up to the street. With the woman guiding him, he put the vehicle in reverse and backed up to the end of the driveway. The woman flung open the rear doors, and with the driver following her, she rushed over to me.

"Did you place the nine-one-one call, sir?" said the young woman who wore glasses and had a headful of auburn hair.

"Yes."

"Okay, what have we got here?"

The name "Sullivan" was stitched into her uniform shirt. Her partner, a solidly-built Black man named "Andrews" knelt on the other side of Lois.

"That guy with no shirt on stabbed her with that pitchfork," I said, as I pointed to it. "There's four punctures."

"What's her name?" Andrews said.

"Lois Maxwell."

"All right, please step back, sir," he said. "We'll take it from here."

I stood up and winced from the pain that shot up the leg the dog had glommed onto.

"What's wrong with your leg?" Sullivan said.

"Dog bite," I replied.

"First things first. There's another unit behind us." She pointed to the picnic table behind me. "Why don't you sit down and take the weight off that leg?"

I started to limp over to the picnic table when I heard another siren. A fire-engine red vehicle turned into the driveway, stopped behind the ambulance, then backed up and parked on the side of the street. Right behind it an LAPD black-and-white rolled to a stop and parked on the other side of the street. Two EMTs jumped out of the emergency vehicle and ran to the end of the driveway, each of them carrying a medical kit.

Two uniformed police officers were right on their heels. One of them wore sergeant stripes. He had short blond hair and a mustache. His partner was younger with no stripes on his shirt, indicating he was more than likely a rookie, or a "boot," in cop-speak. The sergeant asked the EMTs what the situation was. After he got his answer, he turned his head and spoke into a radio transmitter attached to his shoulder. Andrews, the driver of the ambulance, pointed to me and Jacobson, who had now joined me at the picnic table.

The sergeant walked up to us. His name tag said "Brewster." The black uniform fit him like a glove, even with the bulge of the Kevlar vest under his shirt. His complexion was fair, and his blonde hair was neatly trimmed with white sidewalls over his ears. Aviator dark glasses covered his eyes.

"Gentlemen," he said. "I'm going to ask you to remain right where you are. Detectives are on the way. They're going to want to ask you some questions. Okay?" We nodded and he pointed to my leg and the ripped trouser. "What happened to your leg, sir?"

"There's a dog in the house. It bit me."

He looked at both of us for a moment and said, "All right, hang on. One of the EMTs will get to you when they can."

With that, he walked back to where the four paramedics were working on Lois. Sullivan and Andrews, the first pair who'd arrived, had pulled a gurney out of the ambulance. While the second pair of EMTs continued to put pressure on the wounds, Sullivan grabbed Lois under the armpits, Andrews under her knees, and on the count of three, they lifted her onto the gurney, then raised it until it locked in place.

"Can we roll, Sergeant?" Andrews said. "We've gotta get her to an ER."

"How bad is she?" Brewster said.

"She's lost a hell of a lot of blood. We need to boogie."

"All right, let me get some pictures." He pulled out a cell phone and began taking pictures of Lois on the gurney. "What's her name?"

"Lois Maxwell," Andrews replied.

Brewster nodded and said, "Okay, go. Saint Joseph's in Burbank, right?"

"Yup," Andrews said.

He and Sullivan shoved the gurney inside the ambulance and the wheels collapsed as it entered the vehicle. Sullivan and the EMT who had been applying pressure climbed in behind it and Andrews turned to the sergeant.

"We also need her personal effects."

"What do you mean?" the sergeant said.

"Name, address, insurance cards. Saint Joe's always rags on us if someone doesn't have identification with them. The admissions desk is really a pain in the ass."

Brewster turned to us and called out, "You guys know if she has some ID with her?"

I picked up Lois's tote bag off the other bench and said, "Right here."

Brewster walked over and took the tote bag from me.

As he started to walk back to the ambulance I said, "Sergeant, can I ask a favor?

"What?"

"Can you give me her car keys? She drove me here. I should look after the car." I didn't know for certain what the hell they were going to do with Jacobson and me, but I thought it best to see if I could make sure I had wheels when they were done with us.

He thought for a moment and rummaged inside the bag, then held up a key ring. "These them?"

I nodded and he handed me the keys. "Thanks," I said.

Brewster took the bag and stashed it inside the ambulance. Andrews shut the doors, climbed behind the wheel, and with siren blaring and lights flashing, the ambulance barreled down the driveway and peeled off on its way to Burbank.

Brewster told his partner to seal off the driveway with yellow tape. As the boot started back to their unit, the sergeant suggested that the one remaining medic see to my dog bite. He then keyed his radio and informed his superiors as to the status of Lois Maxwell.

The EMT approached me, set his kit down and kneeled in front of me. He looked to be in his thirties, had a thin face with a mustache and a small soul patch under his lower lip. The name "Dawkins" was stitched on the right side of his uniform jersey.

"How you doin'?" he said.

"I've had better days."

"I can imagine. What's your name, sir?"

"Eddie Collins."

"I'm Jack. Let's take a look at what we've got here." He lifted my leg and placed it on the picnic table's bench. "Mind if I cut away the trouser leg, Eddie?"

"Have at it," I said. "The damn things don't fit me right anyway."

He chuckled and began working with a pair of scissors. The bite looked worse than I had thought, and the pain still shot up my leg.

"Have you ever been vaccinated for rabies, sir?" Jack said.

"Not to my knowledge."

"That dog ain't got rabies," Jacobson chimed in with.

"Is it your dog, sir?" Jack said to Jacobson.

"He's my landlord's, and I know for a fact the dog has had all his shots."

The medic turned back to me. "Well, it's not worth the risk. I'd see about getting vaccinated, Eddie."

"Okay."

He cleaned the bite, smeared some salve on it, then wrapped the leg with gauze and tape. He stowed his supplies back in his kit and stood up.

"Keep an eye on that, Eddie," he said, as he handed me a card with pills embedded it. "I've got some pain pill samples for you here, but if it gives you any trouble, find an ER. Okay?"

"Gotcha," I said.

"You're good to go. Try to stay off the leg as much as possible."

And with that he walked back to Sergeant Brewster, who was helping his partner stretch yellow crime scene tape over the width of the driveway. I took advantage of the lull in the action and sent a text to Carla, giving her a short rundown of what had just happened. When I looked up from my phone, I saw Jacobson with his head in his hands. After a moment he slapped one hand down on the table and caught me staring at him.

"What?" he said. "You saw what she did. What was I supposed to do? She pointed the fuckin' gun at me."

"It was full of blanks!"

"Well, how the fuck was I supposed to know that?"

"You could have used that pitchfork and knocked the gun out of her hand," I said. "Instead of stabbing her with it, for crissakes!"

"Fine for you to say. She wasn't after you."

"She's in her eighties, man. We're not talking about Wonder Woman here."

"Shit," he said, as he took his cap off and slammed it down on the table. "What are you gonna tell those detectives?"

"What I saw."

"That it was self-defense, right?"

"That's for somebody else to decide. Not me." I looked at the instructions on the card with the pain pills, pushed one into my hand, then popped it into my mouth, cranked my head back and dry-swallowed it.

Just then a vehicle with a flashing bubble light on the dash pulled into the driveway. It was a plain-wrapped car, an indication that the detectives had arrived. The light went out and the doors opened.

Like the cop duo, there was an age discrepancy between the two detectives. The older one immediately reminded me of Abe Vigoda, the tall lanky actor who'd played "Fish" on the television series *Barney Miller.* He was also "Tessio" in the first rendition of *The Godfather*.

His partner was a young Hispanic man whose suit, unlike his partner's, was neatly pressed. His round face was clean-shaven and his black hair was short and parted on the left side.

Both men wore dark glasses. They ducked under the yellow tape and gave Sergeant Brewster their names. The Abe Vigoda look-alike introduced himself as Osborne and his partner as Gomez.

"So, what have we got?" Osborne said.

"A woman was stabbed with that pitchfork," Brewster said, and pointed to where it lay after I'd pulled it out of Lois's chest and thrown it at Jacobson.

"And where's the body?"

"She was losing a lot of blood. The EMTs said they had to get her to an ER immediately."

"Her name?"

"Lois Maxwell," Brewster said. "I've got several pictures of her." He booted up his cell phone and showed it to Osborne.

He looked at the photos and handed the phone back to Brewster. "Email those to me. And be sure and show them to forensics when they get here."

"Yes, sir," Brewster replied.

Osborne looked in our direction. "Who are those two?"

"The one without the shirt allegedly stabbed her."

"According to who?" Osborne said.

"The guy sitting next to him," Brewster said.

"I see." He took off his glasses, slid them into his shirt pocket and they walked over to us. He reached into the breast pocket of his jacket, pulled out his badge wallet and showed it to us. "Afternoon, gentlemen. I'm Detective Paul Osborne." He gestured to Gomez and continued. "This is my partner, Detective Rudy Gomez. We need to ask you some questions about—"

"It was self-defense," Jacobson blurted out.

Osborne turned to Jacobson with a look of irritation that consumed his entire long face. "What is your name, sir?"

"Burt Jacobson."

"As I was saying, Mr. Jacobson," Osborne went on. "We need to ask you two some questions about what went down here." He pointed to me. "Your name, sir?"

"Eddie Collins."

"Like the ballplayer?"

"Like the ballplayer."

He nodded, then jotted both our names into a notebook he'd taken from an inside pocket of his suit jacket.

"Okay. Tell us what happened," he said, gesturing to me as if to indicate I should go first.

"There was an argument between Lois and Burt here," I said. "She—"

"She pulled a gun and was going to shoot me," Jacobson interrupted.

Osborne held up a hand and said, "I'll get to you in a minute, sir."

"It was self-defense, Detective. I had—"

"Hold it, hold it," Osborne said, raising his hand and cutting him off. He turned to his partner. "Rudy, escort Mr. Jacobson here over to that corral. He's obviously got something to say, and I'm sure he'd be glad to talk to you."

With that, Gomez grabbed Jacobson by the elbow and led him away. Burt looked at me over his shoulder and said, "Tell him the truth, Collins."

Osborne swung his legs over the picnic table bench across from me and sat down. "Okay, Mr. Collins, what do you say we start over?"

"I'm all yours, Detective."

"Terrific. So, tell me. What the hell happened here?"

"Jacobson and Lois Maxwell got into an argument. She pulled a gun. I tried to wrestle it away from her. The gun went off. She knocked me off balance, then climbed over this railing behind me. She made a move toward him with the gun and he stabbed her in the chest with the pitchfork. That's it in a nutshell."

"Just like that?"

"Just like that. She told me the gun was loaded with blanks."

"Did Jacobson know that?"

"No."

"And she still gets stabbed. That's fucked up." He shook his head and made some notes, then looked up at me. "How do you fit into this picture? What's your relationship with the two of them?"

"She's a client of mine. I—"

"Client?" Osborne said.

"Yeah, I'm a licensed private investigator."

He looked up from his notebook and said, "You happen to have your ticket with you?"

I didn't know if I'd thrown down the gauntlet in the inherent distrust that sometimes exists between law enforcement and private investigators, but I dutifully fished out my wallet and handed him my license. He looked at it, then at me and handed it back. "What's your relationship with Jacobson?"

"There is none. She hired me to find him and I did so. They had a financial disagreement that she hoped to settle by meeting with him today. I came along with her for…I don't know…moral support, I guess."

"What sort of financial disagreement?"

I spent the next ten minutes or so telling him the dispute was over a trust fund. That Lois was Jacobson's stepmother, her reluctance to release his funds, his harassment of her.

"Did you know she had a gun in her possession?" Osborne said.

"I did not."

"Where's the gun now?"

"Over there," I said, pointing behind him where the gun and the clip lay. "After she fell to the ground, she dropped the gun. I pulled the pitchfork out of her chest and threw it at Jacobson when he went for the gun. I ejected the clip and the round in the chamber, then tossed them over there."

Osborne turned around, saw the gun, the clip, and the ejected shell. "How about the brass? Where's it at?"

I took my leg off the bench and looked around underneath the picnic table. "Right there," I said, and pointed to the shell casing lying on the ground.

Osborne stood up and peered under the table, then righted himself and hollered over to Brewster. "Sergeant, come over here." Brewster walked up to him and Osborne said, "Take your phone and get pictures of that gun, the clip and the shells." He pointed out the items and Brewster took photos.

I turned when I heard loud voices coming from where Gomez had taken Jacobson. He was arguing with the detective and at one point kicked one of the railings of the corral. Gomez tried to calm him down, but it didn't look like Jacobson was paying him any heed.

Osborne sat down and made some more notes. "So, forensics is going to find your prints on the gun, is that right?"

"That's right."

"And the pitchfork?"

"Correct."

He looked at me for a long moment before saying, "Do you believe Jacobson when he says it was self-defense?"

"Not really. I told him he could have used the fork and knocked the gun out of her hand."

"But you don't dispute the fact that he admits to stabbing her?"

"No, that's what I saw."

After a long pause while he jotted more notes, Osborne stood up, pulled his dark glasses out of his pocket and put them on. "Okay, Collins, here's what's going to happen. I want both of you to come in to the station, file a formal statement and answer some more questions."

"All right," I said.

Jacobson was led over to us. He shrugged off Detective Gomez's arm and got right in my face. "What did you tell him, Collins?"

"What I saw, that's all."

"That it was self-defense, right?"

"Not my call, Burt."

"Man, this is all bullshit!" He stomped off a couple of paces and threw his cap to the ground.

"You need to calm down, sir," Gomez said, as he moved next to him. "We're going to take you in to file a formal statement and answer some more questions."

"Oh, shit, are you arresting me?"

"No, sir," Gomez said. "But a woman has been injured and you yourself admitted that it was you who caused the injury."

"But I told you it was self-defense, man."

"So you did," Gomez said. "But we still need you to come into the station and fill out a formal statement. We will then proceed from there. That incident needs to be fully investigated, and we'd appreciate your full cooperation. Are we clear, sir?"

"We're clear," Jacobson said, as he bent down and picked up his cap. "Can I at least put on a shirt?"

Gomez looked at Osborne, who nodded his approval.

"Absolutely," Gomez said. "Where do you need to go?"

"Upstairs."

"Lead the way," Gomez said, and followed Jacobson into the stable.

I put my leg back on the picnic table bench and Osborne sat across from me. "How long have you had your license?" he said.

"Going on twenty years."

"Really? And you've managed to keep the wolf away from the door?"

"Well, I'm also an actor."

"Oh, yeah? Interesting. That's a tough business, isn't it?"

"Yeah, it has its moments."

We heard a vehicle come up the driveway and stop behind the detectives' car. Two forensics technicians climbed out and Osborne walked over and huddled with them. Jacobson followed Gomez out of the stable; he now wore a dark, red-striped western shirt. The detective led Jacobson to the plain-wrap and put him in the rear seat. The forensics vehicle backed up, waited for Gomez to move the detectives' car, then pulled up to where the yellow tape was stretched across the driveway.

Osborne walked up to me as I raised myself from the picnic table bench. I winced as I tried to put my weight on the leg with the bite. "You going to be all right?" he said.

"Yeah, I'm good."

"I don't think it's a good idea to put you and Jacobson together in one vehicle. You have wheels here?"

"Yeah, I've got the keys to Maxwell's car."

He gave me the address of the Foothill Division in Pacoima and said, "I can trust you to show up there, right?"

I grinned and said, "I'll give you my PI license as insurance."

He chuckled and replied, "After twenty years I guess you can be trusted. But in any case, why don't you follow us?"

With a slight limp, I followed him out to the street. He got into the passenger side of the detectives' car and it waited as I climbed into the VW, familiarized myself with the manual transmission and signaled to Gomez that I was ready to go.

I was led into an interrogation room that contained the usual steel-gray table with one chair on the side facing what I assumed was a one-way mirror. Two similar chairs sat on the other side. The table was bolted to the floor. Welded into the top of it was a metal ring, to which handcuffed perps could be shackled. I'd been in one of these rooms a couple of times over the years, but never handcuffed. Nevertheless, the isolation of these spaces is palpable and foreboding.

My escort was a female officer whose name was Rogers. She asked me if I needed anything. I said a bottle of water would be great. She left and came back in a couple of minutes with a chilled plastic bottle, then said a detective would be with me shortly and left the room.

"Shortly" turned out to be twenty minutes. I expected that. Prevailing police procedure is to let your "perp" sit and sweat for a while. I didn't sweat, but rather took another pain pill for the discomfort inflicted by Bullet, the canine.

During the twenty minutes I called my office, but since it was almost five o'clock, Mavis had left. I sent her a text saying her boss was in the hoosegow and would fill her in when he had the opportunity. Her immediate reply read, *Good grief! What now?* A couple of minutes later Carla called. I told her I was all right and was about ready to expound on what had gone down when Detective Gomez opened the door. He carried a pad and a pen, pulled out a chair across from me and sat down.

"Sorry to keep you waiting, Mr. Collins."

"No problem. This isn't my first rodeo."

"No, I don't suppose. Detective Osborne told me you're a PI. Twenty years under your belt? Is that right?"

"Yup."

"Well, then, you know the drill. I've got a few more questions and then I'll leave you to submit a statement about what happened this afternoon. As detailed as you can get."

"So, you and Osborne play switcheroo with your interviews, is that it?"

"Pretty much. One of us might hear something different." He pulled a small tape recorder from a pocket and laid it on the table. "I'm going to record what you say. Just to corroborate your signed statement. Okay?"

"Fine," I said.

He turned the recorder on, stated the date and time and who was present in the room, and then began. For the next half hour, I related the afternoon's events, blow by blow. Gomez asked me pretty much the same things Osborne had, but he dug in a little more with respect to my encounter with Jacobson. When he got what he needed, he turned off the recorder and slid the pad and pen across the table. It was an official police form. He indicated where I needed to sign and said he'd be back in a few minutes.

"One favor, Detective?"

"Sure," he said. "What do you need?"

"Can someone call Saint Joseph's and ask about the status of Lois Maxwell?"

"I'll see to it," he said, and left the room.

I put pen to paper and after twenty minutes or so had what I thought was the most complete statement of the facts as I knew them. I sipped on the bottle of water and looked up at the one-way glass, assuming that someone was behind it. Sure enough, the door opened and Gomez entered and took a seat. I slid the statement across the table.

"Thank you, Mr. Collins. Let me just take a moment and read this over to see if there's anything that needs clarifying." He did so and said everything looked in order, then glanced up at me. "I'm afraid I have some bad news. Miss Maxwell passed away in the ambulance on the way to the hospital."

I sat in stunned silence.

"From what we were able to learn, a lung was punctured, and an artery was nicked by one of the tines of that pitchfork. There was considerable loss of blood."

I nodded, which was the only response I could muster.

"I'm sorry for your loss. Was she next of kin?"

"No. Just a client. Thanks for the information." I slid my chair back and stood. "What does this do with respect to Jacobson?"

"That's up to the district attorney. He's been arrested and will be held until the DA determines how they want to proceed." He opened the door and held it for me. "Thanks for your cooperation, Mr. Collins. You're free to go."

I shook his outstretched hand and left the room. I didn't see Jacobson. Nor did I wish to. He'd brandished the pitchfork, and the consequences were his alone to deal with.

The sun was low in the horizon as I stepped out of the Foothill Precinct, presenting me with a gloom that was apropos to the information I'd received about Lois. I tried to process what I had witnessed earlier, and it made absolutely no sense. Favoring my left leg, I crawled into her VW and sat for a moment, wondering what the hell I should do with her car. She hadn't told me if she had any family, which made the revelation of Jacobson being her stepson even more surprising. I remembered that one of the parking spaces at my building had recently become vacant with the departure of a tenant. It would suffice until I could figure out some other solution.

I parked the Volkswagen behind my building and went up to my office. I taped a sheet of plastic wrap around my ankle, showered, changed clothes, then sat at my desk with a cold beer and contemplated the events of the afternoon.

Even though I've been in Los Angeles for a number of years playing the Hollywood Hustle, I never cease to be amazed at what can go wrong while trying to create a motion picture. Rain, smog, Santa Ana winds, and every other conceivable weather phenomena conspire against filmmakers. Temperamental stars who don't have the proper bottled water at their fingertips send directors screaming into the night, tearing their hair from its roots. A cantankerous neighbor decides he absolutely *has* to mow his lawn just as an exterior scene next to house is being filmed.

A few months ago I worked on an indie film at Warner Bros. called *Terms of Power*. The financial backers of the project decided to exert their independence and absconded with the money like thieves in the night. Fortunately, another source of financing was found and the film was finished.

And now there was *Burnt Hills*. Efforts by the soundman to get sixty seconds of room tone had been foiled on more than one occasion. Then a bystander fired a gunshot at two actors, wounding one of them and forcing a change in the film's location. Now once again, the production was to be disrupted, this time because of the need for a casting change.

I sipped some beer and stared at the phone on my desk, dreading the call I needed to make. I dialed the number and the call was picked up after two rings.

"This is Preston Bridges."

"Yeah, hi, Preston, this is Eddie Collins."

"Yes, Eddie, what can I do for you?"

I gave him the news of Lois's death. There was a long, dead silence on the other end of the line. After a huge sigh, the *Burnt Hills* production manager said, "Oh, shit."

My sentiments exactly.

25

A lovely spring Saturday would normally provide an opportunity for Carla and me to venture out and enjoy the various avenues of recreation available to us in the Los Angeles Basin. A walk along the beach is always fun. Mingling with the potpourri of people on the boardwalk in Venice gives one a lasting appreciation for one's attempt at normalcy. Even a Dodger dog with a cold beer and nine innings of the nation's pastime in Chavez Ravine offers inexplicable delight—but not on this Saturday.

None of those pursuits presented themselves to us as we sat in my doctor's office waiting to be called in for treatment of a dog bite. A dog bite, of all things! Almost unimaginable to me. Man's best friend isn't supposed to do that. And yet here we were.

Earlier, I'd called the office of Samuel Minh, my Vietnamese doctor, and was heartened to learn that he was on call during the weekend. After being on hold, the good doctor came on the line.

"Hello, Eddie, is everything all right?"

"You're not going to believe this, but I got bit by a dog yesterday afternoon."

"Oh, my God, did you bite him back?"

His attempt at humor was followed by a muffled chortle on his end of the line and a roll of the eyes from me.

"You need new writers, Doc."

"So my nurse tells me. Was this just a nip, or a full-blown chomp?"

"A full-blown chomp."

"Well, then, you better get your private eye buns over here and let me have a look."

And so here we were. After only about five minutes, a nurse stuck her head out of a door and beckoned me to come back. She took my vitals and left me staring at a skeleton on the wall. After a couple of minutes, Doctor Sam came bouncing into the room. If sunny enthusiasm is considered an elixir, the good doctor had it in spades.

He sat down on a stool, rolled it in front of me and looked me in the eye. "I've never had a patient who was bit by a dog. You should be proud that you're the first, Eddie."

He punctuated this declaration with an infectious giggle, then had me sit on an examining table. He asked me which leg. I told him the left. He took off the shoe and sock and gingerly pulled the trouser up to my knee. Bullet had latched onto the fleshy part of my calf. Last night Carla had doused the bite with hydrogen peroxide, put more ointment on it and then followed that with fresh gauze and tape.

The doc carefully removed the dressing, looked at the bite and uttered a soft whistle, like he was in a scene from one of the *Alien* movies and about to discover the habitat of some extraterrestrial demon. There was some slight swelling and a bit of redness around the punctures. "Wow. I'm afraid to ask how this came about," he said, as he tossed the bandage in a trash receptacle.

"All in the line of duty, doc."

"You might want to think about getting a new line of duty."

"I'm too young to retire."

"Yeah, right," he said, and looked at me with disapproval written all over him. "Let me clean it up and put some fresh dressing on it. It doesn't look like any infection has set in. Is it giving you a lot of pain?"

"Some. Not as much as yesterday, though."

"Good." He rummaged around in a cabinet, found what he was looking for, and wheeled his stool back over to me. He cleaned the wound, dried it and smeared some salve on it. "Did this happen in connection to a case of yours, or did you just happen to be walking in the park?"

"A case. I haven't been in a park in ages."

Doctor Sam wrapped new gauze around my leg and secured it with surgical tape. After he put my sock and shoe back on, he said, "Have you ever been vaccinated for rabies?"

"Not that I'm aware of."

"Do you know if the dog has?"

"I don't have a clue, doc."

"Hmm," he murmured, and thought for a moment. "Well, to be on the safe side, I think you should get a series of vaccinations."

"A series?"

"Yes. Four shots. Unfortunately, I don't have the vaccine, so you'll have to go to an emergency facility. There's one real close, on Vine. They're open twenty-four seven. Get the first one today, the second after three days, then another on day seven and the last one in two weeks. Can do?"

"Yeah, I'm working on a movie but I think I can swing it."

"Now that's a better line of duty. I'd stick with that one." To emphasize his point, he uttered another chuckle and wheeled his stool over to a desk and scribbled something on a pad of paper and handed it to me. "That's the address of the place. As I said, they're open around the clock." I stuck the piece of paper in my shirt pocket. "I'll write you a scrip for an antibiotic and an ointment. In the meantime, change the dressing often and try and stay off the leg as much as possible. How long do you have on the movie?"

"Next week, for sure. Maybe longer."

"Come and see me when you're finished. See how it's healing. Okay?"

I nodded, slid my trouser leg back down and got off the table. He handed me the scrips, along with a little plastic bag that contained gauze and surgical tape, then ushered me out the door, said hello to Carla and after I made another appointment, we left the office.

The medical facility was a block away from the iconic, 13-story Capitol Records building. Carla parked her car and as we approached the clinic, I was reminded of the time years ago when I was fairly new in town and didn't yet have insurance. I was forced to go to a hospital emergency room for an ankle that I thought might be broken. Fortunately, it wasn't, but unfortunately it took me the better part of an afternoon to find that out. Everything from whooping cough to broken bones to gunshot wounds had demanded attention. I recalled making a vow to myself to avoid another visit at all costs and bear the burden of whatever ailment I had.

Total Health and Wellness Center on Vine Street was nothing like a hospital ER, but was nevertheless fairly crowded. I presented myself at the intake window, provided proof of insurance and told the receptionist what I was there for and that Doctor Sam Minh had referred me. We took a seat in the waiting room and tried to ignore the glare from two small kids who obviously wanted to be someplace else.

"Why don't you go home?" I said to Carla. "I don't know how long this is going to take. I'll call you when I'm done."

"Nope. I'm stickin' with my man," she said, and draped an arm around my shoulders. One of the kids started to snicker and I turned to him with a scowl that made him change his mind.

After fifteen minutes a nurse stuck her head out of a door and called my name. She led me into a room, once again took my vitals and personal information and said someone would be right in. This time I was left with nothing to stare at except another skeleton, this one displaying the body's circulatory system. I took out my phone and started a crossword puzzle, but didn't get very far.

This doctor was an attractive brunette, hair cut short. The name "Richards" was on a nameplate clipped to her white coat. She wore glasses and flashed a nice smile when she came into the room.

"Hello, Mr. Collins. So, a dog bite?"

"Yeah. Doctor Sam Minh said I probably should have a series of rabies shots."

"First of all, what can you tell me about the dog? Any evidence of it being vaccinated for rabies?"

"I'm not sure," I said, and went on to tell her that the dog belonged to the landlord of a man I'd encountered. "The guy who rented the place said the dog had all his shots, but I'm not sure I believe him."

"I see," she said. "Which leg?"

"The left."

She asked me pull up the trouser leg and then looked at the gauze and tape. "Did Doctor Minh indicate any sign of infection?"

"No," I said. "I just came from his office. He put fresh dressing on it and gave me scrips for some salve and an antibiotic." I showed her the prescriptions. She nodded and handed them back to me.

"Well, normally, I'd like to know more about the dog, but from you've told me, it doesn't sound like that's going to be possible. So, to be on the safe side, we'll start with the vaccinations. Did Doctor Minh fill you in on the number of shots?"

"Yes, he did."

"Great. Let me step out for a moment. I'll be right back."

She left the room and after more glances at veins and arteries of the skeleton on the wall, she returned with a small plastic tray. In it were a syringe and a glass vial. While she slipped into a pair of latex gloves, she told me it was probably best to remove my shirt. I did so and she rolled up my tee shirt's left sleeve, dabbed some alcohol on my upper arm with a small wad of cotton, then filled the vial with the medicine and gave me the shot. She put a band aid on the injection site and I put my shirt on.

"Did Doctor Minh also give you the frequency of the four vaccinations?"

"The third and seventh days, and then two weeks."

"Correct. A day or two on either side is no big deal, but try to stick to that schedule. Keep the bite clean. Try to stay off the leg as much as possible and we'll see you next week. Any questions?"

"Nope. Thanks, doctor."

"You bet," she said, and with that, she left the room. I tucked my shirt into my trousers, nodded to the veins and arteries on the wall and headed for the waiting room.

After a stop to fill the prescriptions, Carla went through a drive-thru for some Mexican food to go. Back at her place, I wasn't much of a conversationalist as we ate, which Carla picked up on right away and didn't press the issue, but rather set about doing laundry. I bussed my dishes and sat down in front of the television. The Dodgers and Mets were playing at the aforementioned Chavez Ravine. I tried to ignore the dull ache of Bullet's bite and concentrate on the boys of spring.

My cell chirped. I muted the TV and saw that the phone's display indicated the call was from Charlie Rivers.

"Protecting and serving on the weekend, Lieutenant?"

"Actually, just cleaning up odds and ends on my desk. But I'm curious about something."

"What's that?

"Seems like every time I look at the blotter and check the previous day's activity, your name comes up. You called nine-one-nine about someone getting stabbed with a pitchfork, for crissakes?"

"Yup. My client, Lois Maxwell. And she died on the way to the ER."

"Oh, man, therein lies a tale, Collins. Fill me in."

And so I did.

"Well," Charlie said. "I'm glad you weren't on the receiving end of the fork. Getting bit by a dog is bad enough. Are you all right?"

"I'm okay."

"I'm actually calling with some news for you."

"Good or bad?"

"Not too good, I'm afraid. The license plate we traced to this Langston Beaumont?"

"Yeah?"

"He's got an alibi for that night at Hollywood and Highland. The SUV in question was at his home. He has a monthly poker game with four other guys and drove there in a second car of his, a Porsche. We contacted the four and they all confirmed Beaumont was with them."

I let loose with a huge sigh and muttered, "Crap."

"Yeah, I know," he said. "However, let's think outside the box a little.

First of all, his poker buddies could be lying. They've all known each other for a long time, so maybe a favor was in play. Secondly, Beaumont isn't married and lives alone, so there's nobody at his address to confirm that the SUV was there. We knocked on some neighborhood doors, but nobody seemed to have noticed whether or not it was there."

"Which means that someone besides him could have been in the SUV at Hollywood and Highland."

"Exactly," Charlie said. "Now, as long as we're outside the box, there's the possibility that an employee or two of Edge Security could have been driving that night and taken the shot at you."

"All good possibilities, Charlie."

"Beaumont has six people working for him in the field, plus two receptionists. We've got two teams of detectives working on getting interviews with those in the field and their whereabouts on the night in question."

"When I scoped out Edge, I saw two of them," I said. "One had blond hair and the other was dark."

"Duly noted," he said. In the background, I heard someone talking to him. "Anyway, we'll keep digging and see what turns up. What does yesterday's event do to your movie?"

"They'll have to replace her."

"Never a dull moment in that business of yours, huh?"

"A thrill a minute. Thanks for the update."

"You got it. Stay away from dogs, and pitchforks while you're at it."

With that, he ended the call. While I was glad to hear that LAPD was still working on the drive-by, I couldn't harbor a great deal of optimism that they'd find whoever took a potshot at Carla and me.

I heard her bustling around in the kitchen, having come out of the laundry room at the rear of the apartment. "Did I hear you on the phone?" she said.

"You did."

"Who was it?"

"Charlie Rivers."

"You need anything from the kitchen?"

"A Coke or something."

"Comin' up." I heard the pop of an aluminum can being opened, and then the sound of ice cubes dropping into a glass. She walked to the sofa and set a tall tumbler of soda on the coffee table, then plopped herself down and folded her legs underneath her.

"What did he want? Any news?"

"Not much. The owner of that SUV they traced has got an alibi."

"Ouch."

I nodded, unmuted the television and picked up the glass of soda. My hand trembled and I set the glass down. Carla saw it, unfolded her legs and scrunched herself next to me. Both arms went around my neck, and she kissed me on the cheek.

"You're still pretty shook up, aren't you?" she said.

"Yeah. I'm not exactly good company."

"Can you get in to see your doctor?"

"It's the weekend. I'll call him on Monday."

"Good." She picked up my glass and handed it to me, then brushed a lock of hair off my forehead. "Thinking about Lois?"

I nodded.

"Wanna talk about it?"

I shrugged. "Not much to say, I guess."

"Come on, Eddie. No clamming up here. What's on your mind?"

"It just doesn't make any sense." I sipped some soda and set the glass on the coffee table. "You, of all people, know how hard the playing field is for women in this town. Rejection. Harassment. A business run by white fat cats with raging libidos. But Lois was a survivor, damn it, hard-nosed, played the game for decades. And then to have it all end in some sort of macabre American Gothic scenario is just too weird for words. And I was there. It happened right in front of me."

"But it wasn't your fault, Eddie."

"Ah, I don't know. I could have taken the gun away from her."

"With a dog hanging onto you?"

"Yeah, there was that." I squeezed the hand that she had slid into mine. She said the gun had blanks in it, for crissakes. That she was just going to scare him."

"Which she could have done with a gun that wasn't loaded. With blanks or not."

"Point taken," I said, and reached for my glass and took a hit of soda. "And then to cap it off, she took a bullet that was apparently meant for me."

"Hey, hey, listen to me. You are not responsible for that either."

"Even though I'm wearing a target?"

"A target that some asshole missed, Eddie. Don't forget that."

I was silent. Just sipped some soda. She was right, of course. But that still didn't ease my mind. Lois Maxwell was gone. I was still here—along with somebody out there that could still be gunning for me. Carla wrapped her arms around me and we sat with our thoughts, watching a man with a bat trying to hit a small ball coming at him at over ninety miles an hour. And I thought I had problems.

The reverie ended when my cell chirped. The screen said the call was from Brad Foster, the first AD on *Burnt Hills*.

"Hey, Brad, this is Eddie."

"I heard the news. What the hell else could go wrong, huh?"

"I shudder to think."

"Are you all right?"

"Yeah, I'm fine. What's up?"

"We're finishing up here in Kern County tomorrow and be back on Monday. Pete's hired someone to replace Lois. A woman by the name of Dorothy Cranston. Do you know her?"

"The name rings a bell."

"Well, anyway, on Tuesday we're going to pick up the scenes Lois had shot. We'll need you at seven."

"I'll be there."

"See you then, Eddie. And I'm sorry you had to go through the stuff with Lois."

"Thanks, Brad. See you on Tuesday." I ended the call and put the phone back in my shirt pocket. "The show must go on, as someone once said."

"So, they've got somebody to replace her?" Carla said.

"Dorothy Cranston. I think I might have worked with her in the past."

She reached for her bottle of water and took a pull. "Getting back into the saddle, so to speak, will be good for you, don't you think?"

"Yup. What's done is done."

"That's my Shamus," she said, and turned my head to her and kissed me.

We held each other and focused on the television. The Dodger with the bat in his hand tried to evade a pitch and took it on the shoulder. As he ambled down to first, the pain in my left leg miraculously dissipated.

26

On Monday morning, Carla dropped me at my office building before heading off to her day's shooting on *Three on a Beat*. I needed a change of clothes and a shower. On the way to my place, we had a brief discussion about when this flitting between two apartments was going to end. Neither of us had changed our minds about us moving in together, but at the same time we agreed that we should wait until my contract on *Burnt Hills* was completed. Since I was the one doing the moving, my forced unemployment would give me more time to concentrate on packing up and vacating my little hole in the wall with its Murphy bed. Helped, of course, by Mavis. When I'd told her of my plan to move in with Carla, she'd practically started drooling over the prospect of having more room for her budding business.

After Carla drove off, I popped into a nearby coffee shop and got myself a large, straight black to go. Before heading upstairs, I opened the door to the building's outside parking spaces. Lois's car was still there, seemingly unmolested. Somehow, I would have to find a way to return it to someone. I wasn't sure who that someone was, but some phone calls definitely needed to be made.

I went back inside and saw my neighbor Lenny Daye waiting for the elevator. A cloudy day is always laid asunder when seeing Lenny. His sartorial choices always leave one wondering if he suffers from nightmares. This morning he wore an orange derby, underneath which was a paisley-on-paisley shirt open dangerously close to his navel. His trousers might have been inspired by Dorothy's yellow brick road.

"Hey, Lenny," I said. "Just coming from morning Mass?"

He laughed and said, "Thousands of comedians looking for work and you're cracking wise. You're a brave man, Eddie."

"Well, you know, I try." The elevator door slid open. We stepped inside, Lenny pushed the button for our floor, and we began the labored ascent.

"Hey, who belongs to that VW in the vacant parking spot?" he said. "Somebody move into the building?"

"It belongs to a client of mine."

"What's it doing here?"

The elevator's rise always took forever, which gave me plenty of time to relay to Lenny the reason for the VW's presence. The car jerked to a stop, the door creaked open, and we stepped out.

"Eddie, are you sure you don't have nine lives? Most people kick up their heels on the weekend and you get bit by a dog? Jesus, Mary and Joseph, my friend, you need to rethink your line of work."

"What, and give up show biz?"

"No, the one where you're channeling Sam Spade."

"Duly noted," I said. Some months back the building's owner had installed new carpet on the floor. Its psychedelic pattern could induce a hangover in the most steadfast teetotaler. I gestured to it and said, "Aren't you afraid of clashing with what you're standing on?"

He glanced down, thought for a moment and said, "Honey, I was here first."

"That you were," I said, and pushed through the door into Collins Investigations.

Mavis hadn't arrived yet and the answering machine wasn't blinking. I went back to my soon-to-be-vacated apartment, stripped down, wrapped more plastic over my wound and took a shower. As I dressed, I heard the front door open.

"Eddie, you here?"

"Yeah, be out in a minute." I grabbed the coffee I'd set on my desk and stepped into her office. Mavis was at her computer staring at the screen. I sat down in one of the chairs in front of her desk and sipped on my coffee. After a moment, she peered over the top of the computer and looked at me. Neither one of us said anything.

"I'd ask you how your weekend was, but I think I know." she finally said.

"I've had better."

"Let me get a cup of coffee going and then fill me in on all the gory details. Emphasis on 'gory.'" She went into her little alcove, and I heard the Keurig start to churn. She then came back to her desk and got an abridged version of the weekend's events before going back into her sanctuary to retrieve her coffee.

"Well, I'm sorry about Lois Maxwell," she said, coming back to her desk. "My God, a pitchfork! What a horror show! What does that do to *Burnt Hills*?"

"They've already hired someone to replace her. I'm called tomorrow at seven to start reshooting the stuff Lois had already done."

"And you're okay with your leg being the way it is?"

"I'll be fine. I'm going to pop over and get my second rabies shot this afternoon."

"What are they going to do with that Jacobson character?"

"I haven't heard. They arrested him. I suppose they'll charge him, despite his claim of self-defense. Involuntary manslaughter or something." I sipped some coffee, and for a moment rued the fact that I hadn't loaded it up with cream. "Looks like that's another trial where I'll be in the witness box."

The phone rang and she picked it up. She listened for a moment, said she wasn't interested and hung up. "I assume you've already renewed your car's warranty, right?"

"They haven't given up yet?"

"Almost every day."

"Why don't you just not answer?"

"And deprive someone in dire need of Collins Investigations?"

"Well, yeah, there is that," I said. "But hey," she said, "speaking of the phone, there is something you should probably do."

"What?"

"Report that dog bite to Animal Control."

"You think so?"

"Yes. We had a neighbor whose dog took a chunk out of our mailman one time. Animal Control came knocking on his door, asking if the dog had been vaccinated for rabies."

"I don't know who the owner is," I said.

"But you have the address, right?"

"Yeah."

"That should be enough for them to find out." She set her coffee down and clicked some keys on her computer. "Let me see if I can find who to call." After a moment she said, "Yeah, I'm on their website." She grabbed a Post-It and jotted down the number. "Here. You better call them."

"Yes, Ma'am."

I took the number from her, grabbed my coffee cup and went into my office. Animal Control answered with the inevitable menu. One of the options had to do with reporting a dog bite. I pushed the key and after a few bars of elevator music, a woman answered. I told her about the bite, said I didn't know the owner of the dog, but did have an address. She took it and said they would look into it.

I pulled my laptop in front of me, deleted three or four emails and thought about how I could deal with Lois's car. She obviously had an agent, but I didn't know if she'd a manager as well. I've never had one, figuring an agent's ten percent was enough of a slice to surrender. I've had conversations with colleagues as to the benefit of having a manager—the argument being that a manager will take a more personal interest in you as a client.

With those thoughts in mind I picked up my cell, brought up the contacts, and punched in the number for Preston Bridges, the production manager for *Burnt Hills*. He picked up after three rings.

"Hey, Eddie, what's up?" His voice sounded like he was in a moving vehicle.

"I'm wondering if Lois had a manager in addition to an agent."

"I'm not sure. Why do ask?"

"Well, I've got her car and I need to find somebody who can take care of it. I drove it away from the scene on Friday. She never mentioned any relatives to me, so I thought if she had a manager they might know if she had close family or friends."

"I'm on the way back from Kern County but let me put in a call to our casting director and get back to you."

"Appreciate it," I said, and hung up.

Coffee cup in hand, I pawed through the beaded curtain into my apartment. I stood in the middle of the small room and realized that packing up my personal belongings was going to be a piece of cake. My wardrobe was far from extensive and moving it would probably require just one trip. DVDs and CDs, on the other hand, presented more of a challenge. My failure to become a clothes horse contrasted sharply with my insane habit of collecting movies and albums.

I set the coffee down and started sliding hangers along the rod in my one and only closet, thinking that there might be an item or two I didn't need anymore. No such thing, I concluded.

Just then my cell went off: Preston Bridges.

"This is Eddie. What'd you find out?"

"Lois did have a manager. Burnett and Associates. Our casting director told me she'd dealt with a man by the name of Michael Powers. Here's the number."

"Hang on. Let me get to some paper." I grabbed my coffee, pushed back through the beads and sat behind my desk. After I picked up a pen and pulled a pad of paper in front of me, I said, "Go ahead."

Preston gave me the number, then said that if I heard of any plans for a funeral or service of some kind to let the production know. I said I would, and we hung up. It was mid-morning, so someone should be in her manager's office. I dialed the number Preston gave me and the phone was answered by a woman with just the hint of a southern accent.

"Burnett and Associates. How can I help you?"

"May I speak with Michael Powers?"

"Who shall I say is calling?"

"My name is Eddie Collins. I'm an actor and have been working with a client of yours, Lois Maxwell. I'm afraid I have some bad news that I think Mr. Powers should hear."

There was a pause on the end of the line and finally the woman said, "Hold on, sir, I'll connect you. I'm sorry. What was the name again?"

"Eddie Collins."

After a moment the call went through. "This is Michael Powers. What can I do for you?"

I told him what had happened over the weekend.

"Oh, my God," he said. I heard a click on the line and figured he had told someone else in the office to pick up.

I told them that I had possession of Lois's car and if they knew of any close family or friends that might be able to deal with the Volkswagen.

"Mr. Collins, can I put you on hold for just a moment? I'll see if we've got anyone to help you."

I put my cell on speaker and sipped on my coffee as I waited. After a couple of moments Powell came back on the line. "Mr. Collins?"

"Yes, sir."

"One of our associates knows of a cousin who lives out in Hemet. Where is the car now?"

"At my office. I'm still working on *Burnt Hills*, but I can leave the keys with my secretary." I gave him the address of my building and the location of Collins Investigations.

"Fine," he said. "The young man's name is Byron Newsom. He can be over to pick up the keys this afternoon."

"Thanks," I said, and ended the call. I then picked up Lois's key chain and walked back into the front office.

"I just spoke to Lois's manager. Michael Powers at Burnett and Associates. They apparently know of a cousin of hers. They're sending over someone by the name of Byron Newsom to pick up her car keys this afternoon. Make sure you see some identification from the guy."

"What are they going to do with the car?"

"That I don't know. The only relative of hers I was made aware of is a stepson, Burt Jacobson. And he's not in a position to help."

"True that," Mavis said.

When I presented myself at Total Health & Wellness for my second rabies shot, the young woman at the receptionist's desk looked at me with what I could only describe as skepticism, but she nevertheless pulled up my name on her computer and told me to have a seat. After a fifteen- minute wait, a blonde nurse summoned me into the inner regions of the clinic. She identified herself as Nancy and remarked on how unusual it was for her to encounter someone who had been bitten by a dog. I replied that it was an anomaly for me as well. She then took my vitals, told me to enjoy the rest of my day and left the room.

Another ten minutes elapsed and an older gentleman entered. He had short black hair with flecks of gray in it. Black, horned-rim glasses sat on his long face. He introduced himself as Doctor Everett. He, too, regarded me as somewhat of a curiosity, having been assaulted by one of our canine friends. I assured him it wasn't by choice, and he said that he was glad to hear it.

He looked at the bite and pronounced that there still was no sign of infection. After he put fresh dressing on it, he gave me another shot, told me to continue taking the antibiotic Doctor Sam had prescribed and said they'd see me in a couple more days.

My medical journey continued with a visit to my shrink. I suppose that isn't the best definition of the good doctor, but since he was helping me deal with this PTSD—which is what he had diagnosed in the wake of the drive-by shooting—the designation seemed appropriate. I gave him the blow-by-blow rendition of the episode with the dog and Lois's death, and I must admit that when I left his office I felt better.

The following morning I drove through the gate of the *Burnt Hills* location with a much stranger feeling swirling in my head than before. Lois Maxwell was gone, replaced by someone named Dorothy Cranston. Odd, I thought, the transitory nature of this crazy business. For a few days a person is indelibly etched into one's consciousness through the means of film. And then in the blink of an eye that same person is gone as the result of a freak display of violence. However, for an actor, I suppose there is small comfort in knowing that your essence is kept intact by the final product of a particular project. I pulled into a parking space, turned off the engine and sat for a moment, lost in thought about that fact, but nevertheless saddened by the physical absence of a colleague, made all the more weird by the realization that I was there to witness her disappearance.

I pulled open the door of my dressing room and saw Chet Cassidy's togs hanging on a clothes rod, beckoning me to don them and become another person. I'd no sooner dropped my bag on the table and picked up the day's call sheet when there was a knock on the door and Cheryl, the PA, stuck her head in.

"Good morning, Eddie."

"Hey, Cheryl."

"Get some breakfast and then Pete wants to talk to the company."

"Roger that," I said.

She paused in the doorway for a moment and said, "You doin' okay?"

"I'm good. Thanks for asking."

"Sorry you had be in the middle of what happened."

"Me too. Pretty strange."

"I've got a cart here for you."

"Thanks." Normally, I would have declined the offer of the ride, but given that my left leg had been the target of a canine on the loose over the weekend, I availed myself of Cheryl's offer. I picked up the sides and call sheet, and climbed into the golf cart.

The soundstage where craft services were set up lacked the usual conviviality. It was obvious that the company had been made aware of what had transpired over the weekend. I straddled a chair at the end of an empty table and looked at the scrambled eggs and bacon before me. I couldn't help but recall sitting across from Lois in this very scenario. Best to let it go, I thought, and bit into a slice of toast.

Pete O'Brien stood by the coffee urns. The director was talking to an elderly lady, and at one point caught my eye and they walked up to me. I sensed that I was about to be introduced to Dorothy Cranston and stood up.

"Good morning, Eddie," Pete said. "I'd like you to meet Dorothy Cranston. This is Eddie Collins, Dorothy. He plays Chet Cassidy, the bartender."

Dorothy set down a plate of food and a cup of coffee and stuck out a hand which I shook. She said, "Hello, Eddie. Pete has told me what happened over the weekend. I'm so sorry to hear about what happened to Lois."

"Yeah, it was quite a shock," I said, and gestured for her to have a seat. She had wispy brown hair with streaks of gray in it. It framed a face with big brown eyes and a soft mouth with just a trace of lipstick. She was dressed in khaki slacks and a brown cardigan sweater. A purse was slung over one shoulder. Sticking out from the top of it was the screenplay for *Burnt Hills*.

"Are you okay, Eddie?" Pete said. "Understand you had a run-in with a dog."

"Yeah, I'm fine, but I now have another opinion of man's best friend."

He chuckled and nodded, then said, 'Well, I'll let you two get acquainted. Dorothy, if you need anything, let us know." With that, he walked off.

She turned back to me and smiled. "I sure wish I was here under different circumstances. It's kind of like being hired as a day-player on a long-running television series. You ever have that feeling?"

"Many times. I know what you mean," I said. "But in any case, put that aside and welcome aboard." She smiled and thanked me. We were silent for a moment as we sipped on our coffees. "Did you know Lois?"

"A little," she said. "Our paths crossed at many auditions over the years. It was always a pleasure to run into her."

I smiled and picked at my scrambled eggs. For the next several minutes we got acquainted, recounted stories about the business and at one point remembered that we had worked together on a movie-of-the-week some years back. She recalled that we'd had just a brief encounter on the set, and both of us laughed when we admitted to each other that neither one of us had ever seen the final product.

I got up to refill our coffee cups and had just returned to my seat when Pete O'Brien stood up in front of the tables that had filled up. He got everybody's attention and said that in case anybody hadn't heard about Lois, he relayed what had happened. He then pointed out Dorothy's presence and welcomed her to the company. When he was through with what was a thinly disguised pep talk, his assistant director took over and said that we'd shoot the first scene within the hour.

Back in Chet Cassidy's trappings and fresh from being painted and powdered, I set foot on the set where Lois and I had done our first scene together. As we worked, I recalled Dorothy's comment about feeling like a day-player on a long-running TV series. Many times in the past I had the feeling that I'd shown up at a formal dinner wearing sweats and sneakers. Dorothy, however, dispelled that notion right off the bat. She had the lines down pat and responded to Pete's direction with sheer professionalism. One almost had to wonder why she didn't land the part in the first place.

For the rest of the week we were a company clicking on all cylinders: no interruptions in the call for room tone, no gunshots from bystanders—in fact, there were none to be seen. Our forced move from one location to another had done away with looky-loos. Since the clinic was open twenty-four seven, I even managed to drop in after work and get my third shot.

By the time Friday afternoon rolled around it looked like I would be wrapped by the end of the day. My last scene again took place in the bar. The set had been dismantled and moved piece by piece from Sunset Ranch. I poured mugs of beer for Bart Kincannon, owner of the valley's largest ranch and Jeremiah Rawlins, the Black owner of another ranch being squeezed by Kincannon. The dispute between the two men was over water rights and this was the first time the two had come face to face.

The set was filled with extras who drank and played cards, typical activities for such drinking establishments of the era. I watched as the conversation between Kincannon and Rawlins continued. It escalated until Sheriff Haynes appeared, separated the two men and the scene ended with a stalemate.

O'Brien did three takes of his master shot, the one that showed the conflict from medium range. He then moved in for coverage of the principals in the scene from different angles. About four-thirty, Brad Foster, the 1st AD, announced that that was a wrap, and Stan Erdman, the sound man, called for sixty seconds of room tone. Given the fact that the set was full of extras, it was extraordinary that only one take was necessary.

After Erdman said he had it, Brad Foster got everyone's attention by shouting, "Everybody, that's a picture wrap for Eddie Collins!" With those words, I was through with *Burnt Hills*, unless any reshoots or dubbing had to be done.

Pete O'Brien walked up to me with an outstretched hand. "Thanks, Eddie, for your good work. And for your patience, considering all the hiccups we've endured. Hope we can do it again sometime."

"You bet, Pete. I'll look forward to it," I said.

The other actors in the scene shook my hand and wished me well.

Over the years and many film shoots, I've never really said goodbye in so many words, because it invariably turned out that I would cross paths with them again down the road.

Case in point: Dorothy Cranston, who stood by the door to the soundstage. I walked up to her and shook the hand she held out.

"It's been a real pleasure meeting and working with you, Eddie."

"Likewise, Dorothy. You've been a trooper, coming in on such short notice."

"Oh, thanks," she said. "But we need to make each other a promise."

"Yeah? What's that?"

"That we actually see the finished product."

We both laughed, hugged each other and vowed that we would.

I signed out with Cheryl and walked back to my trailer. When Chet Cassidy's trappings were back on the clothes rack and I was dressed, I paused for a minute and looked around the room.

Every dressing room on a film shoot manages to evoke memories, both large and small. For instance, there was the one where the toilet didn't work and had to be fixed by a member of the transportation department, which then resulted in an interesting conversation with the teamster about desert flowers. Or there was the one where every morning I found a little basket of snacks on the table and a small bottle of wine in the mini fridge.

The *Burnt Hills* digs were different. The memories that pervaded it were ones that brought on a feeling of melancholia: Lois Maxwell's laugh, Pete O'Brien blowing his top over blown room tone takes, and of course a shot being fired that was meant for me, but unfortunately missed and sadly hit someone else.

I picked up my bag, hit the light switch, and closed the door, hoping those memories would stay there.

But I had a feeling they wouldn't.

27

Saturday morning the three of us were in the middle of the soon-to-be-ex-apartment of Eddie Collins, trying to envision how the space could be converted into a fledging online emporium for the buying and selling of tchotchkes, geegaws and doodads. These are but three definitions for the items my secretary, Mavis Werner, buys and sells on the Internet. One can never be surprised by the trinkets that come through the confines of Collins Investigations. One day it might be Laurel and Hardy bobbleheads, the next Roy Rogers and Dale Evans coffee mugs.

Carla and I had brought bagels, cream cheese and lox. Mavis had pulled my desk chair through the beaded curtain—declaring in no uncertain terms that the beads were history—and now sat, nibbling on a bagel, lost in thought. Carla and I sat across from each other at my tiny breakfast table, watching her and trying to gauge what might be going through her mind.

"What are you thinking, Mavis?" I said.

"That Fritz should haul some collapsible tables up here to put against that wall," she said, as she pointed to the opposite side of the room.

Fritz was her bus-driver husband, who, given his size, could more than likely carry one in each hand.

"You don't want to put a table in front of the Murphy bed," I said.

She turned to me with a look that could melt the cream cheese on her bagel. "Why not? If you think you're going to sneak back here for an occasional nap, Buster, you've got another think coming."

"No, I just thought it would give you another flat surface for your supplies." She thought about that for a moment, and then went back to nibbling on her bagel. "But there's nothing wrong with grabbing a nap now and then," I added.

"You can nap at our place," Carla said. "I don't want you sleeping around in strange places."

"Strange places? I'll have you know that Murphy bed and I have become dear friends over the years," I said.

"Time to give it up, Shamus," Carla said.

"She's right," Mavis said. "But first we'll get the tables up here and then see where they can go. What about those shelves?" She pointed to the ones housing my movie and CD collections.

"The shelves can stay," Carla said. "We don't have room for them."

"So, what happens to the DVDs and CDs?" I said.

"You box them up and put them in storage for the time being," she said. "Then since you're going to have so much time on your hands, we can find something at Ikea and you can put them together."

"Yeah, right," I said. "Be sure to lay in a case of beer while I'm doing it." I found myself feeling a tad wistful thinking about the movie collection I'd amassed. The idea of stashing them in some dank and dark cubicle left me uneasy. I've always found comfort in my ability to pick a Humphrey Bogart or Jack Nicholson film off a shelf and wrap myself in their stellar portrayals of legendary private eyes. "What about the TV and DVD player?" I said.

"We'll put them in the second bedroom," Carla replied. "I think there's a cable connection in there. Then we'll figure out some shelving for the movies and music. Sound like a plan, Stan?"

"I guess," I said, with less enthusiasm than she probably expected.

"Eddie, I know this move is weighing on you, and is going to require some compromising. But we'll work it out. Trust me."

"Okay, boss," I said, and she reached out and squeezed my hand. She was right about the move weighing on me. I wasn't necessarily having second thoughts, but ceding my independent bachelor status was nevertheless going to require change. However, change is good some wise man once said. I wondered if he'd like to help me pack up my life and put some of it in storage.

The discussion then moved on to my one and only easy chair, which I said could sit in my office until a home could be found for it. I suggested Reggie, and they both thought that would be a good idea. Mavis said she could make use of the little table Carla and I were sitting at, and therefore it could stay.

Aside from items already mentioned, that basically left odds and ends and the clothes in my closet. We planned for me and Fritz to pick up some tables from Staples on Sunday, his day off. I said I'd drop into a Home Depot and pick up cardboard boxes. I'd start packing in earnest on Monday.

Mission accomplished for the day, we left the premises, and I persuaded Carla to catch a late-afternoon movie. She checked the venues on her phone and the only one that would work timewise was *Pet Sematary*, based on a Stephen King novel. Not exactly a classic, but with Carla and a tub of buttered popcorn for company, it was perfect.

Fortunately, Fritz owned a pickup that had no trouble handling folding tables. We picked out three six-footers and with the help of a four-wheeled dolly and an eager young Staples salesman, slid them into the bed of the truck. He'd picked me up at Carla's place, so my parking slot at my building was empty. We wrestled the tables inside, then called the ancient elevator. We had to stand them on end in the car before beginning our shuddering ascent.

Fritz's cell phone went off. He looked at the screen and put it to his ear. "Hey, Babe, we're just taking the tables up to the office." Pause. It was no doubt Mavis on the other end. "Yeah, three six-footers," he continued. Another pause. "You and Eddie can figure that out tomorrow. I'll be home in a half hour or so." He ended the call and stowed the phone in a hip pocket.

"Mavis, I assume?"

"Yup. She's dying to get into that apartment of yours."

"Yeah, I know. She's been hinting about me moving in with Carla for weeks."

"So, does this move mean wedding bells will be ringing in the near future?"

"Is that your idea, or Mavis's?"

He laughed and held up his hands in surrender. "Hey, man, just asking the question."

"We haven't talked about it in so many words, but if I did pop the question, I think she'd go for it."

"She's a nice lady. You could do worse."

"I know," I replied.

The elevator lurched to a stop. I punched the button to keep the doors open and we wrestled the tables down the hall to Collins Investigations.

"Wow, that is some serious carpet," Fritz said, as he looked down at the psychedelic display covering the floor.

"Yeah. It doesn't go well with a hangover."

He laughed and I opened the office door. I thought about what Fritz had said a moment earlier. The idea of my and Carla's future together had bounced around in my head. How this move worked out would be the acid test. If two independent, lone wolves could make the adjustment, perhaps it was time to take the plunge.

A bridge to cross, I thought, as we pushed the first table through the soon-to-be extinct beaded curtain.

On Monday morning Mavis was like a kid with a new toy. She pushed tables around, stood back and pondered, then moved them into another configuration. She suggested I strip the Murphy bed and she'd take the sheets home to launder. I told her to keep them, since there were bed linens aplenty where I was going.

I filled two boxes full of DVDs and set them by the elevator. Just as I was about to push the button the door creaked opened, and Lenny Daye stepped out.

He looked at the boxes and said, "What in the world are you doing?"

"I'm moving in with Carla. Mavis is taking over my apartment."

"Oh, my God. Does that mean you're going to be living in sin?"

"Is there any other way, Lenny?"

He burst into laughter and beckoned for me to follow him. "Come with me. You're too old to be schlepping boxes around." He led me into the *Pecs 'n Abs* office, opened a closet door and rolled out a two-wheel dolly. "Use this. You can thank me in the morning when you try and get out of bed."

On the way back from the storage unit I'd rented, I picked up a couple of sandwiches for Mavis and me. As we sat at her desk munching on them, I was suddenly struck with a problem.

"How the hell am I going to get all those clothes down to my car? With that many trips, that elevator is finally going to surrender and quit."

I could sense she thought about it as she finished a bite of her tuna on whole wheat. She swallowed and said, "You know, come to think of it, one day I saw Peggy wheeling a clothes rack into her office."

Peggy was Peggy Stafford, the owner of the Elite Talent Agency, another one of my neighbors.

"She probably has her clients try on different wardrobe items. Knock on her door."

"Good idea." I sucked up some soda and set the cup on the desk. "But first, I'm going to give Reggie a call. See if he's got any use for that chair." I pulled out my cell and punched in his number. Two rings and he picked up.

"Hey, Eddie, how you doin'?"

"I'm good. Hey, listen, let me run something by you. Do you by any chance need an easy chair for your place? Nice and comfy. Yours for the taking."

"Why? Where you goin'?"

"I'm moving in with Carla. Mavis is taking over my apartment for this business she insists on running." I ignored the scowl on her face as I said it.

"No kiddin'? Hey, that's great."

"So, you need a chair?"

"Nope. I really don't have room for it."

"Okay. Just asking. How's things on your end?"

"Good. Bernie's goin' out of town for a couple of days, so I'll have the place to myself."

"Well, don't go wandering around. You never know who might pop up." He broke out in laughter at the running joke we had with him living above a funeral home.

"I'll keep that in mind. Hey, you heard any more from that DA up in Ventura?"

"No, and as a matter of fact, I've been thinking he should be getting in touch with us pretty soon about that trial."

"Yeah, me too. Well, he knows where we're at."

"That he does. Okay, buddy, I'll talk to you soon."

I ended the call and picked up my sandwich. "I think that chair is probably going to go to Goodwill or the Salvation Army."

"Let Fritz know and he'll give you a hand," she said.

Peggy Stafford did indeed have a rolling clothes rack, which she had no problem lending me. I filled it up and managed to get it down to my car. I put the clothes in the trunk and brought the rack back to Peggy. That still meant I'd have to get the clothes up to Carla's condo, but at least there was an elevator that worked properly.

For the rest of the day, I busied myself with filling boxes and making trips to the storage unit. At one point I got a call from Michael Powers at Burnett & Associates, Lois Maxwell's management team. He informed me that there was to be a memorial service for Lois on Wednesday, the day after tomorrow. It would be held at the Wee Kirk o' the Heather in Forest Lawn, Glendale. I told him that I'd be there, and then called Preston Bridges, the production manager on *Burnt Hills*. He said he'd pass the word and make sure that the company would be represented by someone.

I salvaged the one dark suit I owned from its new home in Carla's second bedroom and took it to a One Hour Martinizing outlet. A smattering of her friends attended the service Wednesday morning. Her instructions stipulated that she was to be cremated. A large portrait of her sat next to the urn containing her remains. Preston Bridges was there representing *Burnt Hills*. Several people shared memories of her and the long career she'd had working in Hollywood. An actress who looked to be about Lois's age related one incident where the two of them worked on an episode of the TV show *Mannix*. Apparently, Lois had a piece of business that constantly kept Mike Conners breaking up, which finally resulted in the bit being changed. However, she went on to say that Conners was a good sport about it.

Afterward, as the guests lingered outside the church, Michael Powers introduced me to members of her family that had made arrangements for the service. Somehow, the details of her death had been revealed to them, and I was offered thanks for helping her. I expressed my regrets that my efforts hadn't resulted in a more positive outcome.

The guests gradually dwindled away and as I walked to my car Preston Bridges sidled up next to me.

We shook hands and he said, "How are you, Eddie? That dog bite healed up?"

"Pretty much," I said. "It left me with a new attitude toward man's best friend." We shared a chuckle and stepped to the side of the road as a vehicle passed us on the way out of the cemetery. "How's the shoot going?"

"Good. I think Pete's going to be ready to wrap it in another week or so."

"I'll look forward to seeing it," I said. "Give my best to the gang."

"Will do. And I look forward to working with you again."

We shook hands and climbed into our respective cars. I turned onto Barham and made my way back into Hollywood and the ongoing migration of Eddie Collins.

Later that afternoon I was in the midst of filling another box with DVDS when my cell went off. The screen showed the caller was Reggie.

"You change your mind about that chair?"

"Uh, no, but I need a favor."

"Sure. What's up?"

"I wanna move my air conditioner into the bedroom, but the dang thing's too heavy for me to handle by myself. You got time to give me a hand?"

"No problem. I'm on my way."

"Thanks," he said, and hung up.

Carla was still working, so I sent her a text telling her where I was going, put on my porkpie, and headed out the door.

I found a parking space on the street and walked up the driveway next to Bernie Feldman's mortuary. Reggie's car was parked at the end of the driveway. Shadows had by now claimed half of the exterior stairs to his second-story apartment. I reached the top and knocked on the door.

"Yeah, come on in," I heard him call out from inside. I pushed open the door and saw him sitting at his table at the end of a short hallway.

What I didn't see was that he had company. Two muscle-bound guys who held guns, one of them pointed at Reggie, the other at me. It took me just a few seconds to realize I'd seen them before: outside of Edge Security.

28

The benefits I'd been receiving from my therapist flew out the window, leaving me with a feeling of panic at the sight of guns pointed at Reggie and me. My heart started racing and I had to take deep breaths to calm me down.

When I'd spotted these two guys the other day outside Edge Security, I hadn't been close enough to fully realize their size. Now I did. One of them obviously spent some serious time at a gym. He was blond, his hair close-cropped on top of a chiseled face. He looked to be about six feet tall. Dark brown cargo pants encased legs with bulging thighs and hamstrings. Arms displayed solid biceps that were covered in tattoos that curled over and under muscles and disappeared beneath the sleeves of a black tee shirt. A black sleeveless fishing vest with multiple pockets completed his outfit. He stood to the right of Reggie, an automatic pointed at his head.

In contrast, his companion was dark, swarthy looking. A thin black mustache covered his upper lip, dropping down to a goatee on his chin. Unlike his buddy, he didn't give the impression of being a contender for Mr. Universe, but nevertheless was tall and looked like he could handle himself very well in a dark alley. His piercing dark eyes in a long, narrow face sent a message that he wasn't here on a social call. He, too, wore dark clothes and had an automatic pointed in my direction.

I looked at Reggie seated at the table. He shrugged and said, "They knocked on the door, Eddie."

I nodded and turned to Blondie. "You guys are from Edge Security, right?"

"Don't know what you're talking about, Collins," he said, then gestured with the automatic. "Why don't you have a seat across from your buddy there?"

Before I could sit, Swarthy stopped me and frisked me. When he didn't find a weapon, he said, "No hardware? What the hell kind of private eye are you?"

"Plenty of idiots running around with guns they shouldn't have," I said. "I don't need to add to the stupidity."

"And by that, I suppose you mean me and my partner?"

"Like the man said, 'if the shoe fits, wear it.'"

"You're a real smart-ass, Collins."

"So I've been told."

"Why don't you park it across from your pal there?"

I followed his direction and sat sideways in a chair. "How do you know my name?"

"You're in the Yellow Pages," Swarthy said.

"You work for Langston Beaumont."

"Who the fuck is Langston Beaumont?" he said and looked at his partner. "You know who the hell he's talking about?"

"Haven't got a clue," Blondie said.

"How about Ken Thompson?" I said. "Vic Benedetti?"

"You pulling these names out of your ass, Collins?" Blondie said. "They don't mean a damn thing to either one of us."

"You guys didn't happen to be driving an SUV at Hollywood and Highland a few nights ago?"

"All right, enough with the fuckin' questions!" Swarthy said. He emphasized his statement with a kick to my left leg.

It was the one that had been bit by the dog, and it was still tender. I winced and pulled my legs under the table. His response to my question had struck a nerve. It told me that I'd hit on a subject they didn't want to discuss. A couple pieces of the puzzle started to nudge themselves into place.

"Kickin' a guy when he's sittin' down?" Reggie said. "Kinda chicken-shit, don't you think?"

"Shut the fuck up, Benson," Blondie said. "Or maybe you'd like to stand up and get the same treatment?"

Reggie glared at him for a long moment, open defiance in his eyes. "Okay, so you know my name too, but I ain't in the Yellow Pages. What the hell do you want with us?"

"All in due time," Blondie said. He backed up to where he could look out a window. "It's starting to get dark," he said to his partner. "We ready to do this?"

"Yeah," Swarthy replied. He motioned for Blondie to back up from the window. "Get their cell phones."

Blondie stood in front of Reggie and extended his hand. Reggie just looked at him. "Come on, asshole. Your phone." After a moment, Reggie pulled his cell out of a pocket and tossed it on the table. Blondie picked it up, pocketed it, then extended his hand to me. "Come on. Be smart." I took out my phone and handed it to him. It went into the same pocket.

Swarthy then positioned himself between Reggie and me, gun still trained on both of us. "Here's what's going to happen, guys. The four of us are going to walk down those stairs, you two ahead of us. And I don't want to see any sudden trips or fake stumbles. When we get to the bottom, we walk down the driveway to a van parked across the street. You follow me?"

Reggie and I said nothing.

"I didn't hear you," Swarthy continued.

"Yeah, yeah, we heard you," I said.

The two of them gestured with the barrels of their guns and Reggie and I stood. We walked to the door, and they followed.

Reggie pulled it open and turned back. "I gotta lock it behind me."

"Don't worry about it," Blondie said. "You won't be back."

His comment prompted a glance between Reggie and me. We were in deep trouble.

We got to the bottom of the stairway, which by now was in the shadows of the approaching twilight. I looked behind me and saw both men had their hands in one of their pockets.

"Eyes front, Collins," Swarthy said. "Yes, our hands are full, so let's not see any theatrics. Got it?"

"Got it," I said, and we started for the street.

The sidewalks were empty and there wasn't any traffic. A street T-boned into the one where Bernie Feldman's mortuary was located. Halfway down it I spotted a dark green van.

"Cross the street," Swarthy said. "See the van facing us?"

"Yeah," I said.

"Head for it," he said. "Nice and easy. Just out for a little late afternoon stroll."

We crossed the street and walked up to the van. It was probably fifteen feet long and window-less, save for those in the driver's cab. There wasn't any signage indicating it belonged to Edge Security. They directed us to the rear and Blondie opened two doors. He prodded us into the van, then stepped up after us and shut the doors behind him.

"Okay," he said. "It's time to follow directions. To the letter." He pointed to the floor on the passenger side of the van. "See those holes in the bed?"

I looked to where he pointed. Running the length of the passenger side of the vehicle were two-inch square depressions a couple of inches deep. Each of them had a toggle bar spanning the gap. They were spaced probably a foot and a half apart and looked like they were there to secure cargo or things that one didn't want to slide around and get broken. Two of the depressions had one half of a set of handcuffs secured to the toggle.

"Yeah," I said.

"Park your butts down and put the open cuff on your right wrists. And I want to hear all the clicks. Go ahead."

Reggie and I sat down on the floor, a foot apart from each other. Each of our legs straddled a depression in the bed of the van. Blondie squatted down on an eight-foot-long metal cabinet running along the other side of the van. It had straps threaded through handles on both ends and into cleats in the wall of the van. Also strapped to the wall were two camping flashlights, the ones with fluorescent tubes encased in glass.

We put the cuffs on our right wrists and closed them, then looked over at him.

He slowly shook his head and said, "Come on, Benson, try again. I didn't hear enough clicks."

Realizing he'd been caught, Reggie tightened his cuff.

Blondie got up, leaned over us and checked to see if we'd followed his instructions, then turned his head when Swarthy opened the driver's side door and slid behind the wheel. "They're good to go," he said.

"All right, climb in and let's head out."

"Where are we going?" I said.

"No need for you to know," Blondie said. He duck-walked to the rear and opened the doors, then climbed out and slammed them shut. After a moment, he opened the passenger door to the cab and crawled in. He shut the door. Swarthy fired up the van and it pulled away from the curb.

Both Swarthy and Blondie weren't visible to us because of a partition behind each seat. However, a gap about a foot wide between the two seats allowed us to hear them, but not very clearly. Likewise, I hoped road noise would allow Reggie and me to communicate without them being able to hear us.

Reggie yanked on his set of cuffs but there wasn't any give in them. "Do you know those guys, Eddie?"

I glanced at the cab to see if we were being watched. Seeing that we weren't, I leaned over to Reggie and whispered. "They work for Edge Security. Remember I told you Carla and I were shot at on Hollywood Boulevard the other night?"

"Yeah. These guys did it?"

"I'm not sure, but the license plate of the shooter's SUV was traced to a guy by the name of Langston Beaumont, who runs Edge Security."

"I don't get it. How do you figure they're after you?"

I again looked at the cab, saw we still weren't being watched, and continued. "The other day I scoped out this Edge Security and saw these two guys get out of a company van and go inside. But get this, Reggie. Guess whose car was parked outside the building."

"Whose?"

"Vic Benedetti's."

After a moment, the realization washed across his face. "Aw, Christ, Eddie! One of those creeps from that day up in Piru?"

"You got it."

"Shit! They're going to stop us from testifying, right?"

"It looks like it."

"Damn," he said. "What do we do?"

"Stay cool. And be on our toes."

"Guess we got no choice."

Reggie was correct, but I wished I had another answer for him.

29

Our only view of the outside world was a narrow glimpse through the windshield of the van. The sky had darkened, and I could see illuminated streetlights pass by. We stopped and started, an indication that traffic signals were being adhered to. Gradually, the stops became fewer and then finally ceased altogether. The noise from the tires sounded like we were on a freeway heading to God only knows where, but my guess would probably be north, out of the urban sprawl.

I could feel the van swinging to the right and through the windshield saw the sign pointing to Interstate 14, leading up into the high desert and the communities of Palmdale and Lancaster. A glance at my watch said we'd been on the road for an hour.

At one point Reggie stretched himself across the width of the van. A U-bolt ran through a hasp on a hinge that was screwed into the lid of the locker. He tried to push the bolt through the hasp with his right foot but finally gave up and stomped it on the bed of the vehicle in frustration.

He scooted himself back. "So much for that idea. Any guess where they're taking us?"

"Haven't a clue, but we just got on the Fourteen."

"Where does that go?"

"To Palmdale and Lancaster. We're headed for the high desert, buddy."

"Well, at least it ain't near that cesspool in Piru."

"True that." His comment dredged up a memory from a few months back when the two of us were in the clutches of four demented men that had been making snuff films—a sordid episode that I'd been trying to erase from my mind.

We were silent as the van continued to barrel along. Reggie gave another yank on his handcuff, which resulted in nothing more than a wince of pain. "You know, Eddie, this reminds me of something."

"What?"

"Being cuffed in that hell hole with those four creeps."

"You're right. Maybe we should stop repeating ourselves." Reggie chuckled as the van slowed and Swarthy let loose with a blast from the horn. "But this time we aren't up against rotting wooden slats." To emphasize the point, I yanked on my cuff and was met with the same result as Reggie. "These toggles aren't going to give. You got anything in your pockets that resembles a key?"

He stuck his hand into his left trouser pocket and rummaged around. "Nothing. What about you? Don't you usually carry a ballpoint pen? You could bend the clip off it."

"Well, turns out this is the day I don't have it." Since our right wrists were cuffed, I also reached into my left trouser pocket and ran my fingertips over its contents: tube of lip balm, dental Proxabrush, and a fingernail clipper. I pulled it out and showed it to Reggie. He held out his hand and indicated I should give it to him.

"Wait a minute," I said. "We better stop and think about this."

"What do you mean?"

I stuffed the clipper back in my pocket and glanced toward the two men in the cab, then leaned over and whispered. "Whenever they stop, one or both of those goons will crawl in here with guns. We're basically in a cage. I don't know how we're going to get the drop on them in a confined space like this. Instinct tells me we'd have a better chance out in the open. Wherever the hell that may be."

"Yeah, you're probably right. I sure as heck would like to see what's in that locker, though."

"We'll know soon enough."

Another half hour went by. The van slowed and exited the freeway. We stopped, then made a left, telling me we'd either crossed over or under the 14. The van hit several potholes; we were on a highway that apparently wasn't maintained very well.

Another forty-five minutes elapsed. The van slowed and made a left turn. Stones and gravel peppered the undercarriage of the van.

"A gravel road," Reggie said. "Sounds like we're in the boonies."

"We headed north from your place and given the amount of time we've been in here, I'd say we're definitely up in the high desert someplace."

We rattled along for another ten minutes when Blondie let loose with, "Look out!" We heard a thump. The van skidded to a stop and the two men got out. We heard them having a heated discussion on the shoulder of the road, but I couldn't make out what they were saying. After a couple of minutes, the discussion ended, and they crawled back into the van.

Blondie stuck his head in the space between the two seats and said, "Sorry for the sudden stop, guys. Can you believe it? We hit a fuckin' coyote! Nailed him!" He burst into a raucous laugh. "You two enjoying the ride?"

"Yeah," I said. "Mind telling us where we are?"

"In the desert. You like the desert?"

"Love it," I said. "Why don't you let us out so we can enjoy it."

Blondie let loose with another laugh. "I like you, Collins. You've got a sense of humor. I don't think your buddy has, though. Am I right, Benson?"

"You're a barrel of laughs, asshole," Reggie said. "I'm just trying to contain myself."

Another laugh and he turned to face forward.

"If they hit a coyote we really are out in the boonies," Reggie whispered.

I agreed and we sat silent, trying to absorb the rough road as best we could. After another twenty minutes, we turned right off the gravel and seemed to be driving over a field of some kind. After bumps that were intent on rearranging my spinal column, we finally stopped. Swarthy killed the engine, the two men got out of the cab and after a moment the rear doors flew open.

Swarthy hit us in the face with the beam from a flashlight as Blondie stepped up into the van. "Okay, guys," he said. "Ride's over. Time to go to work."

He unstrapped the two camp lanterns and handed them to Swarthy. Then he duck-walked to the locker, slid out the U-bolt and lifted the lid. He grabbed two shovels and handed them back to his partner. Then he reached in again and pulled out a hoe. Its handle was about four feet in length and the business head was shaped like a claw that tapered into a point, obviously used for breaking up turf. He handed the tool back to Swarthy and dropped the locker's lid, then reached into a pocket and tossed a key to Reggie.

"There ya go, Benson. Unlock your cuff and give the key to your pal."

Reggie unlocked his right wrist and handed the key to me. Blondie had made his way to the rear of the van and climbed out. I unlocked my cuff and exchanged a glance with Reggie. Seeing that the two men were dealing with the equipment they'd unloaded from the van, he pointed to my trouser pocket, and I slid the key into it. Either Blondie was awfully careless, or else he knew Reggie and I weren't coming back to the van. That sobering thought seared itself into my mind as we scooted to the rear of the vehicle and crawled out. Carla's face flashed in front of me. The thought of maybe not ever seeing her again started my heart racing again. There had to be some way for the two of us to get the jump on these goons, but right now I drew a blank.

As we crawled out of the van, a moonlit night greeted us with just a slight trace of a breeze. We were in a pasture, next to a barbed-wire fence with two scraggly trees next to it. Three huge rocks were piled underneath.

Blondie had his hands full with the tools and the camp lanterns. He gestured with his head and said, "Get in front of the van, guys. And don't get it into your heads to take off. My partner's got an itchy trigger finger."

Reggie and I walked to where Swarthy pointed with his gun. Blondie followed and then dropped the tools on the turf in front of us. He set the two camp lanterns five feet apart and turned them on. Their light threw a ghostly aura on the patch of ground in front of us, one that apparently was meant as a grave for the two of us.

Blondie confirmed my suspicion when he said, "If you haven't figured it out by now, you're going to dig a hole. Big enough for both of you. Start where the lanterns are and work your way to the fence. By the looks of the two of you, six feet long should do it." Reggie and I didn't move but changed our minds when Swarthy fired a round into the turf in front of us.

"There's that itchy finger," Blondie said. "Now pick up a goddamn shovel and start digging." He pulled a flashlight from a pocket in his cargo pants and turned it on.

We bent down and each of us grabbed a shovel. I whispered to Reggie, "These things have sharp edges. Aim for something that breaks. Like a leg, or a hand with a gun."

"No need for conversation, guys," Swarthy said. "Get to work."

We positioned ourselves by the lanterns and stuck the shovels in the turf. It was bone dry and hard as a rock.

"You gotta be kiddin'," Reggie said. "You need a backhoe to cut through this stuff."

"Well, guess what, Benson," Blondie said. "Unfortunately, we don't happen to have one. "So, the little one is going to have to do. Pick it up and knock yourself out."

Prophetic words, I thought. If Reggie and I got the chance, we'd oblige them. Granted, we were facing two goons with guns, obviously a disadvantage. But both of us did have a weapon, not to mention a surge of adrenaline. Now all we needed was an opportunity to use them.

Reggie pounded the turf with the sharpened point of the hoe. Clumps of earth came loose. He moved to his left, toward the other lantern— another corner of our intended grave. I followed and dug into the ground with my shovel, tossing the dirt off to my right. After breaking up a sizable amount of turf, Reggie laid the hoe aside and picked up the other shovel and started to dig.

I glanced up at the two men. They still had their guns pointed at us, but Blondie at one point had backed up and sat down on the front bumper of the van. He pulled out a pack of cigarettes and lit one up, then quickly got to his feet when we heard the howl of a coyote, immediately followed by an answer from a second one.

"Hear that?" I said. "You probably killed one of their buddies. I'd watch my back if I were you."

"If I were you," Swarthy said, "I'd shut the fuck up and keep digging."

Blondie laughed, then moved along the driver's side of the van and looked into the dark. "See anything?" Swarthy said.

"Nah," Blondie said, then returned to his seat on the van's bumper and puffed on his cigarette.

"That coyote you guys hit," Reggie said. "Did you drag it off the road?"

"No, we just left it there," Blondie said. "What the fuck kind of stupid question is that? Of course we dragged it off the road."

Reggie and I were shoulder to shoulder. Despite the lack of light, when he turned to me, I could see the trace of a grin on his face. He winked and looked up at Blondie.

"Eddie's right," he said. "You'd better watch your back. Those coyotes have a really good sense of smell. They smell their buddy on you."

I had to bite my lip to keep from grinning. I knew what Reggie was up to. Anything that would distract these two guys and keep them on edge was to our advantage.

"That's bullshit," Blondie said. "How the hell do you know that?"

"I studied up on them when I was in school. They can smell another coyote from a quarter mile away. We've got a nice little breeze going here. They just wanna touch base with a buddy." He bent over and scooped up a shovel full of dirt and threw it to his left. "You can take that to the bank."

I glanced at Blondie. He looked confused and turned to his partner. "Is that true? You think they smell us?"

"Oh, for crissakes," Swarthy said. "Will you pay attention to what you're doing and quit listening to his bullshit?"

Despite the reprimand, Blondie got up from the van's bumper and backed down the driver's side of the vehicle. When he heard another coyote howl, he turned and fired a shot into the air.

"Hey!" Swarthy shouted. "Quit with the goddamn coyotes and get back here!"

Blondie turned around and walked back to where Reggie and I were digging. He looked down at us, his gun in his right hand. "Benson, I think you're full of shit."

"Okay, man," Reggie said. "Don't look at me when one of them starts sniffing up your butthole."

Blondie kicked some dirt on Reggie's feet, backed up and again sat down on the van's bumper. He puffed on his cigarette and kept looking over his left shoulder into the darkness.

A few minutes passed with only the sounds of our shovels interrupting the silence. "So, you guys don't work for Langston Beaumont?" I said, as I filled another shovel full of dirt and tossed it next to me.

"What the hell difference does it make if we do?" Swarthy said. "It's not going to matter to you two in a few minutes."

I returned to my digging and watched the two goons. Blondie puffed on his cigarette and kept glancing over his shoulder. He had demonstrated that he was the more gullible of the two. Swarthy, however proved to be more of an enigma. He hadn't said much, but rather left it to his partner to display their bravado.

"So, what do you two guys do for Edge Security?" I said. "Kidnapping just a sideline?"

Swarthy didn't respond and squatted down on his haunches off to Reggie's left. Blondie stepped on his cigarette butt, stood up and walked up to where Reggie and I were digging.

"What the hell is Edge Security?" he said. "And what makes you think we've got anything to do with whatever the hell it is?"

"Come on, guys. The other day I saw both of you getting out of a van with the company logo on it. You walked right past a silver Mercedes that belongs to one Vic Benedetti, who just happens to be under indictment. Both of us are witnesses to what he and some pals did. So, what did he do? Arrange for the two of you to put a hit out on us?"

"Leave him alone," Swarthy said. "He's just spouting bullshit."

Blondie laughed but stopped when the sound of another coyote howl erupted from the rear of the van. A second quickly followed. Then we heard growling. These critters were too close for comfort.

Our two kidnappers obviously thought so as well. Blondie turned and aimed his flashlight down the length of the van. The beam caught two sets of eyes that glowed in the light.

"Jesus Christ, they're right here!" he yelled.

He started toward the coyotes at the same time that Swarthy rose from his haunches.

I looked at Reggie. His shovel was full of dirt. I nodded and whispered, "Go!"

Shovels in hand, both of us stepped out of the hole we'd been digging and moved toward the two men. Swarthy had just begun to move when Reggie threw his shovel full of dirt in the man's face. He stopped, spit, and tried to brush the dirt away. He fired a round in Reggie's direction, but his eyes couldn't focus, and the shot went wide.

When Blondie heard the shot, he turned and started down the driver's side of the van. I wound up and aimed my shovel at his head. He saw it coming, blocked it with his left arm and screamed in pain as the edge of the tool caught his forearm. I heard what sounded like a bone breaking. I thought the blow would stop him, or at least slow him down, but it didn't. He did, however, lose his grip on his gun and it fell to the ground. Before he could pick it up, I kicked the weapon toward the rear of the van. Blondie grabbed me around the knees and I fell down. He pounced on me and punched me in the face. I grabbed his left arm and twisted. He yelped and I managed to buck him off.

Out of the corner of my eye I saw Reggie and Swarthy rolling around on the ground, wrestling for control of the other gun. Swarthy was on top of him and Reggie wiggled beneath him, trying to get loose.

Blondie wasn't done. Before I could take a step to help my partner, he wrapped his arms around my waist and pushed me toward the barbed wire fence. Both of us tripped and went down when we came to the grave-in-progress. I tried to reach for the hoe Reggie had been using, but Blondie laid his good arm on it before me. He stood, and with the one good arm, raised the hoe over my head. He couldn't wield it very well with one arm and stopped when I placed a solid kick to his groin. Experiencing the pain only we menfolk can describe, he bent over and groaned. I got to my feet and slugged him in the face. He stumbled back and I followed with my fists flying. He careened into the wire fence and writhed as he tried to pull himself off it. I yanked him by the injured arm and slugged him. He stumbled off to his right. I followed, grabbed him by the seat of his cargo pants and with all the strength I could muster rammed his head into one of the large rocks at the foot of the scraggly trees.

That did it. He was out and lay still. Full of rage, I kicked him in the ribs.

I turned around and saw Swarthy and Reggie still grappling for the gun. Somehow, they'd managed to get to their feet and the struggle had now carried them to the front of the van. I picked up my shovel and started toward the two fighters. Swarthy pounded Reggie's hand on the hood of the vehicle until he had possession of the weapon. He backed up a step or two, leveled the gun at Reggie and was about to pull the trigger when I brought my shovel down on his gun hand. The weapon fell to the ground and as he started to bend down to retrieve it, I raised the shovel again and clubbed him on the top of head with the flat side of the tool. The impact was not unlike a watermelon being squashed. He dropped to his knees and then collapsed on the ground. I raised the shovel over my head and landed a blow on his neck, then reared back with the shovel to give him another blow when Reggie stopped me.

"Eddie, he's done, man! Let it go."

Both of us bent over at the waist and tried to catch our breath. After a minute I said, "You know what *deja vu* means?"

"Yeah. Like Yogi Berra said, 'it's *deja vu* all over again'." The tension broke and we broke out in laughter.

"But I'm telling you, Reggie, I'm getting too old for this crap." I found the handcuff key in my pocket and tossed it to him. "Grab those cuffs and let's get these guys trussed up."

He headed for the rear of the van. I pulled out my handkerchief and used it to collect both guns and then put them on the front seat. Both serial numbers were still intact. I grabbed Blondie under the arms and dragged him to the front of the van, then did the same with Swarthy. When Reggie came back with the cuffs, we put them around one of their wrists, and then secured the other cuff to the grill of the van. They were both still out and looked like a couple of raggedy-Andy dolls sprawled in the light from the two camping lanterns.

A single coyote howl pierced the silence of the desert night.

Oddly enough, it no longer sounded very threatening.

30

When Reggie and I retrieved our phones from our kidnappers, we were pleasantly surprised to see that there were sufficient bars for us to use them. It was a testament to the encroachment of cell towers, I guess, but neither one of us complained.

"Call nine-one-one," I said. "And stay on the line."

"Aw, why don't you do it, Eddie? I'm not sure I know what to say."

I caught the sheepish look on his face and said, "I've got to use mine to call Carla. She's left me a slew of messages, so she's probably freaking out by now. Besides, she'll recognize the number."

He handed his phone to me. "Here, you call nine-one-one. I'll stay on the line, and you call Carla with your phone."

"Okay," I said, and took the phone and punched in the numbers. The 911 dispatcher seemed a tad nonplussed when I told her who I was and where I was calling from. I told her I'd leave this line open and that we'd need an ambulance. Her puzzlement abated when I told her that if the responders pinged the cell phone, they'd be able to find us. She said okay, asked for my name, then told me units would be on the way.

It was approaching midnight, but I was sure Carla would jump on a phone call, which she did.

"Eddie? Oh, my God, I've been worried sick! Where are you?"

"Reggie and I are up in the high desert somewhere. We got hijacked by two goons from Edge Security."

"Are you all right?"

"Yeah. I'll probably have a shiner for a few days, but other than that, both of us are okay." I could hear stifled sobbing on the end of the line. "Honey, listen, I know you've been worried, but everything's all right. The two guys who kidnapped us are out of commission and we're waiting for the cops. They'll have a lot of unpacking to do, so it's going to be a while before we get back into Hollywood. But just rest easy and know that I'm okay."

"If you say so. Let me know what happens."

"Do you have to work tomorrow?"

"No, I'm not called."

"Good. Keep your phone handy. Love you."

"I love you, too." And with that we ended the call.

Reggie and I grabbed the two camp lanterns and set them on top of the van, giving the responders some sort of guide to where we were, provided the batteries held up. I told Reggie I'd put the two guns on the front seat and that both serial numbers were intact.

There was nothing to do but wait. A couple of coyote howls pierced the silence. We each had a flashlight and when we caught them in the beam, they skittered away.

"You think they're going to hassle us?" I said.

"Nah," Reggie said. "I think they're just curious."

"By the way, nice play with the warning about the coyote smell. That true?"

"Damned if I know. Sounded pretty convincing, though, didn't it?"

"Animal husbandry. Another Reggie Benson original."

Both of us laughed and turned to the front of the van when we heard a groan from one of our two kidnappers. Swarthy had come to. I squatted down in front of him.

"How's the head?"

He didn't answer me, but just yanked on his handcuff and glared at me for a long moment.

"There's an ambulance on the way," I said.

He coughed and straightened himself up. "What makes you think the cops are going to believe anything you say?"

I stared at him for a moment, forming my thoughts. "Well, for one thing, we were the ones who called nine-one-one. Now, why the hell would we do that if we're the bad guys in this little scenario? Think about that for a minute."

He did and I continued. "And for another thing, when they run the plates on this van, they won't show it being registered to either Eddie Collins or Reggie Benson. Now, are the cops going to believe that we stole this van, drove it into the boonies so we could rough you two up, and then called nine-one-one to turn ourselves in? That shovel scrambled your brains, pal."

As that sunk in, he turned to look at Blondie, who had come to, and did enough moaning to bring on another coyote. He looked around and then yanked on the cuff around his left wrist, which provoked another series of moans.

Reggie knelt in front of him and said, "That arm is probably broken. You're only going to make it worse."

"Fuck you, Benson," he said.

"And to piggyback on what my partner said, unless your guns are stolen, the serial numbers are going to trace them to you guys. If you were planning on being the hotshot kidnappers you think you are, you maybe should have thought of that before you set out. A dumb move, if you ask me."

"Nobody asked you, asshole."

Reggie chuckled and stood up. Another coyote howled and he shined the light on it and turned back to Blondie. "I think this guy wants to come and say hello."

After forty-five minutes, we saw flashing lights approach in the distance. We each grabbed a lantern and began waving them as a signal. Two Los Angeles County Sheriff's units and an ambulance bounced over the turf to where Reggie and I stood, our arms in the air, each holding a lantern.

Both deputies opened the doors of their units and stood behind them, guns drawn. One of them shouted, "Who placed the nine-one-one call?"

"I did," I said. "My name is Eddie Collins. I'm a licensed private investigator." I gestured to Reggie. "This is my associate, Reggie Benson. We're unarmed. There are two men handcuffed to the front grill of this van who need medical attention. Both were armed, and their weapons are on the front seat of the van."

The deputy who asked the question told his partner to check to see if what I said was true. The second deputy walked to the passenger side of the van and said the guns were there. He then moved around to the front of the van and called to his partner.

"We've got two individuals cuffed to the grill, Mike. The EMTs better look at them."

"Roger that," Mike said, and called over his shoulder to the paramedics who stood by the ambulance. "Check 'em out, guys."

The paramedics went to the front of the van, and I could hear them asking Swarthy and Blondie what had happened. After a few minutes, they moved back to Deputy Mike.

"They've both suffered some blunt force trauma," one of them said. "There's a broken arm and they've probably suffered concussions. We'd better get them to a hospital."

"Okay," Deputy Mike said, and then addressed Reggie and me. "Where's the key to their cuffs?"

"Right here," Reggie replied, as he handed him the key.

"You gentlemen move to the front of the van while we secure the two you've allegedly beat up."

I wanted to argue with him regarding his use of the word "allegedly," but figured it best to keep my mouth shut. Reggie and I moved to the front of the van and watched as the second deputy uncuffed Swarthy and Blondie. Then, with Deputy Mike holding his gun on the two kidnappers, the second deputy replaced the cuffs with police-issued restraints. With their hands cuffed behind them, Deputy Mike and his partner escorted Swarthy and Blondie back to the ambulance.

The EMTs helped them up into the vehicle and Mike said to his partner, "Lonnie, you ride with them. Make sure they see your weapon in their faces at all times."

"Roger," Deputy Lonnie said.

"I'll call it in and get some backup out here. Someone will drive your unit back to the station. I'll see you back there."

Deputy Lonnie nodded and climbed into the ambulance. One of the paramedics closed the doors, got in the passenger side, and with lights flashing, the vehicle started off across the field.

Deputy Mike squatted behind the van and jotted down its license plate, then turned to us and said, "All right, gentlemen, why don't you crawl into the back seat of my unit there and let's see if we can make some sense of this scenario."

Reggie and I got into his car and listened as he radioed for backup and a tow truck to haul the van away. He asked his station to run the van's license, then hung up his mic, pulled a notebook from a shirt pocket and turned around to face us.

"Okay," he said. "First things first. Let me see some identification to prove you are who you say you are." Both Reggie and I opened our wallets and showed him our driver's licenses. He jotted them down in his notebook and then looked up at us. "All right. Now what the hell went down out here?"

We started from the beginning and laid out how the kidnapping took place and who we thought Swarthy and Blondie were. At one point his radio crackled and he was given the result of the license plate on the van. Not to my surprise, it was registered to Edge Security under the name Langston Beaumont. We then went on to tell Deputy Mike the connection between Edge Security and Vic Benedetti, which then led to the connection to the other three defendants in the Piru incident. At several points during our story, he shook his head in disbelief, but nevertheless jotted everything down in his notebook. About forty minutes elapsed before we could see lights approaching and were told that that would be all for the time being.

Following the deputy's instructions, three sheriff's unit pulled up, accompanied by a police tow truck. Deputy Mike filled a large plastic evidence bag with the two guns from the front seat of the van. He gave instructions for the shovels, the hoe, and the two camp lanterns to be secured as evidence. Cell phone cameras flashed as a barrage of photos were taken. Satisfied, Mike crawled behind the wheel of his unit and started to drive off, leaving Reggie and me with memories of the horror we had gone through, and the hope that we'd never again be in a similar situation.

We were taken to the Palmdale Sheriff's station, given hot coffee, some ice for my shiner and then were subjected to another hour and a half of questions. At one point a deputy came into the interrogation room and informed our questioners that a trace of the serial numbers on the weapons revealed they were registered to an Alvin Burrows and Rodney Dickinson.

The deputies finally ran out of questions and we ran out of answers. As we were escorted to a sheriff's unit, we saw that the van had been towed into the parking lot of the station. Traffic on the 14 and the I-5 heading into the basin was light. We thanked the deputy when he deposited us at Reggie's place and watched the unit disappear into the night.

We turned and looked at each other and Reggie finally said, "A hell of a night."

"One for the books," I said. "Next time remind me to tell you to move your damn air conditioner by yourself." He laughed and we hugged each other, then he walked up the driveway to the stairs leading to his apartment.

I crawled into my car and headed for Carla's—and now my—condo and what was sure to be the warmest embrace a lucky guy like me could imagine.

31

I set my coffee cup down, picked up the Ziploc bag of ice cubes and placed it over my left eye. The cold caused me to grimace slightly.

"Does it hurt?" Carla asked.

"Only when I wink," I replied, and glanced at her across the kitchen table. The look on her face was not pleasant. "What's the matter?"

"I don't really think this is the time to try and be funny," she said, an edge in her voice that told me my attempt at humor had bombed, big time. "You were kidnapped yesterday and forced to dig your own grave, for god's sake. I fail to grasp the humor in that."

"But it never happened, Carla. I'm sitting right here."

"I can see that, but do you have any idea how I feel when I can't reach you for hours on end?"

"Yes, I do, but you make it sound like it's my fault."

"I know it's not your fault, but this isn't the first time I've been left hanging, wondering where the hell you were. You almost got thrown into Lake Arrowhead a while back. Then four creeps threatened to kill you up in Piru. And now two goons force you to dig your own fucking grave! What's next, Eddie? A nice, clean-cut plain-clothes cop knocks on my door in the middle of the night and I turn over and you're not there? And then that cop asks me to come down to the morgue and identify a body?"

She got up from her chair, took her dishes and dropped them in the sink. One plate broke and she pounded a fist on the counter. She pulled the wastebasket from under the sink and threw the pieces into it, then grabbed a tissue from a box on the counter. She turned back to me and dabbed at one of her eyes.

I looked at her for a long moment as silence filled the kitchen. "Where is this coming from, Carla?"

"Probably from the night someone shot at us, Eddie. I was terrified beyond belief."

"So was I. But after yesterday I think there's proof who was responsible for that."

"And then what?" She blew her nose and tossed the tissue in the waste basket under the sink.

"Come and sit. Please?"

After a moment, she sat across from me. "I'm going to talk to the DA up in Ventura County and tell him what happened," I said. "There's a strong possibility those four creeps are behind efforts to prevent Reggie and me from testifying against them."

"But that doesn't really answer my question. What's next?"

I took a sip of coffee and looked at her for a long moment. She didn't avert her eyes. "What are you saying? I should take down my shingle and close Collins Investigations?"

"No, but do you have to be the answer to everyone's problems?"

"I don't go looking for trouble, Carla, if that's what you're thinking."

She sipped from a glass of orange juice. "Really? What about that key you found in your costume a few months ago? Mavis, Reggie, and I told you to turn the damn thing in, but you didn't listen, and look where it got you."

She had a point, and she knew it. "I'll give you that," I said, "but there's a woman by the name of Barbara McAndrews who finally has some closure about a daughter who was snatched from her and was never seen again. Doesn't that count for something?"

"Yes, of course, but it didn't have to be you riding in on a white horse."

I leaned back in my chair. "What the hell would I do if I were to shut down the office?"

"Last time I checked, your SAG dues are current."

"To do what? Play 'Senator Number Three'? Or 'Man in Uniform'? How about 'Man in Pool Hall'? They don't exactly provide fodder for a demo reel."

"You just worked on your second film in the last six months, Eddie. You and I both know actors who'd be green with envy."

"Granted, but that doesn't mean they're going to keep coming. I need a second source of income." I paused and took a sip of coffee. "Unlike you," I said, and regretted it the minute the words left my mouth. The statement hung in the air like a dense, threatening cloud.

After a moment she said, "So, this is now going to devolve into jealousy on your part? Is that where we're going, Eddie?"

I shook my head. "No, that was a stupid thing to say." I finished the rest of my coffee and looked at her across the table. Her eyes brimmed with tears. "Look," I said. "I had a lot of trouble dealing with an ex-wife who had a good career while I spun my wheels. I couldn't handle it very well and in the end it led to me being kicked out on my ass. You know all that. But this time it's different, Carla. I couldn't be prouder of you for being able to land what looks like a very successful show. That makes me very happy.

"I can deal with the bit parts as long as I have something to fall back on. That's what Collins Investigations gives me. It makes me feel that I'm doing something…oh, I don't know…noble, for lack of a better word. If what I do brings someone peace and order in their lives, then I think that's a good thing. I hope you don't resent me for that."

"No, but it still doesn't help me when I reach out to you and get no response. What am I supposed to do, Eddie?"

The silence was deafening until I reached across the table and took her hands in mine and said, "You know, when I finally fell asleep last night, it didn't last long. I kept seeing coyotes and shovels. They woke me up. Your left arm was draped across my chest. I slowly removed it and sat on the edge of the bed. I held my head in my hands and tried to erase the images. Then I turned around to look at you. You were asleep and had this look on your face, so peaceful and beautiful, no frown or furrowed brow. I burst into tears. Right then I thought that if I was ever to lose you, my life would be shattered beyond repair. Don't ever think for one minute that your face isn't in front of me when I'm in the midst of trying to stay alive. So, all I can say, honey, is hang with me. I love you more than life itself, Carla Rizzoli."

She looked at me. Her dark eyes brimmed with tears, a couple of which rolled down her cheeks when she blinked. Then she got off her chair, came around the table and curled up in my lap. I wrapped my arms around her and felt the tenseness leave her body. Somehow, I knew we were going to be all right.

She kissed me and lightly ran her fingers over my shiner. "I love you too, Eddie Collins. Just make sure you let me know where you're going. All the time, okay?"

"You got it." She kissed me again and I tightened my embrace. "For the record, as far as yesterday is concerned, those two goons probably had a gun to Reggie's head when he called me. If he didn't say what they wanted to hear, he was toast. I had no idea what he was facing."

"Point taken. Is he all right?"

"He's fine. He's a tough little bird."

She got off my lap and took my dishes over to the sink. "You going to talk to that DA today?"

"That's my plan."

"You maybe should also call your doctor."

The look on her face signaled to me that I didn't have room for argument. "Good idea. I'll call him from the office. I've got some pictures in my camera that the DA should see. Mavis can download them and make prints. I'd better check in with her now."

"Okay. I've got some rearranging to do in this place now that I've got a permanent roommate."

"Let's hope he doesn't disappoint," I said.

"I'll make sure he doesn't," she said, and then kissed me.

I picked up my hat and looked back at her before I closed the front door. She had a huge smile, which couldn't have been a better send off.

The door to Collins Investigations was unlocked and Mavis wasn't at her desk, but I quickly remembered she now had taken over what used to be my apartment.

"Mavis?"

"Yeah, back here."

I walked into my office, hung the porkpie on its peg, and saw that the beaded curtain leading to what used to be my lair had been removed. Thus ended an era. I stood in the doorway to my former apartment and looked around. She'd begun to make the place her own: folding tables were set up against one wall, covering Mr. Murphy's bed, I noticed. A shelf unit held rolls of tape, sheets of bubble wrap and a postage scale. What used to be my closet had flattened cardboard boxes leaning up against the back wall. I couldn't deny that the change in the room made me feel a tad wistful, but the decision had been made and I'd have to live with it.

As I walked through the door, she was sealing the bottom seam of one of the boxes with a strip of packing tape. Sitting next to her, awaiting shipment to some expectant buyer were bobbleheads of Laurel and Hardy.

"Good morning," I said. "Looks like you've made yourself at home."

"Big time. I can't tell you how much—" She'd turned to me and stopped when she caught sight of my shiner.

"What does the other guy look like?"

"I don't know for sure. He's behind bars up in Palmdale."

"Okay, I'll bite. Am I going to get another 'Eddie versus the world' story now?"

"Not if you don't want to."

"You know better than that." She pointed me to my easy chair that hadn't yet been moved out, then pulled up a folding chair and sat. "Enlighten me, boss man."

And so I did. When I finished, she slowly shook her head. "Is Reggie all right?"

"He's fine." I held up my digital camera. "I've got some pictures in here that need to be printed out. They're for the DA up in Ventura County."

She took the camera and headed toward her computer. I followed and sat in a chair in front of her desk as she set about downloading the pictures.

"You know, we should figure out something to let you know when somebody's come into the office," I said. "You won't know that if you're back there packing up Laurel and Hardy."

"I've been thinking about that," she said. "We could put a bell on the desk here. One of those ringie-dingie things like they've got in hotels."

"Better yet. We could get somebody to install a button on the outside door that buzzes when it's pressed. Like a doorbell."

"Good idea," she said, as she stood and moved to the printer. The first photo pushed itself out and she picked it up and looked at it. "Who are these two guys?"

"The ones that kidnapped Reggie and me." The second pic started grinding itself into the light of day. She handed me the photo I'd taken of Blondie and Swarthy. Their images were crystal clear.

"Edge Security," she said, as she handed me the second photo. "Is that where they work?"

"That's my assumption," I said. "The sheriff's office up in Palmdale ran the plates of the van they used and the search came back saying it was registered to Edge Security. I scoped the place out and took these pictures. Now look at the third one."

She pulled it out of the printer and said, "A silver Mercedes. What's the connection?"

"It belongs to Victor Benedetti. That name ring a bell?"

"Victor…" She paused a moment and turned to look at me. "Is that one of the guys that waylaid Reggie and you up in Piru?"

"One and the same," I said, as she handed me the third photo. "Now, what the hell do you think Vic Benedetti was doing at Edge Security, two of whose employees wind up trying to kill Reggie and me? Might it have something to do with making sure we don't testify at a certain upcoming trial? What do you think?"

"I think you better talk to that DA," she said, and slid the pictures into a large envelope.

"Bingo," I said, as I stood and took the pictures back to my desk. I found the number for Phil Ainsley at the DA's office in Ventura. Fortunately, he was in, and picked up the phone after a few minutes on hold. I briefed him on what had happened and told him about the photos. I asked if it was possible for me to bring them to him. After a moment during which he checked his schedule, he told me he could see me at two o'clock. I said I'd be there and hung up the phone. It was just a tad before high noon, which gave me plenty of time to make the drive.

The Ventura Freeway was, as usual, clogged, but thinned out as I got further west into Simi Valley. As I drove, I mulled over the earlier conversation I'd had with Carla. She'd been spot on in describing the uncertainties she faced when I was trying to keep myself from harm's way. I couldn't argue with that and knew that I'd feel the same if the roles were reversed. I wrestled with a solution that didn't involve taking down my PI shingle. There didn't seem to be any, as much as thought there might be. Granted, I could perhaps be a little more discriminating in the cases I took on, but at the same time, as I pointed out to her, where a particular investigation led me wasn't always easy to determine. Get Reggie more involved? A possibility. He was younger than me, and always displayed a tougher exterior. Food for thought, I decided, as I exited the 101 into the city of Ventura.

The smell of the ocean filled my nostrils as I climbed out of my car. I was fifteen minutes early, so I found a shaded bench outside the building and soaked up the atmosphere. Spanish architecture pervaded the neighborhood: plenty of red-tiled roofs, and buildings the color of sand.

An attractive Latina receptionist whose nameplate on her desk identified her as Maria Sanchez told me to have a seat after I gave her my name. Her jet-black hair surrounded a very pretty face with dark eyes and a soft mouth with a trace of dimples at the corners. She wore a light green blouse and had a light red scarf tucked under the collar. She flashed me a big smile and pushed a couple of pads on her phone to announce my presence. She said her boss would be right out. And he was.

Phil Ainsley was a man slight of build, about my height and looked to be in his forties. He sported a neatly trimmed dark beard and his hair was short and parted on the left side. He wore two thirds of a three-piece suit, light blue shirt and a tie with subdued red stripes.

He offered me a firm handshake and led me into this office. "You could have emailed those photos you have and saved yourself a drive."

"I thought it better that you hear about what happened from the horse's mouth," I said.

"Yes, perhaps you're right," he said, and gestured for me to have a seat in front of his desk. "Can I offer you anything? Coffee? Water?"

"I'm fine, thanks."

Ainsley's office was quite large. The obligatory certificates hung on a wall behind his desk, which was flanked on either side by tall windows that provided views of the ocean. Law books filled shelves on one wall. He sat down and I pulled the photos out of their envelope. Before I slid them across his desk, I told him how I'd come to learn the owner of the SUV involved in the drive-by shooting Carla and I had experienced, and how it was registered to Langston Beaumont, the owner of Edge Security.

"I found its address and took these pictures," I said, as I pushed the photos across his desk. "Those two individuals are the ones that kidnapped my associate and me. The Palmdale sheriff's station ran a check on the weapons they had and came up with their identities, Alvin Burrows and Rodney Dickinson. I don't know which is which, but they're definitely the two."

He jotted the names down on a pad of paper. "What's the significance of the silver Mercedes?"

"It belongs to Victor Benedetti."

He raised his head and looked at me. "Victor Benedetti, as in...?" He left the sentence hanging.

"As in one of the four that are under indictment for the incident up in Piru."

"And you think he had something to do with what happened to you and Mr. Benson?"

"I'd bet on it. Burrows and Dickinson didn't haul us up into the desert just to get a whiff of some clean air. They were intent on making sure that we weren't going to be around to testify against Benedetti and his three pals."

Ainsley tapped his pen on his desk and looked to his right. "There's nothing to prove what you're suggesting, though."

"Not unless Burrows and Dickinson decided they wanted to start talking."

"Did they give you the impression they'd do that?"

"The blond-haired one seemed to me to be full of bluster. He might."

He leaned back in his chair and took another look at the photos. "All right, let me get hold of the Palmdale station, lay out what you're suggesting, and get somebody up there to sweat them for a while. See what develops."

"Sounds good," I said. "While I'm here, what's the status of the trial for Benedetti and his buddies?"

"Typical legal wrangling. Forbes and Iverson are negotiating plea agreements. Benedetti and Thompson aren't, so there's a lot maneuvering going on. But I'm hopeful that we'll get underway later this month."

"Are they still wearing ankle bracelets?"

"Yes, but if there's any evidence of witness tampering, they come off and they'll be back in custody. From what you've just told me, it might be wise for us to do some investigating. We'll let you know."

"Thanks. I appreciate it."

"Which leads me to say that if you wish, we can assign some security for you and Mr. Benson. To prevent any further incidents like you went through yesterday."

"I think we'll be all right. But thanks for the offer."

He nodded, stood up and extended his hand. We shook and he ushered me out of his office with thanks for bringing the photos to his attention.

I crawled into my car, opened the windows to let some sea air in and sent a text to Carla: *Just ready to leave Ventura. Are you free for dinner?* I watched two skateboarders headed toward the beach and waited for a reply. After a minute or two it came: *I am. What do you have in mind?* I replied: *I'll surprise you.* Her reply: *Bring it on, Shamus!*

I slid the windows up and headed for the 101, hoping that by the time I got to Hollywood I'd come up with something.

32

"…and spring became the summer" …as Neil Diamond sings in his hit song *Sweet Caroline*. So it was with Carla and me. I wouldn't characterize my former studio apartment as a "household," but as the days rolled by, we nevertheless managed to combine all our material possessions into Carla's condo. It seemed to work out just fine. The biggest difference was referring to Carla's home as mine. True, I still had the enclave of Collins Investigations, but now that was only where I went to the "office," where I "went to work." *Three On a Beat*, Carla's television show was on hiatus, so when I was "home," I helped her to unravel the mystery of folding a fitted sheet, for example. We prowled the aisles of Whole Foods together and caught early movie matinees and shared tubs of buttered popcorn. I liked it, and so did she.

Both of us continued appointments with our respective counselors, or "shrinks," as the vernacular calls them. There was a time in the past where I would have scoffed at seeing one, but if Tony Soprano could do it, who was I to argue.

On a Monday morning, after my move was accomplished, I pushed open the door of my office and saw Mavis at her desk, on her computer, frowning.

"What's the matter?"

"You remember Sonny and Cher?"

"'I Got You Babe.' Yeah, why?"

"Some yahoo up in Sacramento won't take my offer on a pair of bobbleheads of the two of them."

"Should I alert the authorities?"

"Ha, ha, smart alec."

I walked into my office, hung the porkpie on its peg and sat behind my desk. Mavis had left a couple of bills awaiting my attention. I pulled my checkbook from a drawer and started writing one with a payment for my SAG-AFTRA dues. I looked up when I saw that she stood in front of my desk.

"I have something for you," she said.

"And what would that be?"

She laid a check in front of me. "Here's my half of the rent on this place."

"I can just deduct it from your salary."

"No, I want to pay you by check. Maybe I can think of some way to write it off as a business expense."

"Good luck with that," I said. But knowing Mavis, she probably would.

May rolled into June, and with it my first outing as a witness in a criminal trial. The defendant was Burt Jacobson, aka Bryce Jesperson. The trial was held in Van Nuys. As I walked to the witness box to be sworn in, I glanced at him. He looked scared, wore an ill-fitting suit, and was represented by a public defender who looked fresh out of law school.

The prosecutor grilled me about the events leading up to Lois Maxwell's death. I stipulated that my fingerprints were on both the gun and the pitchfork and described in detail why that had come to be. On cross examination, Jacobson's attorney tried to get me to admit that his client acted in self-defense. I testified that even if he did enter that plea, it was nevertheless my opinion that even though the gun contained blanks, he could have been knocked it out of her hand with the pitchfork, rather than him stabbing her with it. After about three hours on the stand, I was dismissed.

I'd asked the district attorney to let me know when the jury had reached a decision, so I was in the courtroom when the verdict was handed down.

Jacobson was convicted of voluntary manslaughter and sentenced to the minimum of three years. However, the judge surprised me and everyone else in attendance when he dropped the sentence to probation. While he stipulated that Jacobson did indeed cause the death of Lois Maxwell, he also believed that the defendant was in fear for his life because he was being threatened with what he believed to be a loaded firearm. Jacobson had no previous record and in open court had expressed remorse for what he had done. It was obvious that the judge might have had a twinge of sympathy for him, due to his plea of self-defense. While I was surprised by the decision, I confessed to be in agreement with the judge. Jacobson would have to live with what he did for the rest of his life, which probably would haunt him as much as if were behind bars for three years.

My second foray into the legal jungle happened several weeks later when Reggie and I were called to testify in the trial of the two men who kidnapped us. Prior to the start of the trial, Swarthy and Blondie had been identified as Alvin Burrows and Rodney Dickinson, respectively. I was correct in thinking that Dickinson was full of bluster and might sing like a canary. He admitted that they were hired by Langston Beaumont of Edge Security to prevent us from testifying against the four degenerates who had almost killed us in that ramshackle barn outside of Piru several months back. Under interrogation, Dickinson also confessed to taking a shot at me on the Sunset Ranch set.

A subpoena had been issued for security tapes trained on the front door of the company's office. On camera, Victor Benedetti was seen shaking hands with Beaumont. On the strength of Dickinson's testimony, both he and Burrows, along with Beaumont, were convicted of witness tampering. That led to the four Piru defendants having their bail revoked and spending the last couple of months behind bars.

On the heels of that legal skirmish, Reggie and I were finally called to testify in the trials of the four infamous pornographers. David Forbes and Roger Iverson had negotiated plea agreements and were tried as co-defendants, but separately from Ken Thompson and Victor Benedetti.

Their trial was held in Ventura and was long and brutal. The defendants' lawyers didn't have the veneer of being new to their profession. They were slick, experienced, and put both Reggie and me through our paces. Carla was in the gallery for almost all our testimony, and her presence was a comfort in the wake of being raked over the coals.

Phil Ainsley was first chair for the prosecution and had coached both Reggie and me prior to the trial about how he was going to proceed. He led off by leading the jury through my finding the Pandora key and how it led to my discovery of Meredith Paulson's disappearance and my suspicions of the four men. In the discovery phase of the trial, it was determined that the conversation I had overheard on Ken Thompson's back deck was inadmissible, due to the fact that I had been illegally trespassing on the property. Secondly, it was the judge's opinion that what I heard was hearsay, couldn't be substantiated, and therefore he wouldn't allow it.

Despite that hiccup, what sealed the case for the prosecution was the testimony of David Forbes and Roger Iverson. They admitted that the four men had engaged in the production of snuff films. Their testimony was powerful and led to the conviction of both Ken Thompson and Victor Benedetti. Given the number of victims and the horrendous nature of their crimes, they were sentenced to life without parole.

At long last, Reggie and I then testified at the trial of Forbes and Iverson. Their attorneys also were slick and experienced and tried to sway the jury that Thompson and Benedetti were the ring leaders and that their clients were reluctant participants, at best. But it didn't work. Both men were convicted. Although they testified for the State, they were sentenced to significant prison sentences.

Labor Day appeared, and Carla and I decided we needed to get out of the city. She had gone back to work after her hiatus but had the holiday weekend off. We decided to hit the high seas, well, only as far as Santa Catalina Island, but it was still twenty-six miles over open water.

We booked a Catalina Express ferry out of San Pedro. When it cleared the port, we stood at the stern and Carla started singing and dancing to *'Twenty-six miles across the sea, Santa Catalina is a-waitin' for me. Santa Catalina, the island of romance, romance romance, romance.'* She stopped bopping and said, "Am I going to find romance, Shamus?"

"If you play your cards right," I said, and she snuggled into me. "Okay, trivia time. Who made that song popular?"

Without a beat she said, "The Four Preps."

I looked at her in disbelief. "Damn, how did you know that?"

"I grew up in Henderson, Nevada, for cryin' out loud. What else was there to do but listen to oldies radio?"

We reached the island in an hour's time, accompanied by a school of dolphins swimming alongside the boat. I'd visited Catalina once before, but Carla had never been there. We pulled into Avalon and were amazed at the number of sailboats moored in the bay. To our right sat the iconic circular Avalon Ballroom, the scene of many a Hollywood party back in the day. Houses dotted the steep hillsides above the bay.

We booked a room at the Zane Grey Pueblo Hotel. It was built in 1926 and at one time all the rooms were named after one of the famous author's stories. That wasn't the case now, but it didn't take anything away from the charm of the place.

Our first order of business was to board an open tram for a guided tour of the island. There was a dozen of us, and a grizzled elderly gentleman was our guide. As we started out, he introduced himself as Fred and began his spiel.

"Welcome to Santa Catalina, folks. Our year-round population is roughly forty-two hundred souls. The island is seventy-six square miles, which figures out to about fifty-five people per square mile. Now, for you unfortunate souls from the City of Angels, compare that to two-thousand four-hundred and thirty people per square mile." He turned back to us and said, "So, how many of you ain't goin' back?" His comment provoked laughter from his passengers. "But if you decide you wanna stay you'll have to leave your car on the mainland. Not many of them over here. Not much use for them, really. Get yourself a golf cart and you'll fit right in."

Our tram continued and wound around a bend through rolling hills and grassy fields on both sides of the road. At one point Fred stopped and told us to look off to our left at a peculiar bit of wildlife. Several head of bison grazed in a pasture.

Fred continued, "Now, legend has it that back in the twenties some of them Hollywood fellas transported a few of these critters to the island. They used them in a movie, based on one of Zane Grey's stories. Some say it was *The Vanishing American.* Others say it was *The Thundering Herd.* In any case, the movie company went back to Hollywood when they got done, but the bison stayed. Now there's about a hundred fifty of the shaggy devils. They're well taken of, but if you're out hikin' and run into one of 'em, I'd advise you to turn around and retrace your steps." The tram continued on and Carla vowed never again to have a bison burger.

That evening we had drinks and dinner at the Mt. Ada-Wrigley Mansion. What is now a hotel was once the home of William Wrigley Jr., heir to the chewing gum empire, whose wife Ada oversaw the construction of the place between 1919 and 1921. The Chicago Cubs conducted their spring training on the island from 1921 to 1951. Supposedly, Mr. Wrigley would watch the training from his home on high, and when he felt a player was slacking, ordered them to run up the mountain as a penalty for his lack of effort.

The weekend went by far too quickly, but we had a wonderful time and Carla thoroughly enjoyed herself. I was pleased that we had the time to be together, away from courtrooms and all the misery and depravity that pervaded them. Our little mini vacation seemed to put a spring in our steps and gave us renewed energy to propel us back into the traces of the Hollywood hustle.

Our ferry back to the mainland departed late afternoon. We again stood at the stern of the boat and watched the sun as it began to sink behind the island. The light from it surrounded Carla's mane of jet-black hair, providing her with the semblance of a halo. The look demanded a picture of her against that background. The wind tousled her hair as she mugged for the camera. The moment filled me with feelings of gratitude and sheer joy that she was a part of my life—so much so that I asked her a question that had been bubbling in my head for several days. It was a simple query that required either yes or no for an answer. A huge grin broke out on her face when she said yes, and then threw her arms around me.

EPILOGUE

The ceremony was low-key and took place in the office of a Justice of the Peace in downtown LA. We'd both agreed that pomp and circumstance didn't suit us. My best man was Reggie, who looked splendid—and perhaps a tad uncomfortable—in a new suit. Charlie Rivers was there, along with Morrie Howard, my agent, and a couple of actor buddies I'd had the privilege of knowing for several years.

Carla's two co-stars on *Three on a Beat*, Marsha Bailey and Alison Jackson, were her bridesmaids. Like Carla's, they wore matching light blue dresses, and both had to fight off the onslaught of tears. Mavis and her husband Fritz were also there, and at one point I noticed Mavis also dabbing at her eyes. Carla's parents, Dominic and Helen Rizzoli, drove over from Henderson and both of them beamed when they heard their daughter say "I do" in response to a question from the JP.

But the big surprise and the one that made me choke up when I glanced at her was the attendance of Kelly Robinson, my daughter. Her adoptive parents had put her on a plane and she flew all by herself from Cincinnati to Los Angeles. She had grown and matured into a beautiful young lady, with a striking resemblance to her birth mother. The buttons on my vest almost burst with pride whenever I glanced at her and happened to catch a big smile.

After the ceremony, we adjourned to a reception at a small ballroom in a downtown hotel. A cake was wheeled in, and both of us slobbered over pieces that we tried to feed each other. Toasts followed, most of them serious, although Charlie Rivers delivered a small dose of irreverence, which was met with laughter all around. I'd hired a photographer, and countless pictures were taken of numerous groupings.

At one point in the celebration Kelly sidled up to Carla and me. She had grown to where the top of her head now reached my shoulders. She wrapped us both in a hug and said, "I wish you both all the happiness in the world."

We thanked her and I said, "You know, you can come and visit anytime. In fact, the more the merrier."

"Who knows?" she said. "Maybe I'll come out here and become a famous movie star."

That comment caught me somewhat by surprise. I looked at Carla and she sort of shrugged, as if to say, "Well, why not?"

Carla knew a young guy who worked as a DJ. She'd hired him, and he started spinning discs to start the dancing.

I put my arm around my bride and led her to the middle of the dance floor. "I've got two left feet," I said, "but I'll try not to ruin your new shoes."

"You know the saying 'something old, something new, something borrowed, something blue'?"

"Yeah, so which is which?"

"My dress is blue, this ring on my finger is new, and my shoes are old."

"So what's borrowed?"

"You'll find out later," she said, and smirked, then raised up and kissed me. "Happy, Shamus?"

"More than you'll ever know," I replied.

Truer words were never spoken.

About the Author

Clive Rosengren is a "recovering" actor, whose career spanned more than forty years, eighteen of them pounding many of the same streets as his fictional private eye Eddie Collins. Movie credits include Ed Wood, Soapdish, Cobb, and Bugsy. Among numerous television credits are Seinfeld, Home Improvement, and Cheers, where he played the only person to throw Sam Malone out of his own bar. Rosengren has written five books in the Eddie Collins Mystery series: *Murder Unscripted, Red Desert, Velvet on a Tuesday Afternoon, Martini Shot,* and *Frog in a Bucket.* Books one, two, and five were finalists for the Shamus Award from the Private Eye Writers of America.

www.ingramcontent.com/pod-product-compliance
Lightning Source LLC
Chambersburg PA
CBHW010537100726
47903CB00011B/3033

9 781684 922123